Edited by Franck Extanasié
Translated from French by Edward Gauvin

© 2025 / 2026 by David Catuhe.

DAVID CATUHE

Menilmonea

Experience the story of Menilmonea in the best possible way!

All illustrations from this book are also available as high-resolution images and may be downloaded free of charge using the following link, also embedded in the QR code below.

https://www.davidcatuhe.com/product-page/
menilmonea-illustrations

(All illustrations are entirely handmade by a real human being without any use of AI.)

I

Menilmonea made her way with a firm step through grass glittering with dew, traces of the storm that had blustered through the night before. The heady scent of sodden moss filled the air, adding a hint of coolness to the still-slumbering underbrush. She was in the best of moods, knowing full well as she did that this was the perfect time to dig up roots and especially mushrooms, for the latter always proved chattier and more obliging after a heavy downpour.

She hadn't needed much urging from Tunka to set off into the woods at dawn. With a light heart, she headed for a small clearing usually popular with the spore folk.

Her list for the day consisted primarily of powders for that night's fireworks celebrating the Feast of the Mother. The children, riveted by her tales enlivened with extravagant special effects, awaited these magical moments with almost palpable impatience.

"That said, should I come across willing contributors to my headache ointments, well, beggars can't be choosers," she observed out loud, absentmindedly fiddling with the straps on her wicker basket.

And with a radiant smile, she addressed a group of polka-dotted redcaps that seemed to be waiting for her.

"Good day, dear friends," she began, crouching down gracefully. "I'm looking for a few volunteers. With explosive temperaments, if you know what I mean! And a little bird tells me you'd be just perfect for the job. Am I right?"

After a long pause, she went on with a mischievous smile, her eyes twinkling with age-old connivance.

"Yes, I know. And what's more, it'd be an honor for me, there's no hiding that."

An imperceptible murmur seemed to rise from the ground, a vibration Menilmonea alone could interpret.

"Oh, yes!" she exclaimed, her enthusiasm contagious. "I've been at this for more than five cycles, and what a pleasure it is! One I cherish dearly. At any rate, thanks again, all of you! I'll nestle you here, deep in my basket. It's quite comfy there. I promise to make splendid concoctions that will spread your spores properly about!"

After yet another pause, she rose fluidly to her feet and, with a spring in her step, made unhesitatingly for another promising thicket.

There, in a shady nook barely touched by the morning light, she found a group of mushrooms whose delicate hues blended almost into the gloom. Their caps, of a translucent ivory veined with pale blue, seemed to betray a shyness ill-suited to Menilmonea's needs.

I really must make a convincing case to this bunch, she thought, rolling up her sleeves a little.

In a gentle, reassuring, almost singsong voice, she initiated the conversation. "Well, hello and good day to you! I see several among you are quite ready to be moving on, and as a result, I wanted to invite you to close out your life cycle with a bang! How would you feel about going out in a conflagration, scattering your spores to the whim of the winds? When it comes to spreading your essence to the far-flung corners of the forest, there's nothing else like it!"

Her own lyricism took her by surprise, but she felt it was exactly the right note to strike in motivating this retiring group to come along.

Alas, after far too long a silence, a hint of disappointment crept into her smile. *You can't win 'em all...* She'd stop by again in a few days; by then they'd likely have ripened a little and changed their tune.

The great majority of mature mushrooms were always highly motivated to help. And after a little chitchat, she often managed to coax the uncooperative ones. But it had to be said there was among fungi

also a more traditionalist fringe that preferred to finish off their life cycles in peace and quiet, without frill or flourish. When they died, their spores were borne away on the winds as well, but without the chance to be festive or helpful that she offered.

Why, it's almost selfish of them, she thought. Though she promptly kicked herself for thinking so. Who was she to judge their motivations, how they wished to end their lives?

Convinced she'd have more luck with the roots hidden deep in the clearing, she continued on her way, her basket swaying gently at her hip.

Halfway there, however, she froze. She sensed—or rather, the wood had whispered—that a presence drew near...

II

She wasn't surprised, then, to hear Aureal's voice from the far end of the clearing.

"Yoohoo! Menil! Still talking to your mushrooms? I can hear you telling them your life story all the way from the footpath."

Menilmonea gave an eye roll, of a familiarity tinged with fondness.

"Here to needle me about that again?" she shot back. "Do you think I want to end up all disfigured like our last Healer? Talking to mushrooms lets me know how they'll react when I'm working with them. But you're perfectly aware of all this, aren't you? If I didn't know you so well, I'd think you were just making fun of me."

"Perish the thought!" Aureal retorted, a dazzling smile lighting up her face. "It's just that no one else seems to be able to hear them but you, a fact I find deeply intriguing. Do they speak our tongue?"

Menilmonea knew exactly where this conversation was going, but she decided to play along, shifting her basket on her hip.

"It's more like I hear them all the time, an ongoing song. A melody, but one that stays in the background, never insisting on itself. And when I speak with mushrooms, the song grows more complex. What they want to say to me becomes a part of it. Not in words, really.... Something verging on words while remaining more wild, more intuitive. But through them, I... perceive their intentions, their desires. Tunka says that's called mycomancy."

Menilmonea paused to reflect, then added, "It's a bit like when you try to get a rise out of me without ever quite saying what you mean. I can make out your intent from the way you act and speak. Our communication goes beyond mere words."

"So I'd make an excellent mushroom!" Aureal exclaimed with a tinkling laugh. Then, growing serious again, her gaze softened, and she said, "You know how much you mean to me, Menil. If I keep prodding you to make more discreet use of your gifts, it's only because I don't like it when the village treats you like a misfit because of how you go about your work."

"Those ingrates! They can say what they want!" Menilmonea cried, her cheeks flushing slightly as she lost her temper. "When they're sick and need my remedies, they swallow their words soon enough!"

A silence, weighty with things left unsaid, fell between the two friends, interrupted only by the stirring of leaves.

"Forgive me, Menil. I didn't mean to upset you," Aureal said gently, reaching out a comforting hand.

"I know. Don't worry. Still, were I to rush to a few hasty conclusions, I might be inclined to believe that when you say such things to me, you're almost talking to yourself. As if projecting your own demons," Menilmonea replied, a mocking grin on her lips.

"What do you mean?" Aureal asked, stiffening slightly.

"Let's just say I highly doubt I'm the only one to adopt practices that are... different."

"I have no idea what you're talking about." She broke abruptly away from her friend's inquisitive gaze.

"Well, for example, last night, when we were helping old Mordental find his goat, I got the feeling that the minute we entered the woods, you knew instinctively where to look for it. I noticed a subtle change in you."

Aureal sulked and made no reply, but her fingers toyed nervously with the fringe of her tunic.

"I can tell it bothers you when I bring it up, and I must admit, you're quite the talented actress. But I know you like a twin sister: you didn't stumble on that poor creature by accident. You could sense its

presence."

"I see.... In short, you want me in the oddball club so you won't get lonely, is that it? And as a bonus, I get magic powers when I join, like a welcome gift? Are you sure those mushrooms haven't messed with your head?" said Aureal. Her bravado, however, rang hollow.

"You can lie to me as much as you want, Aureal, but you can't lie to yourself forever."

"I'm sorry I made fun of you earlier, Menil. You're right to needle me back. Still, what you're saying makes no sense. I give you a hard time because I want you to be happy and fit in well at the village. You're my closest friend, and I only want the best for you."

"Thanks. I'm... sorry, too. I didn't mean to make you uncomfortable or get angry at you," Menilmonea murmured, aware she might have taken things too far.

"Let's speak no more of it then! Tunka sent me to help you out and bring back everything we need for tonight's feast. To work!"

Menilmonea nodded, without a word.

The two friends resumed walking through the woods in search of more mushrooms. The weighty silence was broken only by Menilmonea's hushed monologues, her requests lowered to a whisper to avoid Aureal's accusing glances, though her friend now feigned not to care.

After a moment that seemed to stretch out like an eternity, Aureal decided to break the ice at last. "Planning to invite someone for the Feast of the Mother tonight?"

"No, I don't think so. I don't really feel like wasting my time over boys. I think I'll just tell the children our legends with Tunka," said Menilmonea, inspecting a group of silvery mushrooms.

"I'm not trying to start another fight, Menil, but you're already on your thirteenth cycle. Sooner or later, you'll have to fulfill your duty toward the Mother if you ever want your Ascension. You don't want to end up like old Ordine, do you? She's past her fortieth cycle! Wrinkled as a prune!"

At this unflattering description, Menilmonea burst out laughing. "No, of course I don't want to end up like her. But with all due respect to the Mother, I'm just not ready to settle down with a boy, much less bear children for the village. There are so many things to see, do, discover…"

She sighed, gazing off at the horizon.

"Well, I'll tell you one thing for sure—I'm not telling the children any stories tonight!" Aureal exclaimed, a hungry look in her eye and a smile full of promise on her lips.

"Oh, I don't doubt it. In fact, you know what? I'm secretly counting on you to do my duty for me. All it will take is a few more children on top of your own," Menilmonea teased, bending over to gently pluck a bluish mushroom.

"Now there's a fine idea!" her friend laughed, tossing her hair back. "But I'm not sure the Mother would see it that way. And the day she summons me for Ascension, there's no way I'm leaving you behind, you hear? We'll both be by her side, so we can live happily in paradise forever!"

"Yes, Mistress." The mycomanceress nodded, trying to remain as serious as she could.

The girls returned to gathering, chatting about this and that. Now and again, their peals of laughter rang out among the tree trunks, though their conversation did have the unfortunate tendency of circling tirelessly back to the boys on Aureal's meticulously upkept list of potential partners.

III

"I think that about does it!" Menilmonea exclaimed with satisfaction, nestling the last two winterroots in a basket already filled to bursting.

These plants came by their name because when rubbed together, they yielded an icy gel with frankly remarkable properties. The harder you rubbed them, the more piercing the chill they produced. The villagers used winterroot to ease rheumatism, relieve aches and pains, and even preserve foods on the hottest days.

"Lovely! It's back to the village with us, then. If I'm not there soon, Matilda and Ferra will make mincemeat of me," Aureal sighed, straightening her tunic. "We've more than twenty babies at the nursery right now, and three sets of hands are barely enough."

"Twenty already?" Menilmonea's eyes widened in surprise.

"That's right, my dear. Not all of us take our devotion to the Mother as lightly as some," replied Aureal with an exaggerated wink.

"Which just goes to show, you don't really need my contribution."

With a cheery laugh, the two friends left the woods, their steps as one upon the carpet of dead leaves that led the way to their village.

But when they reached the ridge overlooking the valley, their laughter trailed off.

The village lay tranquilly below, nestled at the foot of majestic faraway mountains, its tiled rooftops gilded by the noonday sun.

Aureal let slip an awestruck sigh. "What a wondrous place we call home."

"Oh, yes. The Mother spoils us so…" Menilmonea paused for a moment, uncertain, her gaze lingering on the misty horizon.

"But…?" Aureal asked, a smile at the corner of her lips. "I can tell you were about to say something else."

"But… don't you ever wonder what lies beyond the Mother's crown? Or where the Forbidden Passage leads, for instance?" Menilmonea murmured, a spark of adventure aflicker in her eyes.

Aureal raised an eyebrow, her expression hardening slightly.

"Well, given its name, I'd always figured it best not to pry. Am I right?"

"But aren't you even the least bit curious?" Menilmonea persevered, turning to face her friend. "We've never set foot beyond Gunderki's village. And yet the Mother scattered dozens of villages throughout the world, each with its own Titan. I'd love to visit them all, meet the folk who live there…"

"They're probably just like us, you know," Aureal answered with a shrug. "Gunderki's villagers are no different from Orondoki's. You've seen as much for yourself."

The mycomanceress shot her a playful look, a glint in her eye. "Not exactly like us. I try to pay heed whenever I'm out and about. They don't talk quite the same way, their traditions are slightly different—"

"Don't go quibbling over details," Aureal cut her off with an impatient wave. "In the end, we're all the same. We dwell in our villages, and every six moons, pay a call on a neighboring one to barter some goods. And there you have it. We are the Mother's children, one and all! If there are indeed other villages out there, they must be just like ours. Mayhap one even has a Healer who flirts with blasphemy more often than she ought."

"Oh, I don't know…" Menilmonea trailed off, pensive, one finger absently tracing rings round the handle of her basket.

She was silent for a moment, then said, "Take Tunka: he doesn't simply settle for providing guidance. He instructs us: tells us his story, what the world is like, the origins of our traditions. I know from

Gunderki's Healer that their Titan remains more aloof, acting as a guide but never going beyond. He never encourages his folk to ask questions or explore the way Tunka does."

Aureal snorted, eyes alive with mischief. "Well, he might be right not to. Perhaps Tunka ought not to fill your head with tales. I don't know that the Mother approves of his initiative."

Menilmonea stared daggers at her, suddenly stiffening. "Aureal! Now see who blasphemes! Do you believe one of the Mother's Titans could act in error so?"

"No, of course not," her friend replied with a sly grin, bowing her head ever so slightly in mock contrition. "I simply wonder why you can't just be happy here. You've got everything you could possibly need. And what's more, you've got me! Any other village ought to be so lucky!"

Menilmonea raised her hands in surrender, unable to hold back a fond smile. "Indeed, when you put it like that, I cannot complain. You win!"

"And about time!" Aureal cried, her tinkling laughter echoing in the crystalline air. "Well, I'm off, Menil. Or else I'll be in hot water indeed! I'll drop my basket off at your workshop once the little ones are all safely back home."

"Thank you! You are a true friend. A good day unto you," Menilmonea called out as her heart's sister vanished behind the hedge between the road and the wood's edge, her slender form swallowed up by the greenery.

Alone now, Menilmonea grew lost in thought, her gaze roaming the edge of the village and the mountains that surrounded it like silent guardians.

Aureal must be right, she thought. *Why can't I simply be happy, content with what the Mother has given me, while awaiting Ascension?*

Her own parents, pious and devoted folk, had left to join the Mother before their twenty-fifth cycle—quite the feat, of which she was unsure how to prove worthy.

In the end, it was Tunka's massive shape that stirred her from her thoughts. It was as if a living monument had stepped from between

the houses.

His imposing carapace, covered in countless shimmering flowers and grasses of every color and sort, made its way slowly around the village. No doubt he sought a pleasant spot to hunker down before starting the day's lesson.

A gaggle of children tagged along in his wake, hollering, excited by the prospect of new teachings, their tiny feet hopping impatiently up and down.

Menilmonea smiled, moved by this familiar sight.

She, too, had her work cut out for her.

The mixtures and other decoctions for tonight's festivities weren't about to make themselves, and her mushrooms needed someone to give them all the care they deserved.

IV

The day had sped by. Readying the powders had taken longer than planned. Some mushrooms hadn't needed to be ground up, but in such cases, they had to be dried out before being uprooted, always a delicate process. Menilmonea had only emerged from her workshop minutes before the ceremony began, her hands still stained with colors from her various mixtures.

As usual, Tunka had begun by thanking the Mother for her blessings, urging each and every villager to take part in the feast and celebrate the gifts bestowed upon them.

Menilmonea had barely had time to catch up with Aureal, already hanging from the arm of a charming, broad-shouldered young man en route to where the ball would be.

"See you later, I hope!" her friend cried, radiant in her ballgown.

"Yes! Of course! I'll be sure to swing by the ball after storytime with the children," said Menilmonea, not meaning a word of it. Shimmying about to a festive tune while attempting to decipher the subtleties of mating dances for males her age largely surpassed her abilities. A social exercise she preferred to abstain from whenever she could.

Menilmonea enjoyed Tunka's company a great deal more, and that of children eager to hear the tales of the village founders, their eyes already gleaming with excitement.

Without further ado, she sat herself down by the fire, not far from the Titan. The young ones awaited her with feverish attention, and she had to raise her voice slightly to be heard amidst the ceaseless clamor.

Menilmonea got off to an easy start with several legends about famous village elders, beings whose Ascensions were exceptional, graven in the memories of one and all. She spoke with such ardor that even the adults, distracted at first, drew closer to listen, captivated by her well-chosen words and magical effects. Each story seemed to strengthen the invisible bonds that united the community, a reminder that their lives ran warp and woof on far larger a loom than that of the day-to-day.

Then, in the end, came the highlight of the show. She took a long pause for dramatic effect, then leapt in.

"In the beginning, ours was a virgin world. The forest alone, with its myriad trees, prevailed over the vast expanses beneath the heavens."

A silence engulfed those gathered, already bewitched, as Menilmonea went on, her clear voice borne aloft on the night breeze.

"Many hundreds of cycles ago, the Mother decided it was time for her creation to roam the Earth. That this might be so, she raised majestic Towers at the four corners of the world, instruments of her will, enabling the advent of the Titans. Immense, wise, and immortal, they were incarnations of the Mother's power."

With a gesture precise from years of practice, Menilmonea flung delicate handfuls of flame powder that gave rise to a cluster of little red and yellow glimmers. Swept gently along on the wind, they whirled for a moment like ancient spirits in quiet attendance at her tale, tracing evanescent arabesques in the night.

Then, discreetly, she tossed a choice mixture of roots into the blaze. At a touch from the golden powder, the flames danced with alacrity, casting giant shapes on the ground before the children's wondering eyes.

They let out cries of joy, then all heads turned as one toward Tunka, who lowered his own gargantuan one in respectful acknowledgment, setting the pretty flowers on his shell aquiver.

Menilmonea went on. "But the Mother was not power alone. Love she was as well, and from this love were humans born. She asked the Titans to watch over these newcomers, for they were fragile and mortal."

Seizing upon this solemn moment, she tossed mist powder into the fire. A delicate cloud formed, enveloping her listeners for a brief moment, creating a mystical, ancestral atmosphere.

Shrieks of excitement ran through the audience. The youngest children clung to the elders' tunics. But Menilmonea pursued her noble storyteller's mission undeterred, and went on, her face lit by flames that seemed to obey her every whim.

"The Titans then raised peaceful havens for the human folk in order to protect them, help them grow and multiply."

The children, who knew these legends by heart, awaited the next part with delight. Sparks from the fire found reflection in their wide-open eyes.

"And yet their mortality was not their fate. Not at all! In her infinite generosity, the Mother had offered them the gift of eternity, so that each human worthy of her love might join her through Ascension and dwell by her side in celestial paradise."

Abruptly, Menilmonea crushed two earsplitter mushrooms between her deft hands and a sudden boom rang out, rounding out her tale's dramatic climax and making the audience jump with delight.

"And so it is that for thousands of cycles, under the guardianship of the Titans, humans have lived in harmony with the Mother's precepts, and every village under the heavens is able to grow a little more with each passing day."

One final handful of firepowder, flung masterfully into the flames, informed the audience that it was time to applaud, which they did with wild enthusiasm.

One of the children, with tousled blond curls, raised his hand but had to wait till it was quiet again to ask his question.

"Yes, Amaral? Did you have a question?" Menilmonea inquired, smiling gently.

"Yes, yes! Does Tunka remember when he was born? Mama remembers when I was, but, well… I don't."

A cavernous voice, deep as the ocean, rose up. It was as though the thunder itself spoke, making the very night air shudder.

"Yes. I remember it quite well, in fact," Tunka replied. "I appeared one day, hundreds of cycles ago, at the foot of my Tower. A moment ago, I didn't exist and then, her will be done, I did. I never had the chance to grow up like all of you. The Mother's Tower created me just I am, standing here before you today."

"Oooh!" those gathered exclaimed in unison, transported by this tale from the dawn of time.

Another even younger child shyly raised his hand. His small voice shook slightly.

"Tunka... can you still hear her voice?" he asked, with a hint of hope.

The Titan remained silent for a moment, careful to weigh each word. Then, in a voice suffused with gentle melancholy, he replied, "Alas... no."

He let the silence hover for a moment, as the fire's embers crackled in the darkness, then continued.

"I never heard it again, and yet, I feel it inside me at all times. With every decision I make, every choice for the village, I let myself be guided by the words she spoke to me that day."

A respectful silence fell, then a murmur of admiration rippled through the children, their faces illuminated by newfound reverence.

"What about... us? How did we get here?" asked an innocent little voice, barely audible over the crackling of the flames.

Tunka gave a faint smile, his ancient eyes bright with timeless wisdom.

"As soon as I found a good spot to build my village, the Mother sent one of her guardians. With mysterious invocations, he made the first houses appear, then entrusted me with twelve bodies shrouded in ghostly white. Stiff in a slumber like death, they were, but one so strangely sweet and contented that it raised doubts: was it an awakening they awaited? Or eternal repose?"

Utter silence had fallen over the children, all enthralled by the tale. Every last one held their breath. Even the flames seemed frozen in their flickering, as if better to hear the Titan's words.

"I knew instinctively what I must do. The Mother had endowed me with the power to rouse these bodies and pass on the one true knowledge to them. With my help, the first humans were able to lead their lives, and following the Mother's precepts, beget many descendants who perpetuated their race... and so on and so forth. Until you were born, my children."

Thunderous applause broke out, completely drowning out the crackling flames and the explosions of powder illuminating the night. The children leapt for joy, their eyes agleam with wonder. The parents, amused but resigned, traded annoyed looks, wondering how they would calm this wave of excitement and convince their overstimulated offspring to go to bed.

As the clamor died down and the children rejoined their families, the atmosphere gradually returned to one of hushed tranquility. The fire, now a carpet of glowing embers, let off a mellow, wavering warmth. Menilmonea had remained seated, unmoving, her gaze fixed on the final flames as if hypnotized. In this quiet stillness, Tunka leaned slowly toward her.

"Thank you very much for your help, young lady. You have a true gift for telling our tales."

"Oh, it's nothing, Tunka! I love seeing their excited little faces, but I can't compete with you when you speak of our origins."

The Titan fixed his depthless eyes upon her for a moment before lightly inclining his head. "Why does your smile seem to hide a certain sadness?"

Menilmonea opened her mouth, hesitated, then lowered her eyes, fingers toying nervously with the hem of her tunic.

"I'm not..." She paused at length, searching for her words, before whispering, "I'm sorry, Tunka."

"What is it, my child?"

"I... I don't know. I ought to be happy; I ought to find satisfaction in fulfilling the Mother's precepts. And yet I can't seem to. I feel so... selfish. And different, too."

Tunka waited for a moment before asking in a tender voice, almost a murmur despite his power, "Why different?"

"As you well know, Tunka, I have a gift—or a curse, I can't tell anymore. And it's very obvious that sometimes people talk about me behind my back, whispers that stop the moment they see me."

"But we are all different, my child. I, of all creatures, ought to know."

Menilmonea gave a faint, fragile smile, and a gleam of irony entered her eye. "Yes, but you're the village Titan. The Mother's child."

"We are all the Mother's children. We were all chosen to serve her. She has plans for every last one of us. Even you, despite what you may think."

"But why give me such a gift? Why me? Why have I all these... desires? What am I meant to do?" she exclaimed, a hint of despair in her voice.

Tunka did not answer right away. His gaze grew lost in the starry night, seeking a proper reply in the heavenly vastness. "I cannot speak to your desires, Menilmonea. But as for your gift.... On that, I may perhaps shed some light."

Menilmonea wished to speak, but Tunka went on, his voice growing more somber.

"When your parents set you before me at birth, something happened in me. I still don't quite understand what it was. I don't know if that was the Mother's will... or if it was something else from deep inside. But one thing is certain: I felt a need. A need so strong I could not fight it. I had to take action."

Menilmonea frowned, intrigued. Instinctively, she leaned toward the Titan. "What are you saying?"

"When your parents pressed you close to me—when I gave you my blessing—a fragment of my spirit came loose and fused with your infant body." He paused before continuing. "The only thing I know for certain is that I felt an immense satisfaction once this was accomplished."

Menilmonea wasn't sure she understood what was happening, and her mind reeled at this momentous revelation.

Tunka went on, his gaze never wavering from the young girl's eyes. "I sincerely believe that your capacity to hear the forest, the roots and mushrooms, derives from this incident. Though I lack that gift myself, I think that for some reason, the fragment of myself passed it on to you."

The world seemed to wobble around her. So her power came from… Tunka? She'd had a part of the Titan in her since birth?

"But why didn't you ever say anything? Why did you wait all this time?" she asked, her voice trembling.

"I meant to, more than once. But each time, I told myself it would change nothing." He gazed benevolently at her, infinite tenderness in his immemorial eyes. "But lately, you've looked sadder than ever. I thought that perhaps knowing the truth might help you stop blaming yourself. This gift is no curse, Menilmonea. I believe it is a gift from the Mother."

She shook her head slightly, trying to take in this revelation that turned everything she knew upside down. "I… I don't know what to say or think, really. I'm lost."

Despite everything, she felt a strange lightness inside, as if some invisible burden had subtly been lifted from her shoulders. "I'm grateful you finally told me, Tunka. But still, I wonder… why this gift?"

"Perhaps the Mother knew our healer would be gravely injured, and that the best way to prevent this kind of problem in the future was to give us mycomancy? Honestly, child, I haven't a clue. But my theory doesn't seem wholly absurd. A Healer is an essential role for any village."

Menilmonea nodded slowly, her gaze lost in the final glowing embers of the fire. "True enough…"

They remained that way in silence, watching as the fire slowly went out.

Then, after a long moment, she dared ask the burning question on her lips, her heart pounding madly.

"Am I the only one?"

Tunka let the weighty silence linger before answering.

"No. Another child sparked the same reaction in me and also received a fragment of my spirit. But unlike you, it doesn't seem to have granted her any gifts whatsoever."

"Who was it? It wouldn't be Aureal, would it?" she asked, her eyes suddenly brightening at the idea.

The Titan gently shook its head. The plants on its shell rippled like a miniature sea.

"I cannot tell you. I understand your curiosity, but I don't think knowing would change anything. Besides, whoever this person may be, she surely has no idea what transpired."

Menilmonea took a deep breath, then acquiesced, accepting this limit. "I understand."

"Know simply that I am proud of you. You are an exceptional person. Differences are strengths for those who wear them proudly. You have a rare gift. Wear yours loud and bold. You should thank the Mother for allowing you to serve her so effectively."

Menilmonea lowered her eyes, pensive, absent mindedly tracing patterns in the dirt. "I... I think I just need some time to take this all in. Learning I've a part of you inside me was a shock."

Tunka burst out in deep laughter that shook the ground beneath them, like a rumble of distant thunder.

"Right you are. Get some rest, my child. Sleep on it. Trust me, you'll have greater insight into it tomorrow."

Slowly, Tunka stretched, and his enormous form cast a colossal shadow on the ground, like a living monument.

"And I shall do the same... for I feel sleep overtaking me already." With these words, the Titan rose ever so slowly and headed for the little pond where he liked to sleep, the ground shaking slightly with his every step.

"I can't thank you enough, Tunka!" Menilmonea cried as she watched the titanic figure grow distant against the starry sky.

Really very slowly, that is, she observed silently.

Something in his gait left a strange taste in her mouth, an indescribable impression that troubled her.

And she thought then that she, too, must be tired in mind and body alike after such a long day.

V

Menilmonea dragged herself from sleep with the delectable sensation of not having slept at all. Her mind felt far from rested; in fact, it was buzzing with thoughts that had assailed it until the wee hours of the morn. What Tunka had told her just wouldn't fade away. An obsession lodged in her skull that nothing could shake loose.

She wanted to talk to Aureal.

Now.

But... had she asked Tunka's permission? In the heat of the moment, she'd forgotten about this formality. An oversight she would correct as soon as she was ready.

She pushed back her covers, perched on the edge of the bed, and stretched to rid herself of any stiffness from sleep. The cool air in the house nipped at her skin, a reminder that the fire had gone out in the night. Wasting no time, she grabbed her tunic and quickly pulled it on, shivering slightly at the cold fabric's touch.

She reached for her bag of powders and pulled out two little fire mushrooms whose flaming red caps glowed faintly in the gloom.

Confidently, she took one in each hand and smashed them together. A white-hot light abruptly poured from between her fingers, and the heat spiked. Just before the sting became unbearable, she hurled them into the hearth.

A blast of warm air swept the room.

Flames rose up instantly, dancing frantically up and down the charred log. Satisfied, Menilmonea briefly crouched before the fireplace, watching sparks rise into the air as if they might bring her answers. But this wasn't one of those talking fires.

She straightened up and crossed the room toward her pantry. At first sight, there wasn't much to it: a basic cast-iron trapdoor set into the floor. But this seeming simplicity concealed an ingenious system for preserving food.

She pulled the heavy trapdoor aside and grabbed the pulley's hemp rope. A quick tug, and the mechanism came to life; a bluish glow emanated from the shaft. Her winter powders were still at work, keeping temperatures far below what they naturally would be.

When she plunged her hand into the frigid air, a shiver ran up her arm. She felt around for a moment before pulling out an egg still pearled with condensation from the coolness. Then another, whose immaculate shell reflected the firelight.

Kicking the trapdoor shut with one toe, she plucked a cast-iron skillet from the rack on the way back to the hearth. A knob of fat melted with a pleasing crackle, and soon the aroma of frying eggs filled the room, whetting her appetite.

For a moment, she studied the brilliant yolk quivering in the heat, hypnotized by its perfect roundness. A fleeting thought crossed her mind: *what if Tunka says no?*

She shook her head, shooing the thought away as she might a bothersome fly.

No. She had to be able to discuss this with Aureal.

Instead of savoring her meal, she wolfed it down, washed up quickly, and headed for the spot just outside town where the Titan held audiences with villagers every morning before the children's lessons.

On the way, she ran into the baker, arms laden with bread still warm from the oven, a kindly smile on her face.

"Already up and about, Menilmonea? You're quite the early bird today."

Menilmonea nodded and returned her smile before pressing on, no room in her mind for anything but what she would ask Tunka.

He'd mentioned a second child. He hadn't wanted to say more, but Menilmonea had a hunch it was Aureal. In fact, she was almost sure. Maybe if she told her friend that her own gift came from Tunka, Aureal would finally admit she even had one at all.

But once she got to where she was going, Menilmonea stopped short. The square where their guide received villagers every morning was empty. An eerie absence, almost unreal. Tunka was always there, always ready to listen and give counsel to all who came. And yet, this morning, he was missing.

A few villagers were waiting nearby, looking as puzzled as she was. Among them was the blacksmith, arms crossed over his chest, visibly vexed, his bushy eyebrows joined in a frown over his worried eyes.

Upon seeing Menilmonea, who he knew to be close with the Titan, he walked over and asked apprehensively, "Do you know where our Titan has gone off to this morning?"

He let out a sigh before continuing in a whisper, "I really needed his advice. Marla and I had a bit of a spat last night, and I was hoping he'd help me put things right."

Menilmonea raised an amused eyebrow, smiling slightly despite her concern. "Tunka would surely have told you to start by trying to drink less and listen more."

The blacksmith muttered something under his breath, but there was a glimmer of regret in his eyes. Everyone knew that behind his gruff façade, he was deeply attached to his spouse.

Seeing uncertainty overtake the other villagers' faces, Menilmonea spoke up, trying to hide her own anxiety. "He must still be sleeping. Perhaps last night's revelries wore him out."

There were a few murmurs from the small group, but no one had cause to complain. After all, even a Titan needed a little rest every now and then.

"I'll head over to the pond for a peek," Menilmonea said at last, her heart beating faster than she would've liked.

Without waiting for the others to respond, she turned for the woods, determined to figure out why, for the first time in as long as she could recall, Tunka was absent.

When she reached the pond, she let out a sigh of relief at the sight of the Titan's massive form slumbering peacefully. His immense carapace, covered in moss and wildflowers, seemed one with the surrounding landscape, as if nature itself had adopted him.

But as she drew closer, her relief turned to unease. Tunka wasn't moving. The slow rise and fall of his body that usually betrayed his breathing was so slight now as to be indiscernible. Hesitantly, Menilmonea placed a hand on his rough skin, still warm to the touch but lifeless as stone.

"Tunka?" she called out softly, her voice barely above a whisper.

There was no answer.

She frowned, and almost nonsensically, gave his head a shove. Obviously a Titan several stories high wouldn't budge so easily. But the utter absence of reaction worried her even more. A lump was slowly forming in her stomach.

Something was wrong.

The thought that Tunka might be dead struck her full force. An icy shiver ran down her spine, and at once she banished the absurd thought from her mind with a shake of her head. The Mother's Titans couldn't die; this much she knew. Yet Tunka's unmoving form disturbed her deeply. And with each passing second, foreboding seeped further into her veins, like a slow, depleting poison.

She tried raising her voice, calling out Tunka's name with greater insistence, each time a bit louder than the last.

Nothing.

The idea of tossing a rock at him gave her pause. It was flagrantly disrespectful, but the situation was far too worrisome for such scruples.

She picked up a pebble and threw it at the massive shell. It bounced off harmlessly with a sharp crack that echoed in the silent woods. Tunka remained still.

Frustrated, Menilmonea felt around in her knapsack and pulled out an earsplitter mushroom, its reddish top lightly pulsing between her fingers. Extreme, as her effects went; these mushrooms detonated loudly enough to wake the heaviest sleepers. She crushed one on the ground and held her breath.

A piercing sound rent the air and echoed from the pond like a thunderclap. Panicked birds took off in a flurry of wings, but still Tunka did not move.

Menilmonea's heart was pounding. A very real fear overtook her, rising like the spring tide. Whenever she had doubts, it was Tunka she came to see. He always knew what to say, when to speak and when to listen. His absence left her without bearings, lost in the unknown. He was the pillar on which everything was founded. The villagers were good people, but without Tunka, they were as a ship without a rudder. A wave of panic washed over her, threatening to drown her.

She took a deep breath and felt an invisible vise squeezing her chest, crushing her beneath the weight of dread. For a moment, she stared unseeing at the Titan's unmoving mass, and the desire to collapse to the ground right here and now, to give up on ever understanding, briefly crossed her mind.

She had to find Aureal. Her friend was the only one with enough composure not to sink into hysteria upon learning of the situation.

She hurried to her friend's house, heart hammering in her chest. She placed a hand on the door, about to push it open, then thought better of it. What if Aureal hadn't spent the night alone? The thought made her grimace, and she remained frozen for a moment on the doorstep, undecided. But urgency got the better of her.

She knocked, the sharp raps echoing in the morning silence.

After a few minutes that seemed to last an eternity, the door opened a crack, revealing a sleepy Aureal, still in a nightgown, hair disheveled and looking dazed.

"Menil! Why are you waking me so early? I had a late night, you know," she muttered, stifling a yawn.

Menil didn't wait for her to finish. Striding in briskly past her friend, she uttered in a somber voice, the enormity of her discovery apparent in her eyes, "Aureal, we've got a huge problem."

VI

Menilmonea shut the door behind her, clenching her hands so hard her knuckles whitened. The room was still dark, steeped in nighttime silence. The air inside was tepid, tranquil, in striking contrast with her inner agitation.

Aureal blinked, struggling to make herself fully present. She ran a hand through her tangled hair and walked over to the small hearth where embers still smoldered from the night before.

"A problem? What kind of problem?" she asked with a frown. "You look completely panic-stricken."

"It's Tunka! He won't wake up! I tried shaking him, yelling at him; I even used an earsplitter mushroom. He never budged, never made a sound; I couldn't even tell if he was breathing," she said, voice trembling with fright.

Aureal squinted, still bleary with sleep. She shook her head slowly, trying to think, to arrange events in a comprehensible order. Her gaze slid toward her friend, who seemed about to collapse: Menilmonea's bulging eyes betrayed a visceral terror.

"Hold on… Are you sure he's not just sleeping more soundly than usual?"

Menilmonea shook her head forcefully, her brown locks lashing her pale cheeks. "I'm sure. This isn't normal, Aureal. He won't move. It's like… he's not really there anymore."

Aureal swallowed, with difficulty. The gravity of the situation asserted itself with suffocating slowness. She grabbed a small urn sitting in the hearth and poured warm water from it over some tea leaves, unconsciously trying to slow time, to delay the moment when she'd have to fully face the reality taking shape before her.

"If that's true, we can't keep this to ourselves," she sighed, handing Menilmonea a steaming mug of tea.

Menilmonea took it, gripping it tightly between her chilly hands. The liquid's warmth spread, a soothing wave, through her numb fingers.

"But we can't start a panic for no reason either," she finally declared, calmer now. "The villagers won't know what to do. They won't understand; they'll get scared."

"You're right. I don't know what to tell you," Aureal confessed after a long silence, her gaze lost in the curlicues of steam rising from her mug. "If he doesn't wake up... what then? There's nothing we can do. We're not Titans."

The mycomanceress clenched her fists, looking for an answer. Her mind raced. "Well, we can't just stand here twiddling our thumbs, either! There must be a solution."

Aureal sighed, leaning against the table. She was still staring at her tea and her own blurred reflection on its surface.

"If we alert the village, what'll happen? As you say, they'll panic, and nothing will come of it. Tunka's always been our guide. We all depend on him." Aureal paused once more, then continued in a softer tone, as if attempting to persuade herself. "After all, the Mother knows all, sees all. What if it's not that serious, or even permanent? We should probably wait a bit before we panic."

"Hmm.... You might be right. But I don't really see why the Mother would do this to us. Much less why she'd do this to Tunka."

"Who are we to judge?" asked Aureal, raising her chin slightly with renewed assurance.

"Sure.... But the problem is that the village will wind up figuring out something's not right."

"You could always go stay by his side. If they see you looking after him, we might be able to convince them that everything's normal, and you know what's going on."

"Except I have no idea what's going on!" Menilmonea exclaimed, helplessly waving her hands.

"I never said that'd work forever. At any rate, if Tunka doesn't budge by tonight, then we can all panic. For real."

"I want to believe in your optimism, Aureal. Truly. Even if, deep down inside, I feel like this is a lot more serious than you're admitting."

"Let's give it a try. It's not like we have another option for now, anyway," Aureal concluded with serene resolve.

"Yes. And you're right about one thing. I can see if any of my powders or mushrooms do anything for him, after all..."

"See what happens when you put your mind to it?" Aureal teased, a smile briefly lighting up her worried face. "As for me, I'll hurry to the nursery and tell them I won't be in today. That way, I can test out my theory. If they don't start panicking, that means just explaining that you're looking after Tunka can mitigate the crisis for now."

Once the two friends were ready, they went their separate ways, each determined to carry out their part of the plan. Menilmonea headed for the pond with a heavy heart. The thought of finding the Titan as unresponsive as before made her throat feel tight, but she couldn't afford to lose her composure.

She arrived to find several villagers already gathered around the gigantic carapace, their faces alarmed and confused. An old woman murmured a prayer to the Mother; a child clutched his father's hand, looking lost, wide eyes riveted on the great unmoving mass.

Menilmonea drew a deep breath, doing her utmost to look calm and controlled, arranging her features into a mask of serenity that was the furthest thing from what she felt.

"Everything's fine," she declared in what she hoped was a reassuring voice. "It's nothing serious, I promise. Tunka told me this might happen."

Concerned and skeptical looks converged on her, studying her face as if for the slightest hint of falsehood.

"And... what should we do?" a man asked. He fiddled with the edge of his tunic, nervously tapping one foot on the ground.

"What we've always done, no more and no less," Menilmonea replied, kneeling down beside the Titan. "Go about with your lives as if nothing were the matter. On my end, I'll watch over him to make sure he wakes up as he's meant to."

Some of the villagers seemed uncertain, others relieved by this explanation. But in general, the sense of worry remained palpable. Menilmonea knew she couldn't reassure them forever.

She had to find a solution, and fast.

She waited until the last villagers had left, then breathed deeply, opening her senses to the surrounding forest. She shut her eyes and whispered, "If you know something, if you can help me, then please…"

The song of the forest was perceptible but seemed distant, as if muted by some unseen mist. Menilmonea sensed that nature wished to come to her aid but, powerless before this mystery, knew not what to do for Tunka.

Menilmonea opened her eyes, her heart heavier still. She faced this enigma alone.

Well, not completely alone, she thought after a few minutes of silence, crying out, "Over here, Aureal!"

Her friend had just reached the edge of the pond and couldn't see her from the other side of the gargantuan tortoise.

"Let me guess," Aureal huffed, out of breath. "The forest told you I was coming?"

"Uh-huh. You can't hide anything from me!"

This made them both burst out laughing, and the two friends needed a good laugh to give them the courage to face the problem that was now theirs.

"Do you think the forest can help us?" Aureal asked, serious again.

Menilmonea sighed and shook her head, a stray lock sweeping her forehead.

"I tried, but… even the forest seems powerless. I can hear its song, but it seems distant, uncertain."

A weighty silence fell over the pair of friends. The leaves' rustle, the lapping water, the birdsong… everything seemed normal, and yet something felt strange. The world was holding its breath.

As her gaze slid slowly toward the fringe of trees edging the pond, Menilmonea's eye was drawn by a barely perceptible movement.

"Aureal... do you see that?" she murmured, pointing discreetly at the far shore.

Her friend turned to look, squinting to scrutinize the shadows between the trees. "What are you talking about?"

"Look closer. There are so many animals. I can see rabbits, squirrels, badgers... even a fox, I think. They're watching us."

Aureal tried clumsily to feign surprise, her cheeks flushing a light pink.

"Oh, what a mystery! Animals in the woods, what next? Who'd believe it?" she declaimed in a mock-dramatic tone, posing with one theatrical hand on her breast.

Menilmonea gave her a dark look. "Very funny. Admit it, it's odd. They're all there, unmoving. As if awaiting something."

"Fine, I admit it! It's not normal. But I've never seen our Titan not wake up either. It's a day full of new experiences."

Menilmonea hesitated. For a moment, she eyed the shapes of animals at the wood's edge. This moment seemed one out of time and recalled to her the weighty secret she'd wished to share with her friend.

"Aureal... there's something I have to tell you," she murmured at last.

Her friend frowned, intrigued by the change of tone. "What's that?"

Menilmonea drew a deep breath, for courage. "My mycomancy powers..."

"Yes?"

"They come from Tunka. Last night, he confessed he gave them to me when he blessed me at birth."

Aureal tried to say something, but couldn't find the words. Her eyes searched Menilmonea's, trying to discern some attempt at humor, a jest to lighten the atmosphere.

"Are you for real? Did the Mother ask him to?" she finally burst out, eyes wide open.

Menilmonea shook her head, unsure, her brow furrowing with

concern.

"I don't know. Tunka told me he did it because he felt compelled to, but he didn't know if that need came from the Mother or from himself. That's why he'd never spoken of it to anyone before."

Aureal squinted in thought, pensively plucking at her lower lip with a finger. "But it could only have come from the Mother, right?"

"I don't know. For the first time in his life, Tunka wasn't sure of the answer. And that troubled him, I could tell. I didn't think to ask his permission to share this secret with you, but given his condition, I thought I could let myself."

"*And you were right to!* Goodness, I'm your best friend!" Aureal shouted, waving her hands in the air.

"And how!"

The two friends embraced to give each other both courage and comfort for the task that lay ahead, their intertwined figures reflected in the pond's placid waters.

The rest of the day flew by as Menilmonea threw herself into trying out various remedies. She did her best to stay determined in the face of the Titan's stasis. She applied poultices made from healing mushrooms and prepared decoctions infused with rare plants, but all to no avail. Each failed attempt only served to heighten her feeling of powerlessness, ever greater a weight on her shoulders.

Aureal helped her as best she knew how: passing her ingredients, adjusting dosages, and most of all, steering away curious villagers who'd come by for news. More than once, fretful onlookers turned up to ask if Tunka were doing better. Aureal reassured them as best she could, using her calmest tones to convince them it was all under control.

"He just needs rest," she repeated tirelessly. "Menil is watching over him, everything's fine."

But in her heart of hearts, she knew that nothing at all was fine, and that the future grew darker with each passing hour.

At long last, the afternoon was drawing to an end. The shadows of surrounding trees slipped from the shore, stretching across still waters, and a dull fatigue weighed on the girls' hearts. They had stopped trying. Nothing had worked. The Titan remained frozen in place, his body motionless, no sign of breathing.

Sitting by the water's edge, they gazed at the great unmoving mass, lost in their thoughts.

"So... what do we do now?" said Aureal at last, her voice, barely audible, breaking the silence.

Menilmonea rubbed her face with her hand, weary. There were dark rings under her exhausted eyes.

"I don't know," she admitted.

"We'll have to tell the villagers."

"Yes..."

Then suddenly Menilmonea's gaze brightened. A mysterious glimmer shone from her tired eyes, like a flame reborn from embers. "Hold on, I might have an idea."

Aureal looked up, intrigued, raising a single eyebrow. "Why do I feel like I'm not going to like this? You have that look like when you're about to do something the Mother wouldn't approve of."

"We must go to Gunderki," Menilmonea declared in a firm voice almost humming with barely restrained excitement.

Aureal understood right away, eyes widening slightly. "Their Titan..."

"Yes. If there's anyone who can help, it's him."

Illumined by this unexpected hope, Menilmonea's face now beamed with newfound determination.

Aureal crossed her arms and stared piercingly at her friend before shaking her head with a resigned sigh, half a smile hovering on her lips.

"You know, I get the feeling that despite how serious all this is, part of you is delighted at the excuse to set off on an adventure."

Guilty as charged, Menilmonea opened her mouth to protest, then thought better of it. After a moment's reflection, she gave a light shrug, and a sheepish smile flitted over her face.

"I'd be lying if I said the prospect of a long walk with a good friend dismayed me... though I'd rather it were for some other reason. A reason that doesn't endanger our village."

Aureal gave a faint, tired smile, a mixture of tenderness and worry in her eyes. "Well, let's go tell the villagers, then. You'll just have to keep up the act a bit longer."

"Yes. Obviously this isn't my favorite part, but I think I've come up with something to say to them."

She rose to gather her powders and phials, keeping her friend in suspense, then took her hand as they left the clearing for the village.

On the way, they were silent, each lost in her own thoughts, the only distraction their footfalls crunching on the forest floor.

At last, they reached the foot of the stairs leading to the village square. Menilmonea took a deep breath as she climbed. The invisible burden of deception weighed on her every step. She hated lying to her own people, but she had no choice. Fortunately, her friend was there by her side, her silent presence a pillar to lean on.

The Ascension bell held pride of place in the center of the village, hanging from a frame of carved wood. Its metal, tarnished by time, was scuffed with past tollings, mute witness to the many times the bell had pealed. Usually, it was rung when Tunka called upon someone chosen for Ascension to the Mother, thus marking the moment when they were to leave their loved ones and undertake the long-awaited journey to the sacred Tower. The villagers would then gather to say goodbye and attend their departure with laughter and song. But today, Menilmonea was about to give the ringing of the bell an entirely different meaning.

She seized the mallet hanging from its braided rope, gave Aureal a long look, and after one last breath, confidently struck the bell.

The sound rang out, deep and mighty, rising over the rooftops before being swallowed by the nearby woods, like a call scattered to the four winds.

Little by little, the villagers emerged from their homes and workshops. They flocked to the square, some exchanging worried glances, others already muttering conjectures. Something wasn't right. That much was clear. All gazes turned to Menilmonea as people awaited an explanation, their faces tense with uncertainty.

She summoned her courage and launched in, with more assurance in her voice than she'd have thought she could muster.

"My friends," she began, her voice carrying clearly to the far corners of the square. "There's something you should know. Tunka has fallen into a deep slumber and, despite our efforts, we are unable to wake him. But have no fear. He once told me this moment might come. It is a test the Mother has sent our way, an ordeal meant to strengthen our patience and prove our devotion."

Aureal raised her eyebrows, glancing at her friend. The slant Menilmonea had taken had caught her off guard, but to be fair, it made sense.

Murmurs rippled through the crowd. Some villagers nodded reassuringly, while others exchanged more mistrustful glances, weighing each word they heard.

Menilmonea snuck a furtive peek at her friend for strength, then went on. "Tunka told me what to do should this befall him. Aureal and I are to travel to Gunderki's village to consult him. Usually, such journeys are only undertaken every six moons to barter, but this time, the Mother herself has granted us her permission. This is an exceptional case, a mission necessary for the good of our village."

Aureal tried to convince herself that this blasphemy would be forgiven once everything was back to normal. A rumble—of relief for some, and doubt for others—ran through those assembled.

"We will leave at dawn, and we will return with answers. In the meantime, I ask you not to succumb to worry. Tunka is strong. He will return among us and continue to guide us all toward Ascension."

Menilmonea's gaze swept the gathering. Many folk nodded slowly, satisfied with the explanation. Some still seemed a bit puzzled. Children huddled close to their parents, trying to understand the proceedings.

But just when Menilmonea thought she had won the battle, a deep voice broke the silence.

"What if, despite Gunderki's advice, he doesn't wake up?"

The man who had spoken stepped forward. Greth, a hunter with a face weathered by wind and sun, stared at her with dark, piercing eyes.

"If he doesn't wake up, what then, Healer?" he continued in a sharp tone. "You call it a test, but who's to say it's not a punishment?"

A shiver ran through the crowd and the muttering grew louder, like the wind just before a storm. But Aureal had anticipated this.

She stepped forward confidently to come to her friend's aid.

"So you know better than the Titans now, do you, Greth? Who are you to doubt the words of the Mother's children?" she asked fiercely, eyes flashing with indignation. "The Mother will not abandon us, and I dare hope she will forgive your conduct."

Unsure how to respond, Greth looked sheepish all of a sudden. His shoulders slumped a little, for already, the vast majority of those around him knew that Aureal's words brooked no reply. Of course a Titan would know. That much was obvious.

Then several voices rang out, almost in unison, "Thank you both! We're counting on you!"

Someone in the crowd even began to clap, and soon all those in attendance followed. Even Greth, galvanized by the general atmosphere, applauded heartily, all uncertainty swept away by the communal enthusiasm.

Slowly, Menilmonea unclenched her jaw, which ached with stress, and felt the tension slowly drain from her shoulders.

They'd done it. At least as far as keeping peace in the village went, for the near future.

Tomorrow, they would set out. And if the Mother willed it, they would return... with answers.

VII

They decided to meet at Menilmonea's for the night. After stopping by her own house to grab a bag and a few travel items, Aureal joined her friend, and together they made a light meal before bed.

Menilmonea busied herself at the hearth, mixing herbs in a broth that steamed with intoxicating aromas. Aureal asked, "Tell me, Menil, what will the journey to Gunderki's village be like?"

"It's just shy of a day's walk. A beautiful one, especially after the river crossing. Once over it, we can follow the coast to Gunderki's Tower. The village is located on an inlet, and we must ford a stream to reach it. We should be there before sunset."

"Well, you were dreaming of novelty and adventure. It seems the Mother heard you! As for me, this will be my first such journey."

"Don't fret, I'll take good care of you," Menilmonea teased with a roguish grin.

"You'd better!" Then, after a short pause, Aureal's face darkened slightly. "I just hope Gunderki can give us the answers we need. After my outburst at Greth this afternoon, if we come back empty-handed, I'll go and bury my head in a rabbit hole."

"As you said earlier, my friend: we have no other option. It simply *must* work," Menilmonea said, not entirely convinced herself.

"You're right. The Mother won't abandon us!"

"Everything happens for a reason. Whatever it is, we'll find out!

Even if we have to ask the Mother in person."

Menilmonea knew that such a remark would surely incur her friend's wrath. Nor did Aureal disappoint, for her indignation arrived on its heels, as surely as night follows day.

"Menil! You'll bring us bad luck!" she cried, eyes wide.

The mycomanceress burst out laughing, a crystalline tinkle that echoed through the room.

"My apologies, I intended no disrespect. I merely meant that I would move heaven and earth to save Tunka, and I *pray* to the Mother to grant us her blessings in our endeavor."

"You're incorrigible. Even when you say you're sorry, I can tell you're making fun of me," replied Aureal, shaking her head with a smile of resignation.

They finished their meal in good spirits, trying not to dwell on what might happen should they fail. At least for a while, the warmth of their friendship would keep the shadow of unease at bay.

At dawn's first light, with the village still asleep, they set out in silence. The air was cool, laden with morning dew, and a light mist was rising between the slumbering houses, shrouding the landscape in an ethereal veil. The two friends exchanged a conspiratorial glance before setting off down the path. Their figures gradually faded into the morning mist.

The doubts and worries of the day before seemed to have dissipated, or at least been alleviated, by a restful night's sleep.

Along the way, Menilmonea stopped regularly to inspect the undergrowth, now and again plucking a few specimens she would slip into her bag with almost reverent care. Aureal looked on with a hint of bemused forbearance, arms crossed, foot tapping impatiently on the ground.

"Sure we'll be there before nightfall at this rate?"

"You didn't want to leave, and now you're in such a hurry to get there," Menilmonea replied, feigning indignation.

She finished harvesting a bluish mushroom, since Aureal claimed she'd spent far too long talking to it already, and then set off once more.

The Forbidden
Passage

The
Mother
Crown

Lone
Peak

👑 Gunderki Tower

Gunderki Village 🏠

Orondoki Village 🏠

⛪ Orondoki Tower

👑 Tunka Tower

🏠 Tunka Village

The World
of
Menilmonea

"Not at all! I just want to get this problem sorted out as quickly as possible so we can get back to our old lives," Aureal protested vehemently.

"Admit it, there's something exciting about all this! You and me, alone against the world…"

"Sure, though right now, it's more like you and every mushroom around."

The girls burst out laughing and continued on their way with light hearts, falling naturally into step with each other.

At last, they crossed the river north of the village. Its limpid waters lapped gladly at their ankles. A salt smell grew in the air as they neared the coast, and upon reaching the beach, they decided to take a break. They sat down on the warm sand to enjoy the soothing sound of the waves and savor their meal before moving on.

Prepared as usual, Menilmonea pulled a few eggs from her satchel and began making a fragrant omelet with fresh herbs. Soon, an appetizing aroma wafted through the sea air, and Aureal's stomach began less than discreetly to growl.

"That smells delicious," she admitted, rubbing her hands together in anticipation. "If you lose your gift of mycomancy, you could always try your hand at a market stall."

Menilmonea smiled, but her expression froze slightly as her gaze caught the edge of the woods where they met the shore. There a host of small, bright eyes glinted from the shadows: still, watchful. Rabbits, weasels, birds perching on branches…. They watched the girls with unusual, almost supernatural attention.

"Incredible, isn't it?" whispered Menilmonea, lowering her voice. "Since when have animals been interested in what we do?"

Aureal, who'd followed her friend's gaze, gave a shrug of feigned nonchalance, carefully avoiding Menilmonea's eyes.

"No idea," she replied, biting into a piece of bread. "Maybe they want to learn the recipe for your irresistible omelet."

Menilmonea shot her friend a sidelong glance. She knew Aureal well enough to tell this was an act, that there was something her seeming indifference concealed. But for now, she opted not to press the issue. With a slight sigh, she returned to her makeshift kitchen, casting one last intrigued glance at the silhouetted creatures that continued to observe them from the shadows.

The rest of the journey went smoothly. The way was peaceful, lulled by the sound of the wind in the leaves and the distant rolling of the waves. They walked at a brisk pace, enjoying the scenery and the surrounding calm. As they forged on, daylight began to wane, casting golden glimmers on the path and setting the sky ablaze with fiery hues.

Finally, just before the sun touched the horizon, they reached the ford. Before them stretched the river, lined with reeds quivering in the evening breeze. On the far bank, they could see the first lights of Gunderki's village, kindled one by one like nascent stars.

"Almost there," breathed Menilmonea, overcome by a feeling of relief alloyed with apprehension.

The two girls crossed the river carefully, the gentle current tugging them seaward as they reached the far side. No sooner had they set foot on the bank than they saw a farmer gathering the last sheaves of wheat from his field. He looked up, saw them, and gave a great wave, his face lighting up with a smile.

"Made it already, have you?"

"What do you mean?" asked Menilmonea, frowning.

"Well, you're from Tunka's village, aren't you? Or is it Orodonki's?"

A bit taken aback, the girls exchanged surprised glances before replying, "Er... yes, Tunka, that's right."

The farmer nodded, clearly satisfied, as his cap slipped slightly down his forehead. "Perfect! The Healer will be pleased. She should be at Bell Square. Hurry, go see her!"

Menilmonea and Aureal looked at each other again, surprised by this turn of events.

Nevertheless, they elected to do as they were told and, without a word, headed hesitantly toward the heart of the village, their thoughts whirling like leaves in the wind.

Once at the square, they saw Menara, the Healer, deep in conversation with a gaggle of villagers. Her tone was somber, and the faces around her reflected the general concern. When she saw Menilmonea, her face lit up with a bright smile.

"Menil! It's so good to see you again. We've been waiting anxiously for you!"

"Menara," replied Menilmonea, smiling in return. "This is Aureal."

Menara nodded to Aureal and invited them over. Her colorful shawl fluttered gently in the evening breeze.

"I knew Tunka would sense the problem and send help," she said with conviction. But when she saw the puzzled expressions on the two friends' faces, a furrow of concern crossed her brow. Frowning, she asked, "Tunka did indeed send you, did he not?"

Menilmonea hesitated for a moment before answering carefully. "Yes... in a way. But we really must talk to Gunderki. Tunka is asleep and won't wake up, it seems."

Menara's features froze, and she staggered a little as if from the impact of those words. "By the Mother! Gunderki hasn't woken for several days either. We were discussing what to do next with the rest of the village. We were hoping that the Mother would send us a sign... or that Tunka or Orodonki would sense the problem and send help."

Abruptly overcome by panic, Aureal took a sudden step forward, her face visibly pale. "Wait... Are you telling us Gunderki's asleep too? Our two Titans... both in a deep sleep from which they won't wake?"

She put a hand to her mouth as her gaze darted between Menara and Menilmonea. Her breathing quickened as she desperately sought a rational explanation.

"But... in the name of the Mother, what is going on?" she whispered, voice trembling.

Menara nodded slowly, worry etched on her face. "Come, let us go to the great room. You must be tired after your journey, and a good meal will help us think. We need to figure out what is happening."

Menilmonea and Aureal agreed, still reeling from the revelations. They followed the Healer through the lanes to a large wooden building where several villagers had already gathered. The smell of warm bread and zesty soup filled the air.

They took their places at a long table, and as steaming bowls were served, Menara sat down across them and clasped her wrinkled hands.

"Tell me everything you know about Tunka. How long has he been asleep? Did you notice anything unusual before his slumber?"

Menilmonea exchanged a glance with her friend before answering, trying to gather her thoughts.

"It happened almost all at once," she explained. "On the evening of the Feast of the Mother, he was normal. Although, thinking back, I found his gait particularly slow... even for a giant tortoise. Then, the next morning, he didn't wake up. I tried everything, but none of my powders or preparations had any effect."

Menara paled slightly and nodded.

"It's exactly the same with Gunderki," she said in a grave voice. "Except that it's been five days already. He seems to be asleep, but you can barely tell he's breathing."

Aureal felt a chill run down her spine. The thought that the same ailment could befall two Titans at once was terrifying, as if the universe itself were falling apart.

"Have you noticed any changes in the last five days?" she asked, searching for a glimmer of hope in this increasingly bleak picture.

Menara slowly shook her head. Her eyes reflected deep concern.

"No, nothing noteworthy... well, except perhaps one thing," she admitted after a moment's thought. "The vegetation on Gunderki's back seems to have accelerated its growth. Mosses, ferns, even small flowers have begun blooming faster than usual. He's lying in his usual spot by the river."

Menilmonea frowned, pensive. Slowly she put down her spoon and examined the worried faces around her, searching for an answer that none of them could provide, aware that the mystery was only deepening.

VIII

———

They finished their meal in a silence weighty with unanswered questions. The day's excitement faded away, swallowed by evening's shadows, ceding a palpable tension.

Menara set her cup down gently, the glass squeaking on the polished wood. She looked up at her guests, discreetly scanning the room before leaning toward them, her voice now a barely audible whisper, "Come, spend the night at my house. We can talk in peace, without prying ears. What we have to say need not concern the entire village yet. I've no desire to sow panic."

Menilmonea was not surprised. Menara had always been a cautious woman.

"Good idea," she agreed. "Better if we're somewhere quiet. And to be honest, a good night's rest won't go amiss."

"Perfect," said Menara with a satisfied smile. "I just need to pick up my children from the nursery."

Genuinely interested, Aureal tilted her head to one side, a spark of curiosity in her tired eyes. "Do you have many?"

Menara's face lit up, maternal pride momentarily dispelling the shadows of worry. "Four!"

Aureal whistled admiringly, eyebrows arching in surprise. "Four! Congratulations! The Mother will be proud of you!"

She glanced sideways at Menilmonea with a sly smile. The

implication was clear, but Menilmonea chose to ignore it and continued, "I met your husband last time. Is he with the children?"

Menara straightened her shoulders proudly and gazed up at an invisible horizon. "The Mother called him to her shortly after our youngest's first birthday. He went on ahead of us and must be waiting impatiently for me. I'll join him when my time comes."

She placed her hand on her heart.

"But enough talk about me and my family," said Menara, rising slowly. "I'll go get my little ones and meet you at my house. Go on ahead, it's the one just behind the bell, with the blue shutters."

Aureal sighed and crossed her arms as soon as Menara was out of earshot, lost in thought.

"What an incredible woman. She managed to keep her village together despite her Titan's absence."

"Yes, I like her very much. On my first Touring five cycles ago, she even took me under her wing to share her knowledge with me when I was just starting out as a Healer."

Without another word, the two friends headed for Menara's house.

They didn't have to wait long before she arrived with her cheerful brood, little living stars gravitating around their mother. She greeted them with a kind smile as she opened the door, the wood creaking softly as it welcomed them in.

"Let me see to the little ones, and then I'll be all yours," she added with a wink.

Menilmonea nodded and immediately offered, "I can help you make dinner if you'd like."

"And I can help feed and put the children to bed," added Aureal with a sincere smile.

Menara paused for a moment and gave them a grateful look. "You're so kind. Come, let's go inside, it's getting chilly."

With the children in bed and dinner over, the three women gathered around the fire. The flames wove a cocoon of comforting warmth. Menara watched them for a moment, a burning question on her lips.

"By the Mother! How were you ever able to get away?"

Menilmonea gave a slight smile before replying calmly, "I had to bend the truth a bit. I told the villagers that Tunka had warned me such a moment might come and that, if it did, I should seek advice from Gunderki. That reassured them... and prevented the village from falling into chaos."

Menara nodded slowly, impressed by the mycomanceress' presence of mind. "Well played. Your village needed stability, and you gave them a convincing explanation."

Aureal looked up at the sky. "Let us hope the Mother forgives us such blasphemy."

"Indeed," replied Menilmonea, her gaze dark. "But alas, since Gunderki cannot help us, we have but one option remaining."

Menara frowned. "Orodonki."

"Exactly. If he hasn't been struck by this mysterious affliction as well, perhaps we could go see him with Aureal and ask his advice. After all, we've already made one journey, we might as well make another. Orodonki is... what? Two days away?"

Menara crossed her arms, her thoughts swirling behind her focused gaze. "Yes, just about, but I wonder if it's wise. I could use the notion that 'Tunka warned you' to send one or two strapping young lads to see Orodonki, and in four days we'd have an answer. Meanwhile, you and I could pool our skills and knowledge. I haven't a fraction of your abilities, but I'm still a fairly good Healer. If we can wake Gunderki, everything will be easier."

"I think that's an excellent idea!" Aureal exclaimed before her friend could even open her mouth. "And if I can be of any help to you or the village in the meantime, I'd be happy to!"

Menara replied promptly, a bright smile on her face. "Well, I hadn't dared bring it up, but I've noticed how you handle the children, and I'd love to have your help at the nursery. We're overwhelmed. The village is very devout; we've had a lot of births and quite a few Ascensions recently, so we're a little short-handed when it comes to looking after the little ones."

Without even waiting for Menilmonea to respond, Aureal exclaimed. "Well then, we have a plan!"

Menilmonea burst out laughing when she saw how determined

Aureal was to avoid more traveling. Nonetheless, she nodded with an amused smile.

"I must admit, it's a good plan," she conceded.

The next morning, Menara rose at dawn to tell the village the news. In a voice that left no room for doubt, she explained that Tunka had planned for this moment, and that emissaries must be sent to seek advice from Orodonki. Concerned though they were, the villagers welcomed this explanation with relief. Two volunteers were chosen, and set off within the hour.

The days that followed were spent researching and experimenting. Menilmonea and Menara pooled their knowledge, testing sundry preparations and powders in hopes of waking the sleeping Titan. Each attempt taught them something new, but none produced the desired result.

On the fourth evening, they sat by the hearth in almost utter silence. The only sound was the soft crackle of the flames as they cast flickering shadows on the walls of the house.

Menilmonea sighed as she looked at her hands, worn by long days of work.

"Tomorrow we will have word of Orodonki," she whispered. "Let's hope it's good."

"May the Mother hear you," said the other two in unison.

IX

The next morning, the three women woke up feeling worried. Unable to concentrate on anything else, they decided to wait together in the great room. They were soon joined by other villagers. They talked about this and that, trying to ignore the anxiety that gripped them.

Time seemed to stand still, each minute stretching out endlessly, as if the universe itself were holding its breath. Whispers and forced laughter were a poor defense against the growing unease. Some villagers tried to reassure each other, trading wild guesses about what could be done. Others remained silent, their faces frozen in fear.

In the early afternoon, the door to the Village Hall burst open. The two envoys rushed in, panicked and breathless, their faces marked by exhaustion and despair.

"Orodonki fell asleep!" one panted.

"Before we could reach his village!" exclaimed the other.

A heavy silence fell over the room, quickly replaced by a cacophony of worried voices. The villagers rose brusquely to their feet, faces anguished.

"What will become of us?" someone cried.

"Are we going to die without being able to Ascend?" added another voice.

"Has the Mother abandoned us?" a woman burst out, a sob catching in her throat.

Menara raised her hands to calm the crowd, but her eyes betrayed her own distress. She opened her mouth, but no words came out. She seemed lost, unable to offer a coherent answer.

It was then that Menilmonea spoke, her voice clear and rising above the din, "Tunka said... that if this happened, we should go to the village's Tower to speak directly with the Mother."

Silence fell once more. The revelation had shocked one and all. Floored, Aureal opened her eyes wide.

"What? What was that?" she whispered.

Menara frowned, clearly as perplexed as the others. But, against all odds, those words were enough to calm everyone down. The thought that all was not yet lost held out a glimmer of hope. And for now, that was all they needed.

Menilmonea took a deep breath and added in a tone she hoped was convincing, "All this will soon be resolved. The Mother will come to our aid."

Without another word, she motioned for Aureal and Menara to follow her.

"Yes... that's it! Let's go to my house to prepare for your journey," stammered Menara.

No one said a word on the entire walk home. All this seemed so supernatural that their minds refused to form coherent thoughts. Once there, they sat down at the kitchen table, staring off into space.

Aureal finally broke the silence by asking the burning question. "What was that all about?"

Menilmonea drew a deep breath before answering hesitantly. "I-I don't know, it just felt like the right thing to do."

Menara burst out in a somewhat nervous laugh before adding, "Well, you really are full of surprises. I must admit it worked, and it bought us some time."

Aureal chimed in. "Sure, but... Gunderki's Tower? Really? You do recall the Mother *absolutely* forbids us to even approach the Towers? Tunka's told us that often enough. Only the chosen ones are allowed to enter."

"I'm aware of all that, but let's face it: the Mother doesn't seem to be hearing our prayers. Maybe she doesn't know what's happening to her Titans."

At these words, her two friends' faces turned white as sheets.

"Menil!" Aureal hissed, hunching her shoulders as if to slip unnoticed past their goddess' scrutinizing gaze.

"I know, I know. I'm well aware of what I'm saying. But we must admit that something drastic is afoot. No one can deny it. Nothing like this has ever happened since the Mother brought us into the world and entrusted us to the Titans. Exceptional circumstances call for exceptional measures. I think that if we approach one of her Towers, perhaps she will hear us. Or perhaps we will finally understand why she remains silent."

She paused, letting her words sink in. Her thoughts whirled, torn between the certainty of her intuition and the magnitude of its implications. She knew hers was the right direction, but between knowing and accepting it lay a chasm. She had never been particularly pious, but this was the ultimate blasphemy.

She needed some tea.

She rose and put the kettle on before suggesting, "Some tea would do the two of you good as well."

She took a deep breath, her eyes fixed on the simmering water, then went on. "At any rate, we're backed into a corner. We don't know how to wake the Titans, we don't know where the other villages are... All we have left are the Towers. Aureal, I'd understand completely if you wanted to go back to our village. I would never ask you to sacrifice yourself for me, but I believe I must do this. Should the Mother wish to punish me for it, I'll understand... but I must try. I cannot leave Tunka like this."

Aureal replied right away, tears in her eyes. "Don't be silly! Of course I'll go with you. How could I ever look at myself in the mirror if I let you go about this madness on your own? We shall face this ordeal together, as we have always done."

She paused before adding, more seriously, "And anyway, what other choice do I have? Go home and die of old age without ever making my Ascension?"

Menara looked sadly on in silence for a few moments before sighing. "I-I would like so much to go with you... but I cannot. I cannot abandon my village, let alone my children. They need me here."

Then she added, a glimmer of admiration tinged with melancholy in her eyes. "You are both braver than I could ever be. Facing the unknown, defying the forbidden... Few would have such strength. The Titans themselves would be proud of you."

Her fingers, clutching her dress, tightened for a moment before she said at last, tremblingly, "May the Mother protect you."

Whereupon Menilmonea and Aureal took Menara in their arms, as much to thank her for her support as to comfort themselves.

Menara wiped her nose before going on in a soft voice, "Stay here tonight. You can leave tomorrow, fresh and rested. I'll ready food for you. The Tower is north of here, not even two hours' walk. You can't miss it."

The two friends gratefully accepted. Menilmonea added that she would use the rest of the afternoon to stock up on roots and mushrooms, while Aureal planned to try to relieve her stress with a nice bath.

The evening that ensued was convivial, filled with laughter and shared memories. Menara tried to keep the mood light, avoiding any mention of the next day's departure as best she could. They spoke of the years gone by, the passing seasons, village traditions, even a few amusing anecdotes. The shadow of the next day still loomed, but for a few hours, they were able to forget, and simply enjoy the moment.

X

Silvery flickers of dawn tinged the sky when Menilmonea and Aureal left Menara's house. Before departing, they hugged her tightly to bid her farewell and give themselves courage.

The path they trod was the one taken hundreds of villagers before them had taken to join the Mother through their Ascension, and knowing this lent their steps solemnity. Slowly the still-sleeping village vanished behind them, and they each seemed lost in their thoughts. The only thing to break the silence was Menilmonea's murmuring to certain mushrooms she found by the wayside.

But after a while, Aureal's lengthy silence began to trouble Menilmonea. Paying closer attention to her friend, she noticed that Aureal seemed nervous, glancing frequently over her shoulder, as if something were truly unsettling her.

"Are you well, Aureal?" she asked softly.

Aureal jumped slightly, clearly startled, before stammering, "Y-yes, everything's fine."

Menilmonea raised an eyebrow and said with a smirk, "You've given more convincing performances."

"What do you mean? I'm just afraid of what we'll find in the Tower."

"Aureal, you're like a sister to me. I know you inside out. Tell me what's wrong."

"Menil, cut it out! Everything's fine, I tell you!"

"After all this time, everything we've been through together these last few days, you still won't talk to me? We're about to break one of Mother's greatest taboos, risking who knows what punishment, or worse, and despite all that, you think I'd judge you if you opened your heart to me?"

A long silence set in. Menilmonea gave her friend plenty of time to take the last few steps toward the precipice of truth. At last, Aureal replied softly, without looking up at her, "I'm so sorry. I... I've made fun of you so often all these years. I don't know how to tell you what I want to confess without your hating me."

"I'm not saying I won't tease you for years on end to settle the score, but know this: I will never hate you. I only want to understand what you're going through. I'm here for you. You will not be judged or hated."

"I... I just might have a strange gift too."

Menilmonea pretended to be shocked and opened her eyes wide.

"*What?*" she said, laughing.

"Please, Menil, this is already horribly difficult."

"I'm sorry. I'll keep quiet. Just pretend I have no mouth. Only ears."

"I'm not sure I like that image."

"Mmmhmhmmh..."

"Ha ha! Fine, you win. All right, well... I can... feel animals. Most of the time, it's just a distant clamor, an echo at the fringes of my awareness, like a muffled song I can hear without really listening for it. But sometimes, this murmur becomes clearer, more urgent. It rises, sharpens, and that's when I can feel the animals' will, their curiosity, their fear as well. They don't really talk to me, not with words or images. It's a breath, a vibration, an emotion that... occurs to me. A kind of presence: floating, fleeting. For a long time, I believed it a curse, noise I had to ignore. I did all I could to stifle it, but that never made me any happier. So I live with it, trying not to think about it. And most of the time I manage just fine."

Menil nodded in agreement and opened her arms wide to give her friend a fond hug. Aureal accepted the invitation wholeheartedly.

"I'm still here. See? You're not wanting to be the other weird girl in town? I understand that completely. Honestly, at least this way you were able to fit in. And if you'd told me earlier, you wouldn't have been able to lecture me about being more discreet," she teased with a mischievous grin.

Aureal felt tears welling up in her eyes and took a deep breath before confessing:

"I feel so much better having shared this burden with you. Thank you, Menil."

"And now I know who else received a part of Tunka."

"Yes, apparently I'm part tortoise too," she joked.

The image gave them both a hearty chuckle.

Menilmonea took advantage of the moment to press further, feigning indifference. "So why were you constantly looking over your shoulder?"

Aureal stiffened slightly before admitting in a low voice, "Oh, right. Well... something's been following us for a while. I've an inkling it's the fox you saw at Tunka's pond. I think he was there at the beach, too. I'm almost certain, because unlike all the other animals I can sense around here, he has a very strange 'presence.'"

Menilmonea frowned. "Strange how?"

"I can't sense him at all. I can see he's there because the animals around him are aware of his presence, but to me, he doesn't exist. I can't hear him. He's like... a shadow. And yet, if I look where he's supposed to be, sometimes I can spot him. He's there, but he doesn't make a sound in the other animals' 'song'."

"And he's been following us? You're sure of that?"

Aureal nodded solemnly. "Yes, and the oddest thing of all is that the other animals have no fear of him. You'd think rabbits would be scared of a fox. But no, on the contrary: it's as if his being there soothes them."

Menilmonea peered about, carefully scanning their surroundings. "Is he here now?"

Aureal nodded and pointed to a spot at the edge of the forest. "Yes, right there in the grass, at the edge of the woods."

Menilmonea squinted and stared where her friend was pointing, but the vegetation was too dense. With a shrug, she concluded, "If he'd been hostile, he could have attacked us long ago. Let's keep going but keep our eyes open.

"Or rather, keep your 'gift' open," she said with a grin.

She grabbed several fire mushrooms and twirled them between her fingers before adding with a smirk, "And if he gets too close, I'll roast him."

The rest of their journey went smoothly. The fox was still following them but didn't seem to want to get any closer. When they stopped for another break, Menilmonea tried once more to catch a glimpse of him, but to no avail, despite her friend's directions.

"We're going to have to figure out what he wants," she said at last.

"Yes, you're right. Though I've almost gotten used to his 'shadow.'" Aureal smiled.

"Why, careful there. You're almost waxing philosophical!"

"It must be our adventures. I'm maturing," she shot back with a laugh.

"You see? In the end, leaving the village isn't such a bad thing."

"True, but I won't hide the fact that I can't wait to be home, see Tunka and go back to our quiet lives."

"May the Mother hear you."

"Sure, but... maybe let's try not to draw too much attention to ourselves right now?"

"Ha ha! Indeed, let us avoid incurring her wrath."

They ate the bread and jam that Menara had prepared for them, then set off again.

There was a pleasant scent of moss and damp earth in the air as Menilmonea and Aureal climbed the final hill. The path narrowed as they progressed, eventually dwindling into a simple dirt track lined with tall grass and wildflowers.

Then, all at once, the Tower appeared.

A titanic monolith rose from the heart of the valley below, so tall it seemed to touch the heavens themselves. Its stone walls, streaked with flashes of pure energy, appeared older than the very world. Vines snaked down its sides as if nature itself had birthed this structure.

The two friends stopped dead in their tracks.

Breathless, they tried to take in with their eyes what lay beyond measure. The immensity of the construct overwhelmed them, inducing a faint vertigo like a tightening in their chests. It was a striking testament to the Mother's power.

They knew the Towers were tall. They knew they were ancient. But seeing one before them was an entirely different experience.

"By the Mother..." Aureal whispered.

Menilmonea looked away from her friend for a moment, lips parted, unable to form a thought in the face of this colossal entity.

A long shiver ran down her spine.

"I hope we're not doing something stupid," she finally said, a nervous smile playing on her lips.

Aureal swallowed, then nodded slowly. "Only one way to find out. Besides, you dragged me all the way here. I'm not turning back now."

"Why, it's as if we've switched roles," Menilmonea said with a laugh.

"I'm a devout woman, Menil, you know that. But we've already gone too far in our transgressions; we might as well go all the way and succeed in saving the Titans. Otherwise, we'll have no excuse for our actions."

"That's why I love you, you know? You're my source of energy."

"Exactly! And speaking of energy, were you expecting something this... awe-inspiring?"

"To be honest, I don't even know what I was expecting. But whatever it was, it would never have measured up to the reality."

A respectful silence settled in between them, broken only by the rustling of the wind. High above, the birds looked tiny, their white shapes whirling in a fleeting ballet around the cloud-draped summit.

Aureal ran a hand through her hair, then took a deep breath.

"Well, let's go," she whispered, more to herself than to her friend.

And so, impelled by their combined strength, they set off down the path toward the valley where the Tower stood.

A presence behind them, lurking in the tall grass, was pleasantly surprised.

XI

At long last, the two girls reached the foot of the Tower, draped in a mantle of greenery, a tangle of roots, vines, and thick moss scaling the ancient stone as if in siege. Despite its daunting appearance, time and nature had begun to stake their claim.

A monumental arch yawned before them like a sleeping monster's maw, opening onto a vast dark room, its ceiling lost to shadows. Inside, the architecture was just as spectacular as the Tower itself. Massive pillars, their upper reaches vanishing into the gloom, stood guard on either side of the hall that stretched before them.

Menilmonea narrowed her eyes, peering into the depths of the space. In a pensive voice, she murmured, "It seems the forest has invaded the inside."

Lush vegetation had made the smooth stone walls their own, covering them in a carpet of soft moss. Roots snaked everywhere between cracks and joins; vines fell in curtains of shifting shadow. The smells of earth and undergrowth emanated from the imposing hall.

Something in this fusion of mineral and living matter exuded a strange solemnity that hushed the friends to a whisper.

"Do you think we can go in?" Aureal finally asked.

"I... don't know," Menilmonea dithered. She remained silent for a moment before looking up at her friend, in her eyes mixed glimmers of uncertainty and glee. "And if I'm to call out to the Mother... what should I say? Greetings? 'Milady? Ahem?'"

Aureal giggled, then shrugged. "Not a clue. We're not supposed to talk to her before Ascension. But in any case, we must be respectful."

Still standing on the threshold of the great archway, Menilmonea took a deep breath and, after a moment's hesitation, gathered her resolve. In a timid but steady voice, she called out into the darkness, "Excuse me? With all due respect, we must talk with you... Milady."

The two friends waited for a reply, a sign, anything that might indicate the presence of a goddess. But nothing came. Only the sound of birds could be heard, their distant song breaking the sacred silence of the hall. The pair exchanged glances, torn between perplexity and apprehension.

Aureal smiled, breaking the tension slightly. "Well, first of all, we're not dead, which, given the situation, is a genuine victory."

Menilmonea gave a faint grin before replying, "Do you think we should go in? I think I see a light in the distance."

"Honestly, I don't know. Why aren't there torches to illuminate this place?"

"No idea. But one thing's for sure: we're not going in together."

"How's that?"

"If the Mother, in her wrath, strikes me down for violating her Tower, I want at least to leave this world knowing you're unharmed." Without waiting for her friend's reply, Menilmonea stepped over the threshold.

And immediately crumpled to her knees.

"By all the Titans, Menil!" Aureal was about to dash forward, but the mycomanceress motioned for her to stay put.

"No, wait. I'm fine. I just had this terrible feeling when I stepped inside. I can't hear the forest anymore. Instead, there's a deafening silence."

Aureal frowned. "You can't hear its song anymore?"

"No, not a sound. It was a shock, but I'm fine now."

Without further ado, Aureal reached out to help her up and lead her outside. Menilmonea's face lit up at once.

"Incredible! The song has returned. It's as if the forest isn't allowed inside the Tower."

Aureal glanced about, intrigued. "And yet there are all these vines and creepers right before our eyes!"

Nodding, Menilmonea tried to say a few words to the vines and moss, hoping for a reply, but there was only silence.

"I don't know if they can't hear me or if they don't understand, but at any rate, they're not speaking to me. Still, I can still hear the forest's song, even if it seems distant."

Aureal nodded thoughtfully. "That's odd. We're literally in the middle of a thick wood."

Menilmonea agreed. "Yes, but it's as if the Tower is repelling the song."

She took a deep breath, regaining some semblance of assurance. "Now that I know what to expect, I'll be fine."

Aureal smiled and nodded. "And we also know you're not about to be struck down. I'm going in too."

They crossed the threshold together. Aureal couldn't keep from gagging. "You're right, it's disturbing! I can't sense the animals anymore. As you say, this silence is hard to bear."

They ventured deeper into the growing darkness. Little by little, their eyes adjusted and they began to make out the contours of the room. At the back, untouched by vines and creepers, stood a circular structure. It looked like a great big ring giving off a golden glow.

Intrigued, they approached it. Looking closer, they saw flashes of light racing across its surface, briefly illuminating the air around. A multitude of dots of different sizes and colors hovered gently, as if hung from above. They cast an eerie glow on the stone walls. The air around the ring hummed almost palpably with energy.

Aureal squinted, fascinated. "What is that thing?"

Menilmonea hesitated, then called out again, "Milady?"

Aureal smiled at the absurdity of the question. "Do you think the Mother's a ring?"

Menilmonea sulked, uncertain. "Sorry if I'm a bit lost. However, you seem to know exactly what it is, don't you?"

"Not at all. But I know what it isn't," Aureal said with a laugh.

No sooner had she finished speaking than a disembodied voice rang out. "Come forward, dear Chosen Ones."

Menilmonea couldn't hold back a nervous giggle at her friend's bewildered face. Eyes full of mockery, she whispered, "Well?"

Ignoring the teasing, Aureal stammered, "Is that you, Goddess?"

The voice replied immediately. "I am not the Mother. I am only a Spirit tasked with helping the Chosen Ones on their path to her."

"A spirit? But where are you?" asked Menilmonea.

"Directly before you. I dwell in the ring-shaped structure. Come closer, please. The Mother has entrusted me with the very important mission of showing the Chosen Ones how to invoke the transport runes. This will enable you to join the Mother through your Ascension."

"But we're not here for our Ascension," Aureal said, shrinking her head back into her shoulders.

"What's this? I do not understand. If you didn't come for your Ascension, then why are you here?"

"We need help. Can you communicate with the Mother?"

"I am a Spirit tasked with helping the Chosen Ones on their journey to her. I do not speak to the Mother. That is not my mission. If you are not the Chosen Ones, you should not be here. Please return to your villages."

"Do you have a name, Spirit?" asked Menilmonea.

"I have no name. I am only a Spirit tasked with helping the chosen ones on their journey to her."

Menilmonea turned and took her friend aside. She whispered, "It doesn't seem dangerous."

"Nor very clever."

"No, indeed. However, it is the closest entity to the Mother that we have at our disposal at the moment."

"We could always try interrogating him subtly?"

"Yes, I was thinking the same thing. Let's try asking it for help with the Titans."

Satisfied with their chat, they turned back to the ring, and Menilmonea took the floor. "We are here because our Titans will not wake up. Can you help us?"

"If you are not here for your Ascension, please return to your villages."

"But if we do that, there will never be another Ascension. The Titans are the ones who tell us when we are called. Help us, please."

"If you are not here for your Ascension, please return to your villages."

Just then, Aureal had an idea.

"Mr. Spirit," she began, not daring to look at her friend, though she could hear her stifled laughter quite clearly, "were I here for my Ascension, what would you do?"

"If you are here for your Ascension, please approach the map. Touch the glowing white circle. This will open a passageway from here. Then stand in the golden fluid at the center of the ring and touch the green rune that will appear directly before you. Do not touch any other runes."

Aureal turned back to Menilmonea.

"Hear that?" she whispered.

"Yes, it's... it's unbelievable. We can travel to the Mother."

"Except... she didn't call us." Aureal paused before continuing. "Why did he say not to touch any other runes?"

She turned back to the ring and asked, "What do the other runes represent?"

"The other runes represent all the Titans' Towers. But for your Ascension, you must only invoke the rune of the Mother."

Aureal took Menilmonea by the hand, guiding her back toward the entrance. "I have an idea."

"Yes, I think I'm thinking what you're thinking. It's risky, but less so than going to the Mother's without an invitation. And at least we know that the Towers seem safe."

"Sooner or later, we'll surely come across some Titans who aren't asleep!"

"By Tunka's shell, we must!"

With these words, the girls joined hands and headed for the ring, reinvigorated by their newfound hope.

When they reached the structure, Menilmonea drew a deep breath and solemnly announced, "Spirit, we are ready for our Ascension."

The disembodied voice immediately replied, "Perfect. Please follow my instructions. Approach the map and touch the glowing white circle. Then stand in the golden fluid and touch the green rune that will appear."

With some trepidation, the two friends stepped onto the outer edge of the ring. They spotted the white rune and touched it lightly. At once, the points of light disappeared without a sound.

The two friends exchanged hesitant glances, then stepped over the slight lip that kept the golden fluid contained. It was warm and slightly sticky.

"Like syrup," Aureal remarked, eyeing the viscid substance.

Once in the center of the pool, they were surrounded by numerous runes. Several were red, some orange, and many yellow. And amidst all the others, in the very center, stood a single green rune. One of the orange runes was ringed in white.

Menilmonea frowned and asked, "Does the rune ringed with white represent Gunderki's Tower?"

The spirit replied in an even voice, "I don't know who Gunderki is. The selected rune is the starting point."

The two friends exchanged puzzled glances before turning their attention back to the runes glowing all around.

Menilmonea and Aureal stared. Suddenly, the air seemed denser, almost electric.

"Well," whispered Aureal, "which one do we pick?"

Menilmonea suppressed a shiver before shrugging her shoulders. "Any one except the green one…"

Aureal exhaled slowly and nodded. The green rune glowed gently, as if inviting their touch. They turned their attention back to the orange rune ringed in white. It was clearly pulsing in a different way from all the others.

"Let's try a color that isn't orange," Menilmonea finally said.

"Sounds good to me," said Aureal confidently, and without thinking, she touched a red rune.

Their eyes met, and instinctively they closed their eyes and clenched

their teeth.

A shudder ran through the golden pool. The runes lit up in a hypnotic dance, then vanished.

"You didn't touch the green rune!" exclaimed the spirit. "You must—"

Before it could finish its sentence, the golden fluid suddenly stirred. A wave spread over its surface, as if from a stone tossed into still waters.

Without warning, the world tilted.

A flash of blinding light swallowed them. The ground disappeared beneath their feet. They were overcome by a dizzying falling sensation that snatched a wail from their throats.

Then, silence.

When they opened their eyes again, they were still in the pool.

XII

The walls and massive pillars were lit only faintly, from glimmers cast by the ring's flickering energy. Everything was silent, oppressive. For some unknown reason, the light from outside no longer seemed to illuminate the room.

Menilmonea exchanged a glance with Aureal. She felt her heart pounding fit to burst.

"Are you all right?" she asked in a low voice.

Aureal bobbed her head, though a shiver ran down her spine. "Yes... I think so. I felt like I was falling while staying in place."

Menilmonea gave a slow nod. "Me too... As if... as if the ground had been pulled out from under our feet."

They exchanged glances again, the shadow of a doubt lingering between them. Everything seemed the same as before... but different.

Aureal squinted as she looked around.

"Why can't we see outside? And where did all the vegetation—" She hadn't yet finished her sentence when a deep, calm voice rose from the dark.

"Welcome, dear Chosen Ones. I must admit that your method of arrival is unconventional, but I won't complain. Not after nineteen rotations without an Ascension."

"Spirit, the magic of the ring didn't work," Menilmonea ventured. "We're still in the same place. Though, for some reason that escapes me, the light outside has suddenly dimmed."

"Where, exactly, is this place you claim still to be in?"

"The... middle of the ring?"

"Yes, I can see that. But I have the delightful feeling that this vexes you."

"Let's just say we were hoping to reach another Tower. Perhaps we should try again?"

"Aha! Now I understand the misunderstanding. Actually, you've just arrived. It does so happen that the Towers look very similar and the Mother's transport magic moves you without giving you the sensation of movement."

"So... we're not in Gunderki's Tower anymore?" asked Aureal.

"I don't know who this charming Gunderki is, but what I can guarantee is that you just arrived here. Whence you came, exactly, I cannot say."

The two friends took a moment to digest this information.

"So it worked," Menilmonea whispered. "That's amazing."

"How long did the trip take?" Aureal asked aloud.

"It is instantaneous."

"Then why is it nighttime here?"

"Oh, that... Yes, my Tower had some trouble several rotations ago, and sadly, since then, the door has been... stuck."

"You mean you've been here in the dark for... When you say a rotation, what exactly do you mean?"

"A rotation of the planet."

"Pardon me?" Aureal glanced at Menilmonea to see if she understood what the spirit meant. She deduced from her grimace that Aureal had no idea what a "rotation" or a "planet" was either.

"I see. I haven't been sent the best and brightest, have I? Anyway, we have plenty of time, the Mother's magic must flow back into the ring before you can make your Ascension. Please sit down on the benches provided to either side... And for the Mother's sake, do stop splashing about in the transport fluid."

Without a word, the girls sat meekly down on one of the few benches they could make out in the dim light.

The spirit resumed speaking, visibly delighted to finally have someone with whom to do so. "The world you live on is a planet. That is, a huge sphere of rock, dirt, and water. A rotation is the time it takes for our planet to revolve around the sun. You do know what that is, don't you? The big ball in the sky that hurts your eyes when you look at it?"

"Yes, we know what the sun is," replied Aureal, offended.

"Well, that's something."

To Menilmonea, Aureal whispered, "What's this about planets and balls of dirt?"

"He's one of the Mother's servants, he must know lots of things. And frankly, I find the notion reassuring. I've always wondered, if you walked far enough, whether you'd walk right off the edge."

"Apparently not, if we're to believe Mr. Know-It-All."

"I should point out, for the record, that I can hear you anywhere in this room," the voice chimed in.

"Sorry," replied Aureal, blushing.

"Think nothing of it. Right, then! So, a rotation is used to measure the passage of time, you see? As it's an unchanging cyclical phenomenon, it's very handy for knowing that I've been locked up here *for quite some time*. But how do you measure time, for example? How old are you?"

"I'm ten cycles old," replied Aureal.

"And I'm thirteen," added Menilmonea.

"And how do you know when a cycle ends?"

"When winter returns. It's one cycle when it gets cold again and the first snow falls."

"By the Mother! How primitive. But well, it comes to much the same thing, if less precise. Under such conditions, how do you divide up a cycle? For example, how long is the gestation period for your people?"

"How long between conception and birth, you mean?" Aureal clarified.

"Correct. It's usually a constant."

"About ninety days. We count the days. From the moment the *sun* rises to when it rises again."

"I see. Well, you should know that a rotation lasts about three hundred and sixty-five days."

"Fascinating," Aureal mused.

Menilmonea gave a gentle laugh.

"So you're telling us you've been here for nineteen cycles?" she asked with a hint of pity in her voice.

"Yes, nineteen... cycles. I won't hide the fact that I'm delighted to have visitors. Even if this is the first time anyone has arrived through the ring. Normally, people only use transport magic to leave. In fact, since we've plenty of time, you'll have to tell me how you managed it."

Menilmonea glanced at Aureal, hesitating. Should she tell the Spirit the truth? Aureal caught her gaze and gave the faintest of nods.

"Well... our Titan and the Titans from the neighboring villages have fallen asleep and don't seem to want to wake up. So we decided to go to one of our Towers in the hope of speaking with the Mother."

A silence fell. Then the Spirit replied curtly, "But you can't speak to the Mother. The Mother speaks to you."

There was a pause, as if it were weighing its words before adding, in a voice tinged with nostalgia, "When she saved me and entrusted me with the important mission of guiding the Chosen Ones, I heard her voice. It was... magnificent."

"She saved you?"

"Yes. I can't really remember clearly, but I was dead and she brought me back to life, for she knew I would be proud to serve her. She then entrusted me with an important duty, and I am happy to fulfill it. Although, as you can see, it has grown more challenging of late."

"Were you once human?"

"I don't think so... I'm not sure, but I don't feel like I was. To be honest, I only remember things that are useful for my duties. However, I know things that you seem unaware of. And your people seem so strange to me..." Then, after a slight pause, it went on. "But I'm surprised: how could the Spirit and Guardian of the Tower you came from allow you to do such a thing? Normally, you're only meant to use the rings for Ascension."

"A Guardian? There was only one Spirit in the previous Tower. And it was... polite."

"No Guardian? How... surprising."

"If I may," Menilmonea noted, "you don't seem to have a Guardian here either."

"Oh yes, I do. But he's a bit... flat."

"Where is he?"

"Right behind you, but you can't see him. He's in the shadows."

"I can fix that," said Menilmonea proudly.

She reached into her bag and pulled out two sun roots, rubbing them forcefully together in her left palm straightaway. An intense, somewhat orange glow burst forth at once, bathing the room in a soft golden light that seemed to radiate from her very hand, casting shifting shadows on the massive pillars.

Aureal's eyes widened. "Impressive."

Slowly, the girls turned toward the entrance to the room, and what they saw took their breath away.

Giant boulders completely blocked all passage. Stupendous blocks of stone, covered with cracks and moss, seemed to have been piled there deliberately. There was no way out. No hope of seeing the outside.

"By all the Titans!" Aureal whispered.

"But I still don't see the Guardian."

"Look closer," replied the Spirit.

Menilmonea cautiously stepped forward, her palm wide open, searching for the mysterious Guardian. The flickering light then reflected off a metallic surface protruding from the foot of the rubble. Aureal drew closer in turn, squinting for a better view.

It was an arm. A massive arm made entirely of metal, frozen in a strange position, as if its owner had tried to free himself before being buried by the mass of rock.

Menilmonea knelt down, running a hesitant hand over the smooth, cold surface. She could make out patterns etched into the metal. Ancient runes, intertwined, ran the entire length of the arm. The overall structure was too complex to be a mere artifact. This limb must have belonged to something... or someone.

"By the Mother..." whispered Aureal. "The Guardian! It's—"

"Buried," Menilmonea finished in a tense voice. "The rest of its body must be completely destroyed under that rubble."

A heavy silence fell as the magnitude of their discovery sank in.

"It must have been enormous," whispered Menilmonea.

"Oh yes! He was splendid. Several yards tall. His runes pulsed, glowing with the power of the Mother. He, too, had been saved. She'd given him this body to guard the Tower and guide the Chosen Ones to me."

"But what happened?"

A long silence fell before the spirit replied. Its voice was tinged with unusual gravity. "I don't know... I can't see beyond these walls. But one day, he came running in. He seemed... panicked. He didn't have time to tell me anything before those rocks fell from the sky and crushed him."

Aureal and Menilmonea exchanged worried glances.

"Fell from the sky?" Menilmonea repeated, her throat tight.

"Yes. In an instant, it was all over. The Guardian reached out to me... and then vanished under the stones. The runes on his arms continued to pulse for a few moments, and then... nothing. Since then, I've been here all alone. Waiting." The Spirit paused, as if gauging the impact of his own words. "Until... today."

After another long pause that the two friends did not dare interrupt, the Spirit spoke again. "But back to your story about the sleeping Titans. That's never happened before, I imagine? I understand your reasoning, then. What I don't understand is why you wound up here. The Ascension to join the Mother couldn't be easier in principle. Why, it's child's play. The green rune, and ta-daa! Even you should be able to figure that out, right?"

Aureal lost her temper. "Hey! We're here because we didn't want to be whisked off to the Mother without being invited!"

"And so...? You chose a rune at random? Whatever for?"

Menilmonea was tickled to see her friend so get carried away at the Spirit's mockery. "We're trying to find a Titan who isn't asleep. We hope that, as children of the Mother, they'll be able to guide us."

The Spirit let out something of an amused sigh.

"Yes. Clever of you, in the end. Especially since, even if by some miracle the Mother didn't strike you down when you reached her Tower, once you've Ascended, there's no turning back. Her Tower is the end of the road."

Menilmonea frowned. "What do you mean?"

The Spirit seemed almost perplexed by her question. "Well, if you take a transport ring to the green rune, don't imagine that the Mother will welcome you with feast and fanfare before she gives you a tour of the place. The green rune sends you straight to Ascension."

Aureal paled slightly. "You mean... to heaven, with the Mother, right?"

The Spirit paused before replying in a neutral voice, "Most assuredly."

It seemed to waver for a moment before catching itself. "What I mean is, paradise is a one-way street. Once you're there, you can't come back here to heal your Titans."

"So our plan wasn't so stupid after all," Aureal piped up. "The problem right now is that, of all the Towers out there, we had to end up in your ruined one."

"Young lady! A little respect! I am a servant of the Mother, after all!"

"Exactly," Aureal continued, mischievously. "So it'd be nice if you helped us, wouldn't it? We're doing all this for the Mother's children, after all. We could've been selfish and gone on to Ascension without even being invited, and washed our hands of this entire predicament."

The Spirit seemed to ponder this a moment before replying. "Indeed, indeed... What I can do is show you a rune where it's certain the Titan isn't napping."

Menilmonea raised an eyebrow. "How so?"

The Spirit adopted a more professorial tone. "The colors of the runes indicate the last time they were used. If you pick a yellow rune, you will go to a Tower where the last Ascension took place less than seven days ago."

Aureal nodded, intrigued. "Oh, I see. And orange and red, then?"

"Orange represents one lunar cycle. Red, a full rotation."

The two girls exchanged glances. They finally understood a little better how the Towers worked... and how to avoid making a mistake next time.

The Spirit said, "So I'm guessing my rune was red when you touched it."

"That's right," Menilmonea replied.

"Dark red, even," she added with a laugh. Then, regaining her composure, she said, "Sorry, I meant no offense. I can't imagine what it must be like to be trapped here for so long."

"Don't fret too much about me," the Spirit replied evenly. "I serve the Mother, and that's all that matters. Besides, I think you've likely answered one of my biggest questions."

Menilmonea and Aureal exchanged curious glances.

The Spirit went on, "I've been wondering all this time why the Titan from my village hadn't come to remove the rocks. They're all giants themselves, after all; these stones shouldn't be a problem for them. But... perhaps he's asleep as well."

A brief silence fell over the room as this revelation sank in.

"If you find a solution," the Spirit continued, "promise me you'll come back and help my Titan too. Remember, I am the scarlet red rune!"

The two girls laughed heartily.

As if on cue, the ring began to glow brightly and lightning flashed across its surface once more. The map reappeared with its multitude of dots, one of which was ringed in white.

The spirit then declared, "That's it, the Mother's magic is infusing the transport ring again. You know how it works. I wish you both success in your quest."

The girls thanked the Spirit. Before leaving, Menilmonea asked, "Have you a name?"

A little sadly, the Spirit replied, "I think I did, once... but I can't recall."

And with that, the girls touched the white spot and stood in the

center of the golden fluid. Menilmonea took her friend's hand and, her voice choking with emotion, said, "Thank you, Spirit! You're a good soul."

She touched a yellow rune, and a moment later, the room was once again silent and dark.

XIII

When they opened their eyes again, the golden light of late afternoon filtered through the large archway of this new Tower. Here, the vegetation had yet to assert itself. Only a few intrepid mosses had ventured to colonize the large stone slabs.

Aureal took a deep breath, her voice tinged with a mixture of respect and admiration. "The magic of the Mother... is... incredible."

Menilmonea nodded silently.

As they freed themselves from the transport fluid, a voice rose from the shadows, deep and calm, resonating with astonishing clarity.

"Welcome, dear Chosen Ones." Then, after a pause, "That is, you are here for your Ascension, aren't you? Because in two hundred and forty-two rotations, you are the first ever to arrive through the ring."

The two friends exchanged amused glances, intrigued by the positively exorbitant number of rotations mentioned.

"Alas, dear Spirit, we are not here for our Ascension. Not yet, at least. Actually, we were just passing through. Hope that doesn't cause you too much trouble."

"Oh, you know, I'm starting to get used to exceptions. Just imagine: a little less than a moon ago, I received more than twenty-seven Chosen Ones *all at once!*"

"Twenty-seven people came together?"

"Yes, indeed! Of all ages, too. I've never seen the like. I usually receive about ten travelers per rotation. I can't tell you how chaotic it was! I had to arrange for them to depart in groups. It was quite a bit of trouble, if you must know. But then, the Mother didn't appoint me for no reason, and I must admit, I conducted the operation smoothly! It took almost the whole day, with breaks to recharge the ring, but in the end, everyone was able to leave for their Ascension."

"Impressive," Aureal said, playing along.

"Yes, thank you very much. I quite think so myself."

"And do you know where all these people came from?"

"From the village associated with the Tower, of course! Where else would they be from?"

"Yes, of course. I mean... do you know where that village is?"

"I haven't the faintest idea. I take my task seriously, you know. I don't ask nosy questions."

"How respectable."

"As you say."

"And your Guardian? Might it know where the village is?"

"Perhaps. But first we'd have to find out where he is."

"Has it disappeared?"

"He has indeed. I haven't heard from him in almost half a rotation! Now doesn't that just take the cake! We were both selected by the Mother, after all. He was never very talkative, but he did his share of the work. That said, I'll tell you one thing: he never struck me as being truly invested in his duties, if you know what I mean?"

"I see..."

"At first, he would guide the Chosen Ones to me. It was a great help to everyone, you know? Made things more solemn. Since he left, everything has been dumped on me. And I insist the job be done properly!"

"That's to your credit," replied Aureal, clearly amused by the conversation.

Menilmonea spoke up. "We thank you for your patience, but we won't take up any more of your time. We'd like to get back to the village before nightfall."

"Leaving already, are you? What a shame! In any case, you're a charming pair. It does me good to talk to civilized people. Have a lovely day."

The two friends walked away smiling, their eyes twinkling mischievously.

As they stepped through the door, they gasped. A wave ran through their bodies, and suddenly their connection to their gifts returned, filling their minds once again with a familiar presence. Menilmonea immediately felt the song of the forest humming all around her, while Aureal instinctively brought a hand to her chest as if to absorb this rediscovered sensation.

"That feels good," Menilmonea breathed. "I don't like that empty sensation."

"Tell me about it," replied her friend, massaging her temples. "When I think about it, I can't figure out why the Towers block our gifts like that."

"Right you are. It's truly incomprehensible. Still, it delights me to hear the forest again."

She closed her eyes for a moment, steeping in the ancient murmur, the soft, serene music she found so reassuring. It was a feeling like no other, as if a part of herself had been returned to her.

When she opened her eyes again, she looked around with renewed attention. This Tower was laid out differently. Although its architecture was identical to Gunderki's, its site was quite different. Here, the edifice stood alone on a hillock in a vast meadow where grasses rippled in the breeze. Instead of encircling it as a setting might a gem, the forest began farther down and stretched into the distance. Only a few scattered trees dotted the slope, casting their long shadows in the fading light. A path wound gently toward the edge of the woods.

Menilmonea narrowed her eyes, lost in thought. "I wonder where this Guardian has gone."

Aureal, already scanning the horizon, was quick to answer.

"Not far, actually," she said, indicating a large shape lying halfway down the path to the woods. "Look over there."

Menilmonea looked where her friend was pointing and felt her breath catch in her throat.

A gigantic golem lay there, completely covered in vegetation. Vines had wrapped round its massive limbs, and moss colonized the cracks and crevices of its metal body. Its posture left no room for doubt: it was dead.

The girls slowly descended toward the poor Guardian, stopping when they reached it to drink some water and catch their breath. If this Tower was the same distance from its village that Gunderki's had been, they would reach their destination just before nightfall.

Menilmonea placed a hand on the metal, her fingers gliding over the runes engraved along the torso.

"This alloy is just like the one from the previous Tower," she noted. "The same inscriptions. Except this time, we can see the entire body."

Aureal looked more closely, frowning. "I'm no expert, but... it looks like the head is missing. Or maybe these things just don't have heads?"

Menilmonea, circling the imposing carcass, came to an abrupt halt.

"Here," she whispered, her gaze dark. "It looks like it was... torn off."

Aureal crossed her arms, her face growing stern. "This is starting to add up. First the Titans fall asleep, then a Tower is besieged by boulders, and now a Guardian is slain and beheaded."

She paused, thoughtful, then continued more seriously, "Come to think of it... we didn't see a Guardian at the Tower we started from. Maybe it suffered the same fate."

Menilmonea nodded slowly. "Truly, this is disturbing. Who could have such a grudge against the Mother's creations?"

"Who... or what?" replied Aureal with a slight shudder. "Anyway, I hope I never come across whatever did this. Did you see the size of that golem? Standing up, it must have been over ten feet tall!"

"The other thing that troubles me are all the brambles and moss on its body. That's the only place they grew. Look around! There's nothing but grassland right up to the woods." Menilmonea took a few sips, then added, "And just like in the other Tower, I can sense the presence of these plants... but they don't seem to understand or want to respond to me."

Suddenly, she stopped talking. Something was wrong. A lump

98

formed in her stomach, and she felt a sudden tightness in her chest.

Aureal frowned, worried. "Are you all right? You've gone pale all of a sudden."

Menilmonea put a hand to her chest, as if she couldn't breathe. "I don't understand. I feel… anxious, but I don't know why. It's almost hard to think clearly."

Aureal placed a hand on her shoulder. "Sit down. Let's rest for a while."

Menilmonea shook her head, a lost look in her eyes. "The song… the forest's song has changed. It's… so sad, so melancholy all of a sudden. No, more than that… several emotions are intertwined. I feel anger, but also infinite sadness. It's like… like a mother mourning her lost child. It's unbearable. I don't understand what's happening."

Aureal looked around, searching for an explanation. "Especially since I don't really see what could have caused this sudden change—"

With these words, she tottered slightly and placed a hand on her stomach, eyes wide.

"By all the Titans! The animals have sensed something too. They're scared. They… they're telling us to run, Menil. We must run for the woods. *Now*!"

She shook her friend to snap her out of her trance. "We must leave at once, Menil! Something is coming! Hurry!"

Menilmonea blinked, struggling to reconnect her mind to reality. She stood up hastily, and a sudden cry escaped her lips. "Mother defend us!"

Following her gaze, Aureal turned and saw, in the distance, beyond the Tower, a massive creature emerging from the landscape, like a nightmare woven from leaves, grass, and mushrooms. A misshapen mass, an oblong sphere shot through with eldritch throbbings, was advancing on them, shredding the soil in its wake. Its surface was studded with sinuous vegetal protuberances, like so many moving tendrils seeking to probe their environment. From its center, a dozen inhuman eyes glowed with a sickly light, radiating an ancient, unfathomable madness.

"What is that horror?" whispered Aureal.

"I don't know, but... it's the source of the forest's sadness," replied Menilmonea, her voice trembling.

"Then let's get out of here right away!"

Without another word, the two friends dashed for the woods, running as fast as they could.

"We'll never make it in time!" cried Menilmonea, breathless. "Let's hope the trees protect us!"

"It's our only option!" replied Aureal. "The animals are panicking, pointing me toward the woods. We have to trust them!"

The creature was closing in on them with terrifying speed, tearing up the meadow every time it lurched forward. The din was deafening, a rumble like a raging storm rolling across the land. At least fifteen feet tall, it advanced, thrusting out huge plantlike tentacles that speared brutally into the ground. Every time one of these appendages contracted, it sent clods of earth flying and the monstrous body jerking relentlessly forward. As it advanced, new tendrils reached out, anchoring themselves deeply before yanking the entire body along, while the older ones disintegrated into a cloud of organic particles that hung in the air. Beneath this writhing mass, countless plant-like growths writhed frantically, constantly adjusting its equilibrium.

Running, panting, the two friends didn't dare turn around. They could feel the presence getting closer, much too quickly. The noise had become unbearable, a cacophony of crackling and rumbling that pierced their eardrums.

"It's too fast!" cried Menilmonea, her eyes full of tears. "I'm so sorry I dragged you into this, Aureal!"

They still had a quarter-mile to go till the edge of the woods when Aureal screamed, "Menil! It'll be all right, trust me! Don't stop! Got it? No matter what happens, keep going straight ahead. Don't think! Just keep running!"

Menilmonea could tell from her friend's tone that there was nothing more to say. She knew her inside out, and senseless though it seemed, she knew Aureal had a plan. Something. A way out of this desperate flight.

And just when the creature was only a few hundred yards away, several dozens of wolves burst from the woods in a pack. If she hadn't already been terrified, Menilmonea would undoubtedly have had a panic attack.

The wolves raced past the other way, slavering, eyes riveted on their target, muscles rippling beneath their dark fur. There was something majestic about this savage ballet: as the girls ran for the safety of the woods, these magnificent predators lunged without hesitation toward danger.

At their charge, the entity stopped dead in its tracks.

The girls did not reach the woods so much as collapse into them, legs giving way from strain and fright. Their hearts were pounding, and they had to force themselves to breathe deeply to recover some semblance of control.

They leaned against the rough trunk of a mighty oak and were finally able to get a good look at their pursuer. About sixty feet from the forest's edge, the chimera of plant matter stood completely still atop several thick vines, swaying gently as if in the breeze. Its crazed eyes now seemed tinged with sadness and melancholy.

In front of it, the wolves had formed a semicircle, a living wall of fangs and tensed muscle, their low growls filling the air with palpable tension. Neither side made a move.

Menilmonea, still panting, whispered, "I-I think you saved us."

Aureal shook her head, unable to tear her eyes from the scene before them. "It wasn't really me, but.... Yes, I do think the terror unlocked something. I sensed that I could ask them for help, and... they heard me."

She paused, searching for the right words, then continued in a troubled voice, "I felt something like a wave in the usual tumult, a kind of wave that swept everything else away. And I knew, in some inexplicable way, that everything was going to be okay. I could sense a desire to help us, a certainty that we would be protected. It was... deeply unnerving."

Menilmonea's breathing slowed slightly, and she looked on, worried.

The creature seemed to have calmed. The wolves' growling had died down, leaving only a tense silence. Then, after a few minutes,

the entity spun around in an uncannily fluid motion and went on its way back whence it came, unhurried, as if nothing at all had just happened.

In spite of this, the wolves stayed where they were, still as sentinels, no doubt to ensure the chimera did not change its mind.

In silence, the two friends watched it leave. When it disappeared over the horizon, Menilmonea asked, her breathing still uneven from the stress, "What do you think we should do now?"

Aureal had not taken her eyes from the wolves. "I think they want us to leave as quickly as we can."

Menilmonea scanned the surroundings. "Except we're not on the path anymore. Maybe we can get back to it by following the edge of the forest.... No, wait, I... I think I know where the village is!"

Aureal turned her head toward her, intrigued. "How?"

Menilmonea placed a hand on the oak's bark and closed her eyes for a moment. "The forest.... Its song is still deeply sad, but there's something else. It's as if... it wants to guide us. It's a bit muddled, but I feel like it's pointing the way."

Aureal smiled nervously. "Fine by me. After what we've just been through, nothing can surprise me anymore."

Menilmonea let out a hearty laugh.

"So now we know what destroyed the Guardian," she sighed, tilting her head toward the unlucky golem.

Aureal glanced its way before nodding. "Yes. Mighty as it was, it was no match for... that."

"I wonder if it's the same thing that destroyed the other Guardian."

"The problem with the transport rings is that we have no idea where we are. We could be months away from our village. That said, given how that thing moves, it must be able to reach other Towers fairly easily."

"Right. So let's not hang around. Might as well put as much distance between it and us in case it changes its mind about our fate."

Aureal turned back one last time toward the pack of beasts. In a soft voice, almost a whisper, she said, "Thank you. We will always be indebted to you."

Menilmonea smiled slightly. "I'm glad to see I'm not the only one whispering and getting replies that no one else can hear."

Aureal burst into full-blooded, liberating laughter that momentarily dispelled the weight of accumulated fear. She straightened up, recovering her usual cheerful, determined tone.

"Come on, let's go! I can't wait to slip into a warm bed after a good meal. Now, don't get us lost, okay?"

Menilmonea rolled her eyes, amused. "Yes, Mistress!"

With that, she whispered a few words to the woods and felt the faintest of quiverings in answer. Then, without looking back, she set out toward the village with a confident step.

XIV

The two friends had been walking in the twilight for nearly an hour when a bend in the path at last revealed a village on the horizon. A look of relief briefly crossed their faces, but soon vanished just as quickly.

"Aureal..." whispered Menilmonea, slowing down. "Do you see that? Something's not right."

Aureal narrowed her eyes, scanning the village by dusk's faltering light. The air was heavy, almost still.

"Yes, the houses.... It's like they've been swallowed up. Devoured by vegetation. As if the village has been abandoned for cycles!"

Aureal's gaze took in a door half-hidden beneath thick roots, a broken window whose cracked glass lent daylight's final flickers a sinister edge. A shiver ran down her arms.

"This isn't right," she muttered. "It hasn't simply been abandoned. This is... something else."

"I don't like this at all," Menilmonea whispered, her throat tight. "The spirit of the Tower told us that several villagers went to Ascension less than a moon ago. They must have still been living here before they left, right? How did they cope with all this vegetation?"

Without another word, the girls moved forward slowly and cautiously. Each breath they took seemed to disturb the heavy silence. When they reached the first houses, they knocked nervously on the doors, but to no avail. They glanced furtively through the windows, calling out timorously, "Hello? Is anyone there?"

A mocking silence was their only answer.

As they ventured farther down the deserted lanes, their unease grew. Their footsteps echoed like a trespass on a fragile equilibrium. Upon reaching the center of the village, they came to an abrupt standstill, dumbfounded.

Before them stood a Titan, frozen and forlorn. Petrified. His imposing body was nothing more than cold, unspeaking stone. Yet on his back, vegetation flourished, vibrant, as if thriving on the fertile compost his corpse had become.

Menilmonea swallowed hard, her eyes fixed on the crisscrossing roots and foliage that stretched from the Titan to the houses.

"It's him," she whispered. "He's the one who swallowed everything... or at least what's left of it."

Aureal's face wavered between disbelief and horror. "But... it can't be! Titans are immortal! They are the Mother's children.... Menil? I.... What nightmare is this?"

Her voice broke, and she suddenly collapsed in tears. Her body curled up, racked with uncontrolled sobbing. It wasn't just the pain these discoveries prompted, but also the utter destruction of everything that had sustained, guided, and comforted her since childhood. Her breathing was ragged. She covered her face with her hands to hide the distress caused by this unbearable betrayal.

"Everything I believed in my entire life... all the hymns, the prayers, the stories... Was all of it just... a lie? I don't want to believe that, Menil. I can't..."

Menilmonea crouched down before her friend and took her in her arms. She understood Aureal's pain, though she did not feel it as intensely. Aureal's faith had always been her armor, guiding her in her daily existence.

"Come," Menilmonea whispered softly. "We'll find a house where we can collect our thoughts. We need to eat and get warm."

Aureal nodded, resigned. They settled on a house that the vegetation had largely spared. Inside, the pantry was still well-stocked, as if the owners were about to return at any moment.

Menilmonea lit a fire in the hearth. Its crackle created a pleasant atmosphere that the friends sorely needed. She grabbed an old skillet and fried up a few slices of bacon with some sautéed potatoes, seasoning them with garlic. The smoky smell of grilled fat filled the room, but Aureal remained subdued, staring silently off into space.

"Are you all right?" Menilmonea asked softly.

Aureal was slow to answer. She wrapped her arms around herself as if to contain the turmoil within.

"I don't understand anything anymore, Menil. Where is the Mother? Why does she remain silent in the face of such horrors? I don't understand what's happening. Ever since she created the Titans and our villages, we've led happy lives. Why does everything seem to be falling apart all at once? Why isn't anyone helping us?"

Aureal's voice trembled, betraying the fragility of her shattered certainties. She felt an icy fear at the thought that all she believed to be true might be naught but illusion.

Menilmonea placed a comforting hand on hers. "I don't know, Aureal. I don't understand it either. I don't know what to do, but I promise we'll find out. The best thing for us right now is to get some rest. We'll see things more clearly tomorrow after a good night's sleep."

Aureal looked up at her with teary eyes, jaw quivering. "But what are we going to do, Menil? Keep going from Tower to Tower looking for a Titan who isn't dead or asleep?"

"If there are no other options, then yes! It's up to us! There's no way we're going to let Tunka die like that poor Titan!" Menilmonea declared with fierce determination.

"But... he might already be dead," Aureal whispered. "I'm sorry, Menil, but we may already be doomed. We'll never make our Ascension. One day, we'll disappear into nothingness!"

"No!" the mycomanceress exclaimed. "If we give up, then yes, he'll die, and eventually, so will we. But so long as we keep trying, anything is still possible!"

"Try and understand.... Everything I believe in is gone. It's destroying me from the inside. But you're right.... I'll pull myself

together. We're going to save Tunka! We'll figure out something to do! Even if we must go to every Tower the Mother sets before us." Aureal let out a sigh before adding, more quietly, "If the Mother... is still there."

"Don't say that!" Menilmonea fiercely replied. "Of course she is. We'll figure out what's going on, I promise! Even if we have to go ask her ourselves. Nothing can stop us as long as we're together!"

Aureal gave her a weak but sincere smile.

Menilmonea smiled back before stretching with a hint of amusement. "But to do all that, we need to sleep first."

"And I wouldn't mind a quick wash either," Aureal whispered with a weary sigh.

They didn't dare sleep in the beds upstairs, so as not to further infringe on the privacy of the house's absent owners. And also, no doubt, to stay close to the comforting hearth. Lying on blankets they'd spread out near the dying fire, they struggled with slumber that refused to come. They were exhausted, but their minds kept racing, haunted by the image of the petrified Titan and the uncertainty of what tomorrow would bring. Aureal tossed and turned, shivering despite the warmth of the hearth, while Menilmonea stared at the ceiling, arms crossed, alert to the slightest sound in the weighty silence of the abandoned village.

The next morning, the two friends woke to dawn's pale light gently streaming through the windows. They exchanged a silent glance before mechanically preparing a quick breakfast with the remaining provisions.

"What do we do now?" whispered Aureal, biting into a piece of dry bread.

Menilmonea pondered a moment before replying. "The best thing would probably be to go back to the Tower and try another village. There's nothing keeping us here."

Aureal shivered slightly as she stared off, lost in thought.

"But... what if we come across another monster like that one? I don't know if we'll be able to call upon our friends again so easily."

112

Menilmonea took her hand reassuringly. "This time, we know what to expect. We'll check the surroundings carefully before approaching. The forest will warn us, and then we'll just have to run like mad back to the Tower."

Aureal nodded with a smile and gathered her courage. "All right.... Together, then. Always together."

As they left the house, their eyes lingered on the Ascension bell hanging in the center of the square. Aureal sighed softly, a melancholy expression on her face.

"There's one that will never ring again," she whispered sadly.

But just as the words left her lips, her gaze was drawn to an unusual detail: just behind the bell, on a house overgrown with vegetation, a piece of paper was pinned to the front door with a knife. Her heart raced.

"Menil.... Look over there!"

Menilmonea turned quickly, intrigued. "What is that?"

She quickly went over, took the message gingerly in one hand, and with the other, yanked the knife from where it had been sunk deeply in the wood of the door.

She read aloud, "Ameril, I hope you find this message when you return from the hunt tonight. The Mother heard our prayers. She sent a Guardian. It was incredible! I'll tell you more when you join us! The Guardian gave us permission to go to Opponka's village. This will be my first time there! I couldn't take much with me. Just pack some clothes for yourself. The Guardian said that Opponka and his village will welcome us and help us. I love you. Your Lily."

The two girls stood speechless, staring at each other in amazement. They'd almost missed this crucial message. So the Mother hadn't abandoned them! She was sending Guardians to support the villages. The news was wonderful! Unhoped for, even.

Overcome with sudden joy and renewed hope, they threw themselves into each other's arms, unable to speak for a long moment. But soon, Aureal frowned, realizing something.

"Wait, Menil... We don't even know where this Opponka's village is."

Menilmonea scowled, then smiled softly as she studied the paths leading out of the village.

"Maybe the forest can guide us," she finally said. "If the villagers passed through here, the mushrooms should remember. We'll just have to ask them for directions."

Aureal raised an eyebrow, bemused despite the gravity of the moment. "Sure is handy having a mycomanceress around!"

The girls then went to each of the village's various exits, carefully examining each path. At long last, after several unsuccessful attempts, Menilmonea identified the right one, confirmed by several boletes whom, she said, the sight of so many people passing by had duly impressed.

They were walking on, their hearts much lighter than they'd been the day before, when Aureal stopped dead in her tracks, eyes wide. "Menil... He's back!"

Menilmonea spun around, flooded by a rush of adrenaline. "Who? The plant monster?"

Aureal shook her head. When she replied, her voice held a mixture of astonishment and amusement. "No, the fox. He's back."

"But how? Are we that close to Gunderki's Tower?"

"I have no idea, but he's here, just like on the first leg of the journey. Right at the edge of the trees, in the tall grass."

"That's incredible. We'll have to talk to Opponka about this." Menilmonea turned for a peek at the creature but saw nothing. However, with a cheery smile, she waved toward the tall grass.

"If he wants to follow us, we might as well be polite," she said with a laugh.

The girls continued on their way under the beautiful midmorning sun. However, a few clouds were gathering on the horizon. Aureal pouted. "I hope the village isn't too far away, or we'll end up drenched."

Menilmonea thought for a moment before replying. "If it's anything like where we're from, the farthest village away was three days' walk."

Aureal shrugged, a satisfied smile on her lips. "In the end, we did well to stock up on eggs and dried meat before leaving. It looks like we're going to be on the road for several days."

The mycomanceress looked concerned. "You know, we've been gone for eight days already. I hope the people back home are holding up."

Aureal stopped dead in her tracks and frowned. "Eight days? Are you sure?"

"Er... yes. Why do you seem so worried all of a sudden?"

"Menil, I'm late! I haven't had my half-moon blood, and I should have two days ago. I'm always as regular as the seasons. Once every fourteen days! Fifteen, if I'm really off."

"But... then does that... are you..."

"No, that's just it! I didn't take poor Oldemar home after the Feast of the Mother. I even thought of you when I was wondering if I wanted to spend the rest of my life with him. He's nice, but not very interesting, except for his muscles."

"But how can this be?"

"I don't know! It's odd indeed. Anyway, I'm not pregnant, unless you can become pregnant these days without dallying with a boy. Which... well at this point, I wouldn't even be surprised," she concluded with a laugh.

"Look, we'll see. If I've counted right, I should get my half-moon blood in two days."

"At any rate, I'm not about to complain. Most of the time I have such terrible stomach cramps, I could do without it."

"Sure, but let's keep an eye on it, okay?"

"Yes, Healer!"

The pair exchanged a winking glance and continued on their way.

The journey continued without incident. With every step, the landscape unfolded, alternating between dense forests and sun-drenched clearings. The air was crisp, and despite growing fatigue, the girls' motivation remained intact. Finally, as the day began to draw to a close, a silhouette appeared on the horizon: the village.

The two friends slowed down instinctively and eyed the outlines of the first houses with a mixture of excitement and apprehension. The place seemed untouched, a far cry from the desolation of the previous one.

Aureal took a deep breath, turning to Menilmonea.

"This time it'll work out," she said with resolve. "We're finally going to find a Titan who can help us."

Menilmonea nodded, a smile forming on her lips. "Yes.... This time, we'll get answers."

XV

Night was falling when Aureal and Menilmonea reached Opponka's village. To their surprise, the atmosphere was almost festive.

Villagers hoisted furniture from one house to another, laughter echoed through the winding lanes, and people sat at tables before their thatched-roof houses, drinking beer and singing cheerfully. The mouthwatering aromas of warm bread and grilled meat wafted through the air, mingling with the woody scent of torches lighting streets paved with stones the passing years had polished to a high shine.

The two friends looked at each other, puzzled. After the grueling days they'd just been through, they found this sudden change in atmosphere unnerving. Dust from their travels still clung to their clothes, and fatigue lined their faces. However, they had no time to dwell on their thoughts, for a loud, warm voice now hailed them vigorously.

"You, youngsters! Help me carry these chairs! We need to take them over there, to the other side!"

A middle-aged woman, her gray hair tied back in a loose bun and a friendly smile on her lips, was waving insistently at them. Her stained apron bore witness to a day's hard work. Taken aback, Menilmonea and Aureal exchanged a questioning glance before letting themselves be swept up in the energy all around. Instead of overthinking things, they grabbed the carved wooden chairs and followed the woman to a bustling house where other villagers were busy in a well-orchestrated ballet.

"Put them in back. Thank you, girls!" said the woman, wiping her shiny forehead with the back of her sleeve. "Oh, by the way, remind me of your names again? With all the new arrivals the day before yesterday, I haven't got everyone straight in my head yet."

Aureal and Menilmonea briefly froze, their hands lingering on the backs of the chairs, before introducing themselves a bit hesitantly.

"We didn't arrive the day before yesterday," Menilmonea clarified, almost apologetically, her voice betraying a slight nervousness.

The woman raised a bushy eyebrow, clearly baffled. Lines showed on her forehead. "What's all this now?"

"We've only just arrived, ma'am," explained the mycomanceress, nervously smoothing her dusty tunic.

"You're from Maronoki's village, aren't you?"

"No, we're from Tunka's village," replied Aureal.

A veil of doubt passed over the woman's face. Her hands froze on the apron she was adjusting. "Whatever do you mean? What are you going on about? Weren't you with the exiles?"

"No, ma'am," Aureal murmured.

The woman shook her head, visibly intrigued, setting a few silver strands of hair that had escaped her bun aflutter. "Oh, how very strange this all seems to me! Opponka never mentioned anything of the sort. Well, go see Abigail, our Healer. Tell her your story, she might be interested. She's in the community hall, right off the central square. And take this chance to eat something, you poor dears! You look exhausted."

For a moment, Menilmonea took in the hustle and bustle of the village, the laughter that rang out like sparks in the falling night, and sighed with a gentle, almost melancholy smile. "This village is full of good cheer."

Aureal nodded and her gaze grew briefly lost in the stream of busy villagers.

"Yes, it reminds me of home. Before... before all this," she murmured, her voice tinged with sorrowful nostalgia.

The girls crossed the cobbled square, lit by lanterns hung from carved wooden posts that evoked serpentine shapes, and reached the great room. Larger than the other structures, it flaunted a slate roof and a massive door adorned with symbols. Inside, several families were already seated at tables for supper. Some wore clothes slightly different from those of the Opponka's people—probably the exiles from Maronoki.

A few curious glances turned briefly toward them, studying their clothes and worn faces, but everyone soon returned to their conversations and activities. A friendly hubbub filled the space, mingling with the appetizing smell of steaming soup that made the two friends' mouths water. Candlelight flickered on the tables, bathing the villagers' tired but smiling faces in a golden glow.

Aureal spotted a child with tousled red hair passing by, a chunk of bread in hand. She called out to him softly, "Excuse me, do you know where Abigail is?"

With a bite of his bread, the boy pointed to a table a little farther off, near the imposing stone hearth where a comforting fire crackled and two women seemed to be deep in conversation.

The girls made their way through the bustling crowd to join them, and Menilmonea cleared her throat to get their attention before speaking.

"Excuse me for disturbing you. My name is Menilmonea, and this is my friend Aureal. This may sound a little crazy, but we come from a village you've probably never heard of."

After this introduction, the two women at the table looked at them, taken aback.

"You're not from Maronoki?" asked the taller of the two, glancing questioningly at the other woman.

Smaller, and with drawn features, she now shook her head slightly. "I don't think so. I don't know these two girls."

The taller woman, frowned slightly before speaking. Her gray eyes scrutinized the newcomers with a mixture of curiosity and suspicion. "Well, fancy that! It seems the Mother has no shortage of surprises."

She motioned for them to sit down and pushed away the remains of her meal. "Make yourselves comfortable, girls. We'll bring you something to eat, and you'll tell me all about it."

The taller woman had an imposing presence despite her slender frame, and an aura of wisdom that immediately inspired trust.

"I am Abigail, the village Healer," she said. She pointed to the woman seated beside her. "And this is Aboren. She was the Healer in Maronoki. And you? Where exactly are you from? And more importantly... how did you get here?"

Abigail's fingers, adorned with wooden rings engraved with esoteric symbols, tapped gently on the table. Aboren, older but with a lively, intelligent gaze, watched the two girls with undisguised curiosity. Her wrinkled hands clung tightly to a clay cup from which wafted an herbal aroma.

Before replying, Menilmonea took a deep breath, nervously fingering the leather cord that fastened her tunic. "We come from the village of Tunka. We left eight days ago. Our Titan would not wake up, so we went to seek help."

Without stopping, almost without breathing, Menilmonea told them about their journey from Tower to Tower, until they arrived at the village of the dead Titan and found the letter.

Abigail and Aboren were speechless, captivated by this extraordinary tale. The magnitude of what they had just learned far exceeded anything they could have imagined. The silence that followed was broken only by the crackling of the fire and the distant conversations of the other villagers.

Then, after a brief moment, Abigail suddenly exclaimed, her eyes shining with excitement, "By the Mother, we live in incredible times! If someone had told me I would meet girls like you before my Ascension... How brave you are!"

Her eyes lighting up with sincere admiration, she went on. "Opponka will be happy to answer your questions tomorrow morning. It's a little late to bother him now, and I've a feeling you wouldn't mind a cozy bed."

Aureal, who had remained relatively silent during her friend's story and could no longer hold back her questions, spoke up and addressed

Aboren directly. "Your Titan... How did he turn to stone? How did your village become overgrown with vegetation?"

The Healer let out a slight sigh. Her shoulders sagged slightly under the weight of her memories, and then she spoke in a voice tinged with sadness.

"A little less than a moon ago, the Mother summoned an exceptional number of our villagers. Our village has always had many Ascensions, but never so many in a single day. To tell the truth, one of our eldest grandmothers had been called a week earlier, and then her entire bloodline received the call. All those older than eight cycles were chosen. This rare phenomenon left us amazed. Old Marlene, who was nearing thirty-five, had seemed destined to remain among us until the end, or so we all thought. But the Mother's ways are inscrutable, and who knows what Marlene whispered to her in prayer? In any event, she managed to leave with her children and grandchildren.

"We organized a great feast for their departure, of course. We were all so proud of them. Unfortunately, the very next morning, our Titan began showing clear signs of weakness. He headed for his favorite resting place, as was sometimes his wont, to recover... Except this time, he never got up. And just like your Tunka, he remained frozen in that endless sleep. But unlike you, none of us dared lift a finger. We waited, in doubt. Every last one of us hoped for a miracle, thinking our prayers might suffice. Some suggested going to seek help, but fear of blasphemy and respect for tradition were stronger than our will to act."

She shook her head slightly and gave a sad smile. "Oh, don't blush, I'm not judging you. I was one of those who wished to leave... but I lacked your strength of character. Fear held me back, as it did so many others."

Aboren's gaze wandered for a moment, contemplating the dancing flames in the hearth, before she continued in a firmer voice. "Ten days ago, Maronoki stopped breathing altogether... and began turning to stone. The vegetation on his back was already surprisingly lush, but from that moment on, it spread everywhere, as if possessed of a will of its own. We didn't dare do a thing. After all, it was our Titan's body..."

She paused, took a sip of her herbal tea, then added in a calmer voice, "We prayed to the Mother day and night. We asked her to send us a sign, a message. We were desperate.... Our village was going to disappear, and we with it. And then, at last, we were heard. Three days ago, a Guardian arrived at our village. When it first appeared, we all froze, eyes wide with wonder and fear. Some even fell to their knees, murmuring prayers or thanks to the Mother. It was imposing, made entirely of metal, covered with glowing runes that gave off an unearthly bluish light. It spoke little, but every word it uttered resonated like a promise of survival. No one had ever seen a Guardian before. To us, it was the most beautiful thing that had ever happened. We were saved."

Aboren stared at Menilmonea and Aureal, her dark eyes conveying both fear of the recent past and relief at the present. "The Guardian told us the Mother had given us permission to join Opponka and settle here. So we all left, taking what we could with us. Opponka knew we were coming, and the village had begun preparations to take us in.... And here we are. A new life begins, even if the memory of poor Maronoki will haunt us forever."

Menilmonea frowned slightly before she asked, her voice betraying a hint of apprehension, "And the Guardian? Did it go?"

Aboren nodded, and a strand of gray hair fell across her wrinkled forehead. "Yes. No sooner had we set off than we saw it heading for another village farther west. I wonder if it came from Maronoki's Tower."

Menilmonea exchanged a troubled glance with Aureal, their thoughts seeming to converge in an eloquent silence, before murmuring, "Alas, I think not. We came across the Guardian from your Tower during our journey. Only it was... dead."

"Dead?" Abigail's eyes widened. "How can that be?"

"Destroyed, actually," Menilmonea clarified somberly. "We think the plant monster did it. Our world is changing at a demented pace. Titans are dying, Guardians being demolished by entities from who knows where.... Something dreadful is underway, and we don't know what."

She sighed, a shudder running visibly through her tired body, then she lifted her chin with a glimmer of hope in her eyes, her fingers unconsciously clutching the edge of the polished wooden table.

"But all that is behind us now! I am so happy to have found your village. Opponka will guide us!"

On that hopeful note, the four parted. Abigail escorted the girls to a small house nearby. After quickly washing off the dust of their journey, they both soon fell into a deep, dreamless sleep.

XVI

Dawn was already breaking when Menilmonea opened her eyes. After a long night of deep, restful sleep, she felt full of new energy. She sat up with a start, then turned toward Aureal, who was still buried under her blankets and sleeping soundly. Menilmonea softly called out her name several times before she finally stirred, slowly emerging from sleep.

"Already up?" she mumbled.

"Yes! As are you, now," replied Menilmonea, a mischievous smile playing on her lips. "Come, up with you. We must go see Opponka!"

Aureal grumbled before pushing back her blankets and dawdling her way to wakefulness. "Are you afraid he'll fall asleep before we see him?"

"Bite your tongue! It's just that Abigail and Aboren are likely already awake and waiting for us in the great room."

Aureal nodded, quickly braiding her hair. "Just give me a few moments to freshen up. I look like an old bear."

"There is indeed much of an old bear in you!"

The two friends got ready, humming happily, delighted to have achieved their goal at last. Once Aureal was satisfied with her appearance, they headed for the village square.

In the great room, the warmth of the hearth contrasted with the morning cool. The aromas of warm bread and steaming milk enveloped the girls as they walked through the door. They saw Aboren serving children breakfast. The two friends gave her a great big wave, and she pointed to a table at the back where the village Healer was sitting.

"Ah, at last!" exclaimed Abigail, laughing when she saw them. "I was wondering if you two had been struck by your Titan's curse."

"We slept so soundly," said Menilmonea, sitting down. "We can't thank you enough for your hospitality. But all is well. We're here and ready to go see Opponka."

"He'll be delighted to meet you. I mentioned you briefly this morning. Why don't we have a bite to eat before we go see him?"

As the four shared a meal, the atmosphere seemed both merry and restless. The girls knew that this day would mark the long-awaited beginning of a return to normalcy.

After their meal, all four left the great room and headed north of the village. Opponka, an enormous snake with scales covered in vegetation, lay coiled among several houses, his imposing body stretched out in the shade of their roofs. His appearance was fascinating, his sheer size majestic. He inspired both respect and, admittedly, a certain wariness.

As the girls approached, his black eyes fell on them, and a soft, almost amused hiss could be heard.

"So! The exiles from the other side of the world have arrived," he declared in a vibrant, cavernous voice.

The girls bowed respectfully before speaking.

"Opponka, we have come to see you about an important matter," Menilmonea explained. "Do you know Tunka, the Titan of our village?"

Silence fell as the serpent scrutinized them with his piercing eyes. Then, with a slow movement, he shook his head slightly.

"No. Titans rarely come into contact with one another. And never with those from such distant villages. In fact, I must commend you on your astonishing bravery. There are many your epic journey would have deterred." He paused. "Surprising, as well, that the Guardians you encountered were destroyed or missing.... I will not conceal the fact that I find this dismaying."

Menilmonea drew a deep breath. "But then… do you know why Tunka refuses to wake?"

As Opponka bowed his massive head slightly, a glimmer from fathomless depths lit his eye. "Alas, no, my children. I know nothing of the evil that has befallen your Titan. I have not spoken to the Mother since I was born. Like all my brethren. When Maronoki died, I simply felt that I had to prepare my village for the arrival of the people from his. I know this intuition issued from the Mother, but I cannot ask her for more."

A feeling of utter disillusion swept through the girls' hearts. The air seemed to stand still around them, and the leaden weight of the revelation landed upon their shoulders. Menilmonea felt a shiver run down her spine, while Aureal looked down, eyes misting over. Their last hope had just been extinguished.

"Then… what should we do?" Aureal finally asked in a broken voice.

Opponka studied them at length, his eyes sad yet suffused with kindness. When at last he spoke, his voice was as soft as could be.

"It would be best if you stayed here. If what happened to Maronoki is anything to go by, poor Tunka will be dead within a month, and his village will disappear with him."

Menilmonea gasped. Her throat felt tight, and a dull pain coiled round her soul. She felt Aureal's hand find hers. They couldn't save their home, their friends… everything they had ever known.

The very idea was unbearable.

Upon seeing their distress, Opponka tried to comfort them. "Don't despair. Look what has happened here. The Mother sent a Guardian to guide the villagers."

Menilmonea looked at him, eyes glistening with tears. "Yes, but alas…. The two other Titans in the villages nearest ours are also asleep. Where are those villagers to go?"

Opponka sighed, sensing the anguish that lay heavy in the air. "You must trust in the Mother, my children. She loves us and will look after us all."

Menilmonea, eyes still blurred with tears, timidly raised her head. "Perhaps they could come here? We could go back and find them by

retracing our steps."

Aureal shook her head. "I thought about that, but... I can't re-member Gunderki's rune at all! There were hundreds of them."

Menilmonea clenched her fists, desperate. "We'll visit every last one if we have to."

Opponka gazed at them before letting out another sigh. "Alas, even if you could perform such a miracle, I cannot allow more villagers to come here. Already we must find ways to take in those who have, rearranging our crops and our homes. We won't be able to cope with more waves of inhabitants for several cycles."

Menilmonea and Aureal exchanged glances. They had nothing left. Not even a lead. With their throats still tight, they bowed to the Titan one last time.

"Thank you for your honesty, Opponka," Menilmonea murmured.

"May the Mother watch over you," he replied simply.

They withdrew slowly, shoulders slumped, hearts heavy. Neither of them spoke a word until they had left the place behind.

"What now?" Aureal finally whispered.

"I don't know," replied Menilmonea. "I'm lost. I thought.... I don't know what I thought. I hoped for something else. At least... a clue about what to do."

"We must pray to the Mother."

"Yes, of course."

They stopped at the edge of a low wall facing the mountains. The wind had risen and was tossing about a few blades of dry grass.

"Maybe we could just... take a break?" suggested Aureal. "Help out here, settle in the newcomers, take some time to think about what we can do. We're exhausted, Menil. We'll see things more clearly if we stop rushing around."

Menilmonea didn't answer right away. She gazed at the village: its roofs, its people. She knew she didn't like the idea. But she also knew that Aureal was right.

"All right," she sighed. "But just for a little while. Till we catch our breath."

They spent the rest of the day cleaning, moving furniture, and arranging living spaces in the village's houses. They pitched in as best they could amid the hectic villagers, lending a hand here, repairing a shutter there, keeping busy so as not to think.

When evening came, they helped serve supper, then finally sat themselves down at a table not far from the great hearth. Their movements were slow, their muscles weary, but the silence between them was placid, almost mellow. No solutions, not yet. But some peace, at least.

Suddenly, Aureal grimaced and leaned forward slightly, one hand on her stomach.

"Are you all right?" asked Menilmonea, raising an eyebrow.

"Bad cramp! But don't worry, I think that's good news," Aureal replied with a half-smile. "Although I can't explain the four-day delay. How about you, by the way?"

"Nothing yet, but any day now. I can feel it."

"It seems all is finally as it should be."

"Something's looking up, at least."

With that, Abigail joined them, a steaming bowl in her hands. She looked on kindly for a moment before addressing them.

"I'm very sorry Opponka couldn't help you," she said softly. "But consider this your home, for as long as you wish it so."

Moved, Menilmonea and Aureal exchanged glances, then turned to her with sincere smiles.

"Thank you, Abigail. Really. It means a lot to us," said Aureal.

"We must admit, we feel fairly lost," Menilmonea added. "We never imagined that even a Titan couldn't help us."

Abigail nodded slowly. "I understand. In your shoes, I'd feel just as helpless. But don't lose hope. I will pray to the Mother to send a Guardian to your village. It might not happen today, but she watches over us all, even in silence."

The girls thanked her again, and then, feeling an onslaught of exhaustion, quietly withdrew. They didn't have the strength to think any more that night.

Once in their room, they took a moment to tend to themselves. They needed it more than anything. And as they were washing up,

Menilmonea broke the silence.

"Do you think we should go home?" she asked in a low voice. "I can't bring myself to believe we're safe here when our people must be lost and panicking. We could at least go back and tell them what we know."

Aureal remained silent for a few seconds, then slowly nodded. "You're right. I agree. And we could all pray together for the Mother to send us a Guardian. The real problem is: how are we going to get back? I have no idea which rune to choose."

"I've been thinking about it. We know that Gunderki's Tower was orange. There weren't that many that color; most were yellow and a few red. We'll need a piece of paper to write down the ones we've tried and work our way through by process of elimination. It could take several days, so we'll need to bring enough food and water. Moreover, I recall that the rune was surrounded only by other orange ones, which should further narrow our options."

"Yes, that's true.... You're absolutely right! It could work. Menil, you're a genius!"

Menilmonea smiled slightly. It wasn't a solution, but at least it gave them a new goal. And that was better than doing nothing.

The next morning, they went down to the great room as soon as they were ready and found Abigail and Aboren near the fireplace, busy assigning the first tasks of the day. The girls approached and took the Healers aside.

"Good morning. We wanted to let you know that we've made up our minds. We're going home."

"Oh?" said Aboren, a little surprised.

"We've committed so much blasphemy already that another journey won't make things much worse when we're up for judgment," added Aureal with a sly grin.

The other two Healers burst out laughing.

"We'll miss you," said Abigail, regaining her seriousness. "And truly, I understand. Were I in your shoes, I would feel just as torn. I sincerely hope the Mother sends a Guardian to your village. I will pray for it."

"You have our sincerest thanks," said Menilmonea. "For every-thing. And please thank Opponka for us as well."

"Be careful on your way out, though," added Aboren. "The fewer people who see you leave, the better for everyone. Tempers are running high with all that's taken place recently."

"Understood," replied Aureal. "This time, we won't make any grand speeches in the village square."

"Speaking of which, which way is it to Opponka's Tower?" asked Menilmonea.

"Take the road to the east, behind the Village Hall. No one will see you there."

The girls exchanged a few more smiles with the Healers, stocked up on provisions, and took their leave, their hearts already set on the road home.

XVII

Day had barely dawned, and the village was bathed in a pale, muted light. All lay in torpor still, as if the houses had not yet fully stirred from the night. As planned, Menilmonea and Aureal left the great room quietly, their bags filled with provisions Abigail and Aboren had offered. They had encountered few villagers on their way down, which was just as well.

No sooner were they on the path than they noticed the vegetation became denser, soon obscuring their figures. The murmurs of the village faded away behind them, replaced by the unassuming song of birds flitting among the treetops.

The girls hadn't gotten far at all when Aureal said in a low voice with a mischievous grin, "Looks like he was waiting for us."

Menilmonea narrowed her eyes. "The fox?"

"Yes. His usual spot."

Menilmonea smiled softly. "At any rate, he offers no disruption to the forest's song. So it's fine by me."

"Me too," admitted Aureal, moving forward slowly. "I think I've even grown fond of him. A bit like old Mordental's dogs... but more distant and almost invisible."

"At least we don't have to feed him!" Menilmonea added, an impish gleam in her eye.

They kept up their pace for nearly four hours, in the shade of the tall hazel trees that met in almost a vault above, sieving the light in a kaleidoscope of shifting glimmers. The atmosphere was peaceful, punctuated only by the rustle of wind in the leaves.

Finally, the massive shape of Opponka's Tower loomed among the tree trunks, familiar in its strangeness. It looked almost exactly like the other Towers: the same impressive verticality, the same moss-covered stones. Nestled in dense growth, the foot of the Tower stood partially concealed by a snarl of thick vines and twisted brambles, as if nature had, as before, attempted to reclaim its own.

Menilmonea paused briefly, studying the clearing they would have to cross to reach the wooded fringe around the Tower.

"We'll have to venture out into the open," she muttered, squinting.

She remained silent for a moment, listening to the sounds of the wood. But nothing seemed amiss. No tension, no warning signs.

"The song of the forest is at peace. Soothing, even."

"The birds don't seem worried either," confirmed Aureal, scanning the treetops. "They're still twittering. If they sensed a threat, they'd have flown long ago."

"Then let's go. But run. Best not to linger out there, beyond cover."

"You read my mind," Aureal replied with a knowing smile.

Without a moment's hesitation, the two friends set off for the Tower, their footsteps gliding over the damp grass, their breathing measured, their senses alert.

As they drew closer, Menilmonea slowed ever so slightly. Something was wrong. She frowned and scanned the surroundings. Then she spotted it.

"Look!" she hissed.

The Tower's Guardian, or what was left of it, lay unmoving at the foot of the edifice. His body was covered with thick vines, moss, and brambles, as if the vegetation had slowly digested him. No more light shone from his runes. He was nothing more now than a lifeless shape caught in the forest's green embrace.

"What a shame," Aureal whispered, heart heavy. "I would've loved to speak with him. He might have been able to tell us how to get back."

"Yes, that would have been very helpful! But still... I have a plan. I think."

Aureal raised an eyebrow, intrigued. "I'm all ears."

"I took some ink and parchment from our room before we left. We'll enter the transport ring, and I'll try to note down the layout of the runes and their colors."

"Excellent idea. Since we already know where we are, that should give us a good reference point."

"Exactly. What's more, we know that a few hours' walk south of here is the Tower we came through. Logically, then, the ring should show a yellow rune under that Tower. Which will provide us with a direction. We'll know which way north is."

"That's perfect! You're so smart, Menil!"

"Thank you," said Menilmonea, pretending to blush.

"Then all we have to do is make a list of the orange runes and keep only the ones that come in threes, which should greatly narrow down our options. And thanks to your map, we can cross them off as we go along."

"Let's hope Mother is with us! And that we find our Tower soon."

"I believe, Menil! I believe we will! It's just like you said: we'll be all right, as long as we're together. The two of us... alone against the world!"

The two friends joined hands and entered the Tower. The atmosphere inside was as peculiar as ever, as if within these walls, time itself was reluctant to pass.

"Ouch! I don't know if I'll ever get used to that." Aureal grimaced.

"Me neither," replied Menilmonea, rubbing her temples, eyes half-closed.

Aureal sighed softly. "Careful. Three... two... one..."

"Welcome, Chosen Ones," a deep voice rang out, its echo reverberating throughout the chamber.

"Regular as clockwork," Aureal said with a mocking smile.

This made the two friends burst into titters, momentarily dispelling the tension of their bizarre odyssey.

"Might I inquire as to what's so amusing?" the same voice intoned with ill-concealed annoyance.

Menilmonea straightened up immediately, a bit embarrassed. "We're sorry. We didn't mean to offend you."

"No harm done." The voice was gentler now. "But you are the first to not ask me who I am."

"You are the Spirit of the transport ring," Menilmonea replied simply.

"No—well, yes! But how did you know? What sorcery is this?"

"It's a long story," replied Menilmonea. "But we're not here for our Ascension."

"Ah, well, that reassures me somewhat. You do seem too young for it. You're what... twenty rotations at most?"

"Come now!" exclaimed Aureal. "We're not that old. I'm barely ten cycles, and Menil is thirteen."

"Ah yes, yes... Of course. I always forget about that acceleration business," the Spirit muttered under its breath. There was a brief pause. "Why *are* you here, then? This is no fit place for villagers. People don't come just to pass the time."

"Oh, we know all that, dear Spirit. We're trying to return to our village," Menilmonea said as delicately as she could.

"Er... the village you just came from?"

"No, that one wasn't ours. We came through another Tower."

"Excuse me… I need to sit down."

"Can you even?" asked Aureal, surprised.

"No. That was just a figure of speech, silly girl."

"Oh."

"So… am I to understand you travel between Towers as you please?"

"Yes. Sort of... but honestly, it's not for the pleasure of disobeying the Mother," replied Menilmonea.

"Ah, well, that's all right then," replied the Spirit with a hint of irony.

"Don't make fun. We're desperately trying to save our Titan, who refuses to wake up."

"Oh. And… have you found a solution?"

"Alas, no," said Aureal. "We're just going back to be with our people and pray to the Mother to send us a Guardian."

"If she sends you mine, tell her I'm getting impatient. He set out a few moons ago and left me here all alone to handle the Ascensions... and apparently mere passersby as well."

"I don't want to upset you," said Menilmonea softly, "but... we saw your Guardian. It's lying right outside the entrance to your Tower. Dead"

"What do you mean... dead?"

"Alas, yes. I'm sorry... But if it truly left only a few moons ago, I don't understand why it is already covered in vegetation."

"What are you talking about? The Guardians are the Mother's most powerful children! Not very talkative, I'll admit, but I don't see what could harm them. They are made of metal, after all!"

"Yes, we're as lost as you are," Aureal sighed. "Not to further lower your morale, but the world is in turmoil: the Titans are lost to slumber, and one of them has even died in a nearby village. The Guardians are disappearing or dying. By the Mother, it's a nightmare!"

"Yes... indeed," the Spirit replied pensively. "As a result, your little transgression seems very minor now. And between us, apart from judging you, I have no power here. I can see you, hear you, and guide you, but I cannot prevent you from using the ring."

"Good to know." Menilmonea grinned. "Perhaps you could even help us find our village?"

"Find your...? As in, 'We left like idiots without making sure we knew the way back'?"

"I wouldn't have put it quite like that, but... more or less, yes."

"With help like yours, your Titan's off to a good start," the Spirit grumbled sarcastically.

"Hey! It's not like anyone ever taught us how to handle this!" Aureal protested. "We're just making it up as we go along. You think we wanted any of this? You think we're not heartbroken to see everything we believed in crumbling around us?"

"Don't be offended. I'm just saying that from an outside perspective, there's room for improvement."

"In any case, we've exhausted all our options," said Menilmonea.

"Even Opponka can't help us."

"Opponka?"

"The Titan of your Tower! Don't you know him?"

"Embarrassingly enough, I wasn't in the ring when he was born. I arrived when his village was founded."

"And where did you come from?"

"If I knew... I shouldn't even talk about it, but this end-of-the-world atmosphere seems like the right time..." He paused at length. "I have no memory of what I was before I came here. But I'm sure I had a life."

"How so?" asked Menilmonea.

"I have... flashes. I see images, trees, forests... But that's all. I spend all my free time—and I have plenty of it—trying to remember. I don't know if I'm dreaming my past or making it up. But I'm sure I wasn't born here."

"Why didn't you ask the Mother?"

"We don't talk to the Mother. When I appeared here, she spoke to me. I was amazed... and since then, I've *wanted* to serve her. Well... I think I want to."

"That verges on blasphemy, my dear," Aureal smirked.

"Yes, I thought your little club looked like such fun, so why not join?"

"Ha ha." Menilmonea rolled her eyes.

"And you haven't tried talking to your Guardian about it?" Aureal continued.

"Oh no! Guardians speak to the Mother; they're extremely close to her. I would never dare question my sacred mission with the Guardian."

"You mean you could have... died? He might have... killed you?"

"I have no idea, but when in doubt, I don't want to anger the Mother. I do still want to serve her..."

"But?" Menilmonea pressed.

"But I have my doubts. I don't understand who I am, and it's driving me batty!"

"I understand. I, too, have some difficulties with my faith," said

Menilmonea softly.

"With everything going on, who could blame you?" Aureal chimed in.

The two friends exchanged a knowing and sympathetic glance.

"Thank you. I'm so glad you're here," whispered Menilmonea. Then, to the Spirit, "To tell you the truth, I even went so far as to consider blasphemy and ask the Mother herself to save our Titan."

"Ho ho! And what stopped you, apart from the fear of a horrible death at her hands? Which, if you ask me, would be justified," the Spirit snickered.

"Actually, it's mainly because one of your, er... counterparts told us that there was no coming back from Ascension. That it's a one-way trip."

"Yes, indeed, well put. But... if I may say so, and do wish to see her, there is a fairly simple solution."

"Without risking her 'just' punishment?"

"Ha ha! No, but I get the impression you consider that an acceptable risk."

"Well, it's not our first choice either, you know," Aureal grumbled.

"But let's say we agree," said Menilmonea cautiously. Then, more to herself, "If it can save Tunka..."

"Well, as the other Spirit told you, if you go to the green rune, it's straight to Ascension. But nothing is stopping you from doing as you did to reach this spot. You could choose one of the Towers closest to the Mother's... and go to meet your fate on foot."

The two friends were stunned. The solution was so obvious!

"But why help us? It's not really your mission," asked Aureal.

"True, but there's nothing that says I shouldn't, either. And, well... I don't know, I like you. It's been so long since I've had a real conversation."

"In any case, you have our thanks. And if I may ask... what is the Mother's Tower like? Is it like this?" asked Menilmonea.

"No idea, my dear. If I've ever been, I can't recall."

"Thanks again, ever so much. You're a dear."

"Hoo hoo! Don't flatter me. But you're right, I'm not such a bad sort."

Without further ado, the girls selected the white dot on the map and stepped into the transport fluid. Before them, the map of all the Towers lit up.

"So, let's see what we have around this green rune..." whispered Menilmonea.

"What do you think of that one? At a glance, it looks the closest," suggested Aureal.

Menilmonea pointed to a yellow rune ringed in white. "Yes, I agree. And since this is where we are, that means the Tower just below must be Maronoki's."

Then she addressed the Spirit. "It looks like this map has north at the top, doesn't it?"

"That's right."

"Perfect! And since Maronoki is about a day, maybe a day and a half from here, I'd say the Tower we want to choose would be three days, maybe four at most, from the Mother's."

"I can handle that," Aureal said.

The two friends joined hands.

"Thank you again, Spirit! I hope you remember who you were!" said Menilmonea warmly.

With that, she touched the rune she had selected.

XVIII

A flash of lightning split the sky as the two girls reappeared in the center of the new Tower. They stepped quickly from the transport fluid. The stone floor vibrated slightly with each thunderclap.

The architecture all around was identical to that of the other Towers, although here it had a wilder feel to it. The entrance itself was partly covered over with thick vines, tangled brambles, and vibrant yellow flowers that seemed to stretch slowly toward the transport ring as if trying to embrace or absorb it. The air was charged with electricity, and an unseen, almost palpable tension hovered in the room.

Menilmonea shivered. "Feels like we've come at a bad time."

But before Aureal had time to reply, a somber voice deep as a chasm boomed throughout the chamber. "How dare you use transport magic for anything other than Ascension? Who are you?"

The voice reverberated among the massive columns, which seemed to intensify its tone of accusation. Aureal straightened up and stammered a reply, thrown off by such a cold, brusque welcome.

"We apologize, Spirit. We were simply passing through, nothing more. We have no intention of meddling with anything here."

"Passing through? To where? No! Out of the question. You have disobeyed the sacred rules. You will pay for your offense."

Slowly, Menilmonea raised her hands in a conciliatory gesture. Her voice was calm despite the mayhem in her heart. "Don't take this the wrong way, Spirit. We understand your wrath. Should our presence vex you, we shall leave at once. We have no wish to disturb the peace of this place."

"I don't think so. You will stay right where you are. And you will explain yourselves. Quickly."

Aureal narrowed her eyes, a hint of defiance in her voice. "And how are you going to stop us? You can't really keep us from leaving."

The Spirit's response was icy, almost jubilant. "Me? No. But... that can."

A low rumbling, heavier and more menacing than the thunder outside, could be heard from a corner of the room. The walls themselves seemed to thrum with the sinister sound.

The two friends froze. Then, slowly, they turned their heads toward the source of the noise. A massive figure emerged from the darkness: a metal body covered in runes that glowed with a soft blue light.

Menilmonea paled. She squinted, staring once, then again to get a good look at the approaching figure. It looked... wounded. One arm hung limply at its side, and its gait was anything but smooth. It seemed to be dragging itself along rather than actually walking.

"It... it's hurt," she whispered, both fascinated and concerned.

"Yes," the solemn voice confirmed. "The Guardian has fought many battles outside to defend this Tower."

Aureal scowled and asked skeptically, "Against whom?"

"Against evil! The Mother's enemies. Demons!"

There was a long silence. Finally, Aureal said, with a bitter smile, "You have no idea, do you?"

Without waiting for a reply, Menilmonea grabbed her hand and whispered, "Let's go."

They rushed toward the arch, but against all odds, the golem leapt forward with a nimbleness that nothing in its previous pace had led them to expect. In an instant, its imposing mass blocked the exit, a living wall risen between them and freedom.

"By Tunka's shell!" Aureal swore. Panic put a quaver in her voice.

"If he catches us, we're done for," whispered Menilmonea, her eyes riveted on the metal colossus.

The girls hurriedly retreated toward the ring, trying to keep as much distance as they could between themselves and the Guardian, which had resumed its slow, relentless march, each step echoing like a countdown.

"I think I have an idea," said Menilmonea, a feverish gleam in her eye.

"For defeating that thing?" asked Aureal, incredulous.

"It does seem tricky," said the Spirit, mocking as ever. "Allow yourselves to be caught so we can discuss this like civilized people."

"Do you trust me?" Menilmonea asked her friend, without taking her eyes off the Guardian.

"Completely! I'd trust you with my life."

"Well, now's your chance to."

"I wouldn't do... whatever it is you're planning," said the Spirit with an invisible grin. "The Guardian is a son of the Mother. He cannot be harmed. Especially not by such wee little things as yourselves."

Menilmonea rummaged around in her bag and pulled out several grayish, spongy mushrooms. She handed half of them to Aureal.

"Now, do exactly as I say, all right? Don't think. Just do what I tell you to, in the order I tell you to."

"Sure, but whatever it is, we have to do it now!" said Aureal, glancing anxiously at the giant only a few strides away.

"When I say to, crush these mushrooms in your hand, count to three, and throw them where that thing will put its left foot. Got it? Crush, count, toss: left foot. Meanwhile, I'll do the same for the right."

Aureal nodded, a determined expression on her face.

"You're going to throw mushroom mush at him?" the Spirit sneered. "I can't wait. This will be simply enthralling."

"Crush!" Menilmonea ordered.

Both friends did so simultaneously. No sooner were they crushed than the mushrooms transformed, their invisible alchemy at work, into a sticky substance with silvery sparkles, like rubber brought to life. The temperature rose sharply, and at the end of the stipulated three seconds, the girls hurled the jelly-like mixture right into the

Guardian's path.

It placed its left foot squarely where Aureal's mixture had landed, and instantly, it was stuck. A terrible metallic groaning rang out as it tried to free itself. Its leg seemed to have welded itself to the stone floor. Taken by surprise, it wobbled and had to quickly pivot its other leg to stay balanced, thus narrowly dodging Menilmonea's attack.

"Wahoo! Did you see that?" cried Aureal. "That's amazing! Well, Spirit? Still think it's so enthralling?"

"What?! What sorcery is this?" the voice roared, furious.

The golem emitted shrill metallic grinding noises, its runes glowing brighter and brighter from the strain of its movements.

"They're glue mushrooms," replied Menilmonea proudly. "They can stick a table to the ceiling!"

Then she looked toward the exit. "Let's hurry! I'm not sure it'll hold him for much longer."

Indeed, the guard's foot, though still trapped in the adhesive substance, was slowly starting to lift. Thousands of tiny, resistant fibers stretched out, clinging tenaciously to the floor, refusing to give way.

The two friends cautiously skirted the golem, then ran headlong for the exit, breathless, legs shaking, hoping the creature would not free itself in time. In her haste, Aureal dropped her satchel, the thud of its fall punctuated by a muffled curse.

"No, don't stop!" cried Menilmonea. "We'll manage without it!"

They passed through the archway without stopping, racing onward at full speed. The transition was the same as ever: a wave of nausea struck them as their gifts returned, but they ignored it.

"The animals... They're telling me it'll be okay! I don't know how, but it'll... be okay..." Aureal panted. "We have to keep running!"

"Yes, the forest's song is reassuring too!" said Menilmonea. "It worked last time! Let's get to the edge of the wood, over there!"

The Tower stood in the center of a vast meadow, surrounded by a dense, looming wood. As far as the eye could see, there were only trees, a sea of deep, ancient, almost mystical greenery.

The girls had gone no more than a few yards when a deafening crash sounded behind them, followed by a blood-curdling metallic clang.

"It broke free!" cried Menilmonea, glancing over her shoulder. "By the Mother—it jumped! It's going to land right on us!"

"Don't look, keep running!" shouted Aureal, without turning around.

The guard soared up into the air, its trajectory perfectly calculated to intercept them, while the Spirit's voice echoed one last time, laden with vengeful satisfaction. "Go on, fools! Run! No one escapes the Mother's justice!"

The golem cleared the arch at breakneck speed.

And then it was as if it had hit an invisible wall. Its massive body halted mid-flight, stopped short by some monumental force. A harrowing clamor of crushed metal burst out in the air, immediately followed by a hellish screeching as the golem's joints screamed and bent from the violence of the impact. The ground shook from the force of the collision. Startled by the sudden noise, the girls stopped dead in their tracks and turned around.

The sight that met their eyes defied belief: the golem was completely entangled in a swarm of vines, thick tendrils, and gnarled roots that seemed to have surged forth from the vegetation covering the outside of the arch. This dense, living web of plant life had sprung shut on the golem like a trap of nature, leaving it no chance of escape. Red flowers dotted this mesh of living links, adding an almost poetic touch to the brutal masterpiece.

The colossus tried to free itself, runes glowing blinding blue from effort. Each movement caused new vines to appear, thicker and more numerous. They sprang up from every direction, wrapping themselves around him. They slipped into the gaps in its armor, insinuated themselves into the joints of its body, and tightened their grip with inexorable force.

A sickening sound rang out, both organic and metallic, like an overripe fruit being crushed by an unyielding weight. The two friends shuddered in unison.

"It's... dead." Menilmonea let out a held breath. "The runes have gone out."

"I-I can't believe it," Aureal murmured, still in shock. "Did the forest do that?"

"I don't know," replied Menilmonea, troubled. "If so, its song hasn't changed at all. It's as peaceful and serene as ever. Nothing like... that. I'll go closer to see if those vines will speak to me."

"Are you sure?" asked Aureal, hesitantly.

"Yes. I think the animals are right. We have nothing to fear. And anyway, the Guardian is dead."

They cautiously approached the giant crucified on its scaffolding of plants. Menilmonea whispered a few words, hoping for a response.

A heavy silence fell, broken only by the rustle of wind in the tall grass.

"No, they... don't want to talk to me. Or... they can't."

Aureal tore her gaze away from the metal remains and turned abruptly toward the Tower, her pragmatism taking over. "Let's fetch my bag, then. Our provisions are in there, and the fewer roots I'm forced to eat, the better."

Menilmonea gave her a quick grin, then nodded silently and followed.

As Aureal was gathering her belongings inside the Tower, she was unable to resist the temptation to call out, "Well, Spirit? You seem a lot less arrogant all of a sudden."

Its voice, now shaking, rang out faintly like a distant echo. "You're monsters! You've destroyed a child of the Mother. She will banish you to the abyss for this blasphemy!"

Menilmonea and Aureal exchanged a foreboding glance. Without a word, they turned on their heels and walked away.

Upon reaching the edge of the woods, Menilmonea asked gently, "Are you all right?"

"Yes," replied Aureal, the hesitation evident in her voice. "I just hope the Spirit's wrong."

"Do you want to go back?"

"No, no. We didn't do all this for nothing. And besides... if the Mother's anything like what we've been told, she'll forgive us."

Menilmonea didn't answer, but she could sense her friend's inner

turmoil. She took Aureal in her arms, and they remained like that for a few moments, comforting each other in a silence charged with tension and tenderness.

Then Menilmonea stepped back gently and, a new spark of curiosity in her voice, asked, "How did the animals know that all would be well?"

"I don't know," Aureal admitted. "I can't communicate with them directly. I sense things more than I converse, really. And they seem to pick up on my stress, my emotional state, reacting accordingly. But..."

"Yes?" Menilmonea encouraged.

"But I have a vague feeling that the fox was the one who told them everything would be all right," Aureal replied, eyes narrowing slightly. "I'm not sure, but... that seems to have come from him."

"He's here already?" Surprised, Menilmonea peered around. "How is that even possible?"

"I don't know either," replied Aureal, troubled. "But yes, he's here. The background hum is very different when he's around."

"The more time goes by, the more I think that fox wants to help us," Menilmonea murmured thoughtfully.

"Ha! You think so too? That's a relief. I feel the same way, but I didn't want to sound like a madwoman for telling you," Aureal admitted with a nervous titter.

"With all we've seen, I think we crossed the line into madness a few days ago," replied Menilmonea, a puckish grin playing on her lips.

Aureal let out a hearty laugh.

"Well, I propose we camp here for the night," said the mycomanceress.

She pointed to a majestic oak whose roots formed a perfectly acceptable natural shelter.

"We'll build a nice fire, have a bite to eat, and rest up. Tomorrow, we'll set off for the Mother's Tower!"

XIX

The first rays of sunlight gently brushed Menilmonea's eyelids, drawing her from peaceful slumber. The rich smell of humus and rotting leaves filled her nostrils. Around her, the forest was bathed in golden light, the leaves' dancing shadows making arabesques on the carpet of moss that had served as her bed. The night had been mild.

Aureal, too, had woken. She stretched out her arms above her head, her tousled hair cascading over her shoulders.

"That was... delightful," she sighed, half-closing her eyes. "Sleeping under the stars, lulled by the hoots of tawny owls, the skittering of tiny paws, the whispering of wings.... It was like a lullaby."

"I wholeheartedly agree," said Menilmonea, already crouching near the dying embers of their campfire. "The song of the forest at night is an incredible experience. I've never slept so well. Despite all that awaits us, I feel relaxed."

She rummaged around in her satchel and pulled out two glowing red fire mushrooms. Calmly, precisely, she rubbed them together and tossed them into the embers. A sudden light flared, and with a whoosh, the flames sprang back to life, frolicking joyfully as if in greeting.

Menilmonea then took out some carefully wrapped eggs and cooked them in a small skillet, tossing in a pinch of dried herbs. At once, a pleasant aroma filled the air, rousing their still-sleepy taste buds. Having made herself a mug of herbal tea, Aureal dunked a bit of stale bread there to soften it.

"So what's the plan, then?" asked Aureal, pulling out the bread and biting into it.

"We head for the sun," Menilmonea answered, pointing east with her chin. "Due east. If all goes well, the Mother's Tower will be visible on the horizon. If it's as tall as those of the Titans, we can use it to find our way."

"Well done, Mistress! I like it when you have a plan."

Once they'd struck camp, the two friends set out once more, treading softly on the carpet of damp leaves in the undergrowth. The walk was pleasant: the ground yielding underfoot; the morning light, as filtered through the trees, a gentle gloom.

For nearly three hours, they made good progress, chatting quietly, sharing memories and speculating about what they might find when they reached their destination.

Then, without warning, the forest ended.

At the foot of a steep slope lay a deep valley, seemingly gouged from the surrounding sylvan mass.

But it wasn't the geography that shocked them speechless.

The valley was completely carpeted in mushrooms. And not just any mushrooms: colossal fungi, some as tall as the oldest trees in the forest. Their caps formed a colorful canopy of improbable shapes and intoxicating colors. Some were translucent, seeming to capture the light and make it dance in iridescent shimmers. Others, slender as marble columns, wore tapering bell-shaped caps.

"By the Mother...." whispered Menilmonea, mouth agape.

"It's... incredible," Aureal breathed, eyes wide with wonder. "As if someone cast a spell on the trees, turning them into mushrooms of every color."

"I-I want to talk to them," said Menilmonea. Her face seemed scarcely wide enough to contain her smile.

"You'll have a hard time fitting those in your bag," Aureal jested.

"That's for sure," said Menilmonea, laughing. "But I want to know who they are, what this mind-boggling valley is, why they're so tall!"

"Or maybe the question is... why are ours so small?" Aureal

contributed with a sly grin.

"I wonder if their power is commensurate with their size. Imagine: an ear-splitter tall as a house!"

"I'm not sure I want to," replied Aureal, laughing in turn.

The two friends began descending cautiously toward the valley, feeling both apprehensive and excited.

Halfway down, Aureal grabbed Menilmonea by the arm to stop her.

"The animals.... They're different here. They're not... afraid. It's something else. I'm not sure how to interpret their feelings."

"They're reverential, aren't they?" Menilmonea suggested.

"Exactly! How do you know?"

"The song. It's completely different here. Full of... deference. Esteem." Her voice fell to a whisper. "It's so strange."

"Yes... this place is steeped in history," Aureal whispered back. "Something important happened here."

"Indeed. Let's try not to disturb the peace."

The girls advanced respectfully into the forest of mushrooms. The air, thick with musky scents borne on a host of floating spores, seemed to hum around them.

Menilmonea stopped for a moment, her mouth half open.

The song had changed.

Vague melody no more, it was now rich and complex symphony, almost personal. She could hear voices, individual echoes in this invisible choir. Each mushroom seemed to have its own timbre, its own breath. It was overwhelming.

"You're behaving oddly," Aureal murmured, giving her a look full of tenderness. "Like you're... elsewhere. You hear something, don't you?"

Menilmonea nodded slowly, her eyes wide with the intensity of what she was experiencing.

"It's unbelievable," she whispered. "Such a vast song, so ancient... and I can hear them all! One at a time, and all at once."

Aureal remained silent, moved by her friend's sincerity. She felt, deep within herself, that something sacred was happening.

The deeper they ventured into the heart of the mycelian wood, the more supernatural the atmosphere became. A soft iridescent light filtered through the tall caps of the giant mushrooms, creating dancing haloes. A crystalline sound, discreet at first, could be heard in the distance. The burble of running water.

"Let's get closer," said Menilmonea. "We can sit down over there. I'd like to try speaking to one of those giant mushrooms."

They set their belongings down by the river, on a generous carpet of welcoming moss. A bright yellow fungal giant proudly stood a few steps away, as big around at its base as the trunk of a tree.

Menilmonea approached it slowly, reverently, and placed her palm against its stem. Instantly, her body was wracked by a violent spasm. Her head fell back, her pointy hat tumbling to the ground, eyes rolling upward into their sockets. Aureal rushed toward her, but Menilmonea raised a reassuring hand to indicate that everything was fine.

Aureal hesitated, unnerved. But then changed her mind and stepped back, watching her friend anxiously. Menilmonea entered a deep trance. Slowly, her body rose from the ground, levitating slightly over the grass. Her breathing seemed suspended, her expression caught between ecstasy and intense concentration.

Her whisper, when it came, was barely audible, almost guttural. "Everything will be all right.... Don't worry. They're… friendly. Trust me... Rest. I can tell this will take quite some time…"

Aureal remained frozen, speechless. Time stretched out, strange and burdensome.

At long last, she drifted off, trying to make herself useful: perhaps Menil might enjoy some herbal tea when she came to? Aureal set about building a fire to prepare it.

But there was no dry wood to be found. No bushes, no branches... nothing. It was all just grass, moss, and spores. Aureal felt her frustration mount within. Time went by, and still her friend floated, arrested in this enigmatic state. Aureal's anxiety grew with each passing minute, coiling around her stomach like a too-tight rope. What if Menilmonea didn't come back? What if she couldn't break the spell that was keeping her in stasis?

Just as Aureal was starting to really go round in circles, consumed by worry, a movement drew her eye. A host of animals had cautiously approached. Rabbits, weasels, colorful birds, even a few deer with large, gentle eyes. They all stood at a distance, silent, forming a circle around her.

Aureal looked at them, her heart aching. "If I hadn't spent so much time refusing my gift, maybe I... could understand you better now. Maybe I could tell you how lost and terrified I feel."

She paused for a moment, her throat tight, before going on. "Menil was so right to embrace her power. And I was so foolish. I just hope... I hope she can control it enough so it doesn't destroy her. I-I couldn't bear to lose her."

She shuddered. Suddenly, a gentle, unexpected warmth enveloped her. An almost palpable wave of affection, empathy.

The animals understood her. There could be no doubt. They were here for her; she was important to them.

"Thank you for being here," whispered Aureal, moved. "I don't know if I deserve you. I can't even build my friend a fire."

At these words, the animals scattered quietly, as if understanding their mission. A bit surprised, Aureal watched them walk off, but strangely enough, she felt their presence still, almost close enough to touch.

She watched as they came back moments later. Some were carrying small twigs, others larger pieces of wood. Deer approached with their antlers bearing branches, which they carefully deposited at Aureal's feet.

She had enough to make fires for weeks.

Speechless, she stood there for a moment, hands trembling.

"Thank... thank you so much, my friends," she stammered, misty-eyed.

Slowly, she approached them. Not a one moved away. In fact, they seemed almost to invite her nearer. She held out a hesitant hand and gently placed it on a doe's warm flank. At once, a wave of affection washed over her, so powerful it took her breath away. She sensed something, a message silent but clear. *Everything will be all right.*

"Thank you. I-I don't know what to say. This is all so new.... I ignored your song for so long. I dismissed it as noise, without trying to look more deeply. To distance myself from its richness... and above all from everything it implied. I've been such a fool. I don't deserve to have you here for me."

At these words, a subtle transformation took place in her perception. The animals looked at each other, as if a single shiver had passed through them all.

And from within this gathering, she felt a new energy, an almost solemn respect that seemed to converge on one of their own. The circle around her opened to let an imposing grizzly bear pass through.

The creature advanced slowly, solemnly, its impressive bulk casting a broad shadow on the moss. Aureal should have been terrified, paralyzed before this force of nature. But no, not at all.

A strange feeling of peace came over her. Of absolute safety. This was no predator, not right now. It was a friend and a protector.

She stood there, mouth agape, hands clasped over her chest, overwhelmed by an encounter that stood outside of time. She knew now she was no longer alone. She knew now she never had been.

She reached out a hand toward the great beast's thick fur. The moment her fingers touched him, she heard it as clearly as if the bear had spoken. *We are here for you. You have nothing to fear.*

They weren't really words, but she knew with absolute certainty that this was the message they all wished to convey.

"But why? Why me? Why so much... kindness?" she whispered, overwhelmed.

The answer exploded in her head, as clear as the one before. *Because you are the bearer of hope. Because you, in your quest, shall also aid us. Because you are good of heart.*

"I-I don't understand. Do you want to talk to the Mother, too?"

No sooner did she utter that name than the animals' song grew troubled, filled with sudden, almost rageful tension.

The bear turned its head slightly toward her, and in the unambivalent silence, she perceived a thought as clear as the sun in the summer sky. *The only Mother who has ever existed is Nature itself.*

"I see…. I didn't mean to upset you. This is all so new to me," she stammered, sincerely contrite. "I'm a bit lost…"

At once, the song subsided to its former self, appeased by her humility.

"It's getting dark," she said, as if to swiftly change the subject. "I hope everything's all right with Menil. As for me, I'm going to build a fire. Unlike all of you, I don't have any fur, and it's starting to get chilly."

Aureal walked over to her friend's floating form and, as gently as she could, undid her satchel. She'd seen Menilmonea fiddle with her fire mushrooms often enough to know which ones they were. Aureal took two, examined them carefully, and then, with all the concentration she could muster, crushed them together before tossing them onto the small pile of branches she'd readied.

She sat down beside the growing flames. To her surprise, the bear came and lay down right behind her, breathing quietly, reassuringly. She turned her head toward him, thanked him tenderly with a glance, and began to make herbal tea.

She felt serene. The crackling of the fire lulled her gently. And before the water in her iron jug had time to boil, she'd fallen asleep, leaning against the side of her new companion.

Satisfied, the animals took their leave one by one and went back to their business. Only the grizzly bear remained motionless and peaceful beside Aureal.

XX

When Menilmonea emerged from her stasis at last and opened her eyes, daylight had already begun to wane. An orange glow dappled the leaves, and the scent of evening gently crept among the trunks. There was a storm in the air, with a downpour undoubtedly on the way. Menilmonea blinked several times, still sluggish, her body heavy with the strange torpor from which she was slow to emerge.

She stretched slightly, her muscles protesting for a moment. Casting about for her friend, she came upon a scene that took her mind quite a while to process.

Aureal was fast asleep, curled up against the imposing bulk of a grizzly bear.

The creature must have been twice her size, but that didn't seem to bother her in the least. Quite the opposite: she looked at peace.

The animal's muzzle quivered slightly with each deep and lulling breath, and its thick hide rose and fell with serene deliberation. A campfire crackled nearby.

Once Menilmonea's mind had accepted the bear's presence, a second puzzle awaited: there was another pile of wood near the fire, with enough branches to build a whole cabin or two. She couldn't understand how Aureal had managed to gather so much wood in such a short time. Or, for that matter, how she'd managed to tame a grizzly bear.

As Menilmonea approached on tiptoe, both to avoid waking her friend and out of caution over the imposing creature, she listened intently, alert to the slightest movement. The grizzly bear opened one eye, watched her at length, let out a low growl—a sound closer to contentment than annoyance—then gently lowered its eyelid and drifted back to sleep.

Menilmonea took this as implicit permission and sat down with care, quietly crossing her legs.

Reflexively, she reached for her bag, but her palm met only the moss-covered ground. She frowned, looking around, panic rising in her chest.

"Where did that damn thing go?"

At last, her eyes settled on it, resting against Aureal, half hidden in her new cushion's thick fur.

She crawled forward on all fours, trying not to wake Aureal or disturb the slumbering beast. But a twig snapped under her knee.

Aureal stirred slightly, then abruptly came to, her eyes lighting up at the sight of her friend.

"By the Mother! You're safe!" she cried, forgetting all restraint as she threw herself into Menilmonea's arms.

The embrace was as energetic as it was welcome. The bear let out a satisfied yawn.

"It was an incredible experience," whispered Menilmonea, briefly slumping against her. "I'll tell you everything, but right now, I'm hungrier than I've ever been in my life."

"I'm on it," Aureal replied without missing a beat.

"Perfect. Because on top of that, I also have an irresistible urge to pee. I'll leave you to the kitchen. Be right back!" she said, getting up with a little sigh. Then she changed her mind, turning to Aureal with a curious smile. "By the way, what happened to you while I was communing with the mushrooms?"

Aureal shrugged with a mischievous look. "I opened myself up to my gift!"

Menilmonea's eyes widened, genuinely moved.

"I'm so proud of you! And did you make a new friend?" she asked, indicating the grizzly bear with her chin.

"Exactly. Several, even. They helped me gather wood, as you can see!" Aureal replied with a little wink, pointing to the impressive pile of branches.

Menilmonea gave a gentle laugh.

"Well, yours was a busy day!" she shouted as she ran toward the river.

Aureal smiled mirthfully, grabbed the pan by the fire, and threw in a few slices of bacon that had been carefully wrapped in a fern leaf. Soon, a familiar sizzling filled the evening air, and a delicious smell began to waft about.

The grizzly bear twitched an ear. Then a paw. He sniffed the air. Slowly, he rose partway, eyes still half-shut, snout pointed panward.

Aureal burst out laughing. "I'm not sure I have enough for all three of us."

She stared at him for a moment, eyes sparkling with merriment.

"What's your name, anyway, my friend?" she asked gently.

Promptly, a sentence popped into her head, as clear as if it had been her own. *I am the bear of this territory.*

"I see, so... no name. No problem. May I give you one?"

I don't see why not, the voice replied in her mind, accompanied by a low growl, almost of indifference.

Aureal thought for a moment, distractedly tapping the handle of the pan. "I'll call you Grumf. It sounds a little like the noise you just made."

Feeling proud of herself, she turned the bacon slices over, whistling. But suddenly her face froze, her mind returning to a recent memory.

"Come to think of it... Earlier, you called me a 'bearer of hope'. What did that mean?"

The answer came quickly, full of profound respect. *Nature's Sentinel thinks you can help him.*

"Nature's Sentinel? Who's that? And how can I help him?"

He will introduce himself to you when the time is right. He will guide you.

"But what does he look like?"

He can take on any shape he wishes.

Aureal remained silent for a few seconds, deep in thought. "He wouldn't take on the form of a fox, would he?

He has, yes.

Back from the river, Menilmonea caught the end of the one-sided conversation. "Was that you asking him who the fox was?"

Aureal turned to her, looking pensive. "Yes, but I'm not sure of the answer. To tell the truth, he's not very talkative, but... it sounds like Grumf calls him Nature's Sentinel. And apparently he needs our help."

Menilmonea sighed softly and sat down beside her friend. "Well! What a great many changes. Speaking of which, do you know how to talk to our fox? How to find out what he needs, or how to help him?"

Aureal shrugged with a pensive pout. "Apparently, he'll come to us when he needs to."

Menilmonea gave a slight smile. "So be it, then. We've got enough to keep ourselves busy, don't we?"

She gave Aureal a conspiratorial wink, then said playfully, "So this charming fellow is named Grumf, eh?"

"Yes, but only as of just now. I found 'Bear-of-this-territory' a bit too formal."

"Ha ha! Just so. Oh, by the way, my half-moon blood came. Two days late. I'm quite glad. I was starting to get anxious too."

"I don't know if it's just the stress of traveling, or…"

"Most likely. I've never had this issue before, and I've been fertile since my seventh cycle. Still, it's disturbing that our bodies have been so out of sync since we left."

"Well, now things are back to normal, so: one less problem! But apart from that, what happened to you?"

Menilmonea took a moment to gather her thoughts. "By all the Titans! It was intense. The moment I touched that chanterelle's stem, I felt like I'd been projected from my own body. I was in communion with all the other mushrooms around. It wasn't like the song of the forest. It was more like a vast conversation with thousands of voices, some louder than others. They welcomed me. They recognized me."

"Recognized?"

"Yes. These are the first mushrooms this world ever bore. They are extremely old, Aureal. Hundreds of cycles. In fact, they call themselves the Elders. The mushrooms found near us, and all over the continent, are their children. Descended from spores scattered by the world. The spores told them about me. About my gift."

"Wait... did you say continent?"

"Ah, yes. Well, do you remember what the spirit told us about the 'planet'?"

"Yes, I'd be hard-pressed to forget."

"Well, our planet is covered by enormous oceans of unfathomable depth. And on these oceans is a mass of land: the continent."

"We live on an island?"

"Yes, in a way. But a very, very large one. The Elders think it's possible that other continents exist, but they're not sure. No spores from other continents have ever reached them."

"Well... This journey will at least have helped advance our understanding of the world. I never saw beyond our own village."

Menilmonea burst out in a hearty laugh. "The Elders are the first mushrooms, then. They were born on this soil after an epic battle. A struggle between Nature's Primals... and the Others."

Aureal frowned. "Primals? Others?"

"Yes, the whole story is quite staggering, I agree. For example, the Ancients literally grew from the bodies of these Primals. They don't know exactly who the Primals were, but they fought here to defend Nature against the Others. The latter were able to use forbidden magic dangerous to the forest. Nature, also called Gaia, then deployed the Primals to prevent the Others from doing harm. The battle was an epic one, but apparently, the Others eventually won. Using their sorcery, they managed to destroy the Primals. And many cycles after their tragic end, Gaia brought forth the Ancients as a testimony to the memory of these vanished beings."

Aureal was speechless. "But... what about the Others? Where are they? Who are they?"

"That's where it gets harder to take. They're in their fortress, east of here."

Aureal paled slightly. "You mean...?"

"Yes. It seems we are indeed talking about the Mother's Tower."

There was a long silence.

"I don't understand," Aureal whispered. "The Mother created this world, didn't she?"

Aureal paused, as if a piece of a gigantic puzzle had just fallen into place.

"Yes?" asked Menilmonea. "Is there something you found out?"

"Earlier, when I mentioned the Mother to Grumf, his response was cold. Almost scathing. For him, the only Mother is Nature."

Menilmonea nodded slowly. "The more I think about it, the more I believe that the Mother's true nature is not the one Tunka taught us."

Aureal sighed deeply, then let herself fall back into the grass, arms outstretched.

"I really wish we'd brought some brandy from the village. I wouldn't mind a drink right now. But anyway! To sum up, the first mushrooms and even the animals believe that the Mother is not the true creator of our world, but a usurper. And this entity, or her minions, fought Gaia's defenders right here, winning by some obscure means?"

"I'm afraid so, yes."

"But who or what is this Gaia?"

"According to the Elders, she is the creator of everything. The First to Be, before all else. It is her song I hear."

"That sounds an awful lot like what Tunka told us about the Mother, doesn't it? Except for the singing part, of course."

"I don't know, Aureal. I'm confused. The Elders told me in no uncertain terms that the Mother is not a goddess. Merely an impostor."

"By all the Titans! At any rate, I suppose we'll see when we get there."

A heavy silence followed. Both girls remained still, their thoughts in disarray, their gazes lost in the void. The crackling of the fire and Grumf's steady breathing were the only sounds to disturb this listlessness.

Then, after a moment, Menilmonea spoke softly. "There's one last thing. They told me we could see a genuine artifact of the Others. A magical weapon they used to defeat the Primals: a sphere of negation."

Aureal sat up, intrigued. "A magical object? Here?"

"Yes. If you follow the river east, you'll come to a place where nothing grows. And in the middle of it lies the sphere. Animals, plants... nothing survives within its baleful influence. The Elders have asked me to help them get rid of it. They consider this object an offense to Nature and the Primals' memory. They believe that since we can enter the Towers, we can also approach the sphere and take it far away from here."

Aureal grew pale once more. "The Towers.... What have they to do with the sphere's magic?"

"The Elders are convinced that the magic of the Towers and that of the artifact are one and the same. According to them, nothing can enter the Towers for the same reason."

"Nothing except us, apparently."

"Exactly. And that would also explain why our gifts cease working in the Towers. The magic of negation would block them."

"Heavens! What a tale! Well, it won't cost us anything to go have a look."

The rest of the evening passed peacefully, lulled by a light rain that the giant mushroom's cap, their shelter for the night, was broad enough to ward off. The two friends spent a long time speculating on the true natures of the Mother and Gaia without coming any closer to understanding.

They also discussed what they might say to the Mother should she really turn out to be as they had been brought up to believe. How could they ask her forgiveness for their transgressions while also begging her to save Tunka and the sleeping Titans?

What if their goddess had been nothing but an impostor? What to do then?

But simply talking did them good, offering them an anchor in the maelstrom their lives had now become.

Eventually, they drifted off, both huddled up against the warm fur of their ursine protector.

XXI

The night had been mild and restful. A fine rain still fell on the mushroom caps, creating a peaceful, almost hypnotic atmosphere. When Aureal opened her eyes, Menilmonea was already busy by the fire, intently preparing an omelet.

"Good morning, Aureal! Did you sleep well? I had another excellent night. I slept like a log."

Aureal stretched lethargically, a lazy smile on her lips. "By Tunka's shell, I couldn't agree more! Grumf makes an excellent pillow."

The bear grumbled, looking slightly offended.

"Let's eat, freshen up a bit, head for the sphere, and see what can be done when we get there. How's that sound for a plan?"

"Yes, Mistress! Perfect. Anyway, it'll get us closer to the Tower. And it'll give us a chance to take a closer look at negation magic. If the Mother isn't our goddess, we might as well learn more about her abilities before leaping into her arms."

A broad smile lit up Menilmonea's face. "Why, whatever happened to my dear Aureal? The homey sort with the well-ordered life.... Who are you, madam?"

"Oh, I don't know.... We can all change, can't we? I feel good, that's all. Ever since accepting who I am, I've felt at peace with myself. And ready to commit all manner of lunacy, with you by my side."

"So be it!"

Once ready, they struck camp and followed the river eastward. Loyal and imposing, the grizzly brought up the rear with his massive bulk.

"Do you know why Grumf wants to come with us? It doesn't seem like we're in any danger. Could you ask him?"

"Oh, no need. He understands you very well, even if you can't hear him. Basically, the Sentinel wants to make sure nothing bad befalls us."

"But where is this Sentinel? Do you still sense the fox following us?"

"No... I haven't 'seen' him for a while."

"I do hope he'll consent to talk to us someday. He's very intriguing."

"You're telling me! Grumf says the time will come soon enough."

"You're a bear of a philosophical bent, dear Grumf. But then... what dangers could we be facing? Not the plant monster again, surely?"

Aureal remained silent for a moment. "He says, and I quote: 'Nothing in particular.' Our dear friend isn't the most talkative fellow. I did warn you."

"We'll see, then. In any case, walking beside a protector twenty times our weight combined is rather reassuring."

For an hour, the landscape remained hopelessly unchanged, a blend of mossy soil and a host of humongous fungal colossi tall as trees in an ancient wood. Then, all at once, everything was different. The river continued peaceably on its way, but now it flowed through a peculiar clearing where nothing at all grew save for sparse, yellowish grass, as if resigned to survive in a place from which the rest of the vegetable kingdom had withdrawn.

The clearing formed a perfect circle just over sixty feet across, as if drawn with a compass. And occupying its exact center was the sphere of negation. It was the size of a small pumpkin and seemed to be made entirely of silver or some bright gray metal. It glowed faintly in the dim light of the cloudy sky, as if radiating its own energy. An eerie silence seemed to preside over the area. The air was much heavier and denser here than in the wood.

The friends slowed their pace and stopped at the edge of the sphere's baleful influence. Grumf wrinkled his muzzle, nostrils quivering, and seemed particularly on edge.

Menilmonea took a deep breath, trying to hide the growing anxiety slowly creeping over her.

"I'll go have a look. There's no need for both of us to risk it."

Aureal stared at her intently, face tense with apprehension. "Please be careful. If you have any doubts, come right back, all right?"

"Yes. I'll be very careful." With that, Menilmonea entered the area and immediately felt the familiar shock of her gift becoming inaccessible. She raised her head and loudly declared, "All is well, it's just like when we enter a Tower. I can't hear the singing anymore, but other than that, I feel fine as usual."

"Good!" replied Aureal, her voice slightly tense. "Let's take it slow."

Menilmonea advanced toward the sphere, commenting aloud, "There's nothing out of the ordinary. The grass isn't very lush, but apart from the absence of my gift, it could be any meadow."

She took a few more steps toward the sphere. "It looks like it's vibrating. I'll try to touch it."

"Are you sure?" Aureal could no longer hide her concern.

"Not at all! But if we're to move it, I don't see that we have much choice." After a few seconds of hesitation, she said, now more intrigued than fearful, "Strange… It's shiny, like the blades of the swords our blacksmith makes, but there's no reflection. Yet it looks smooth, as if polished to a high shine. All right, I'm going to touch it."

Slowly she reached out with her finger, shutting her eyes and clenching her teeth instinctively. As soon as she felt its cold touch, she quickly snatched her hand back. Straightaway, she said, "It really does feel like a ball of metal, maybe silver, but it's vibrating and doesn't reflect its surroundings."

Aureal tried to lighten the mood with a mocking quip. "Wait a moment and see what happens to your finger. It might rot and fall off!"

Menilmonea rolled her eyes. "How lovely. I do appreciate the moral support. For now, my finger seems to be staunchly resisting rot."

After a long moment of cautious waiting, Menilmonea continued in a relieved tone, "Well, it seems this sphere definitely does not cause rot in those who touch it."

"Wonderful news!" replied Aureal, relieved.

The rain had picked up again a few moments earlier, and now a thunderclap boomed in the distance, startling the two friends.

"We ought to wait for the storm to pass before trying to move it. Do you think it's heavy?" asked Aureal, staring doubtfully at the sphere from a distance.

Menilmonea frowned. "Let me... try to lift it."

She stepped forward hesitantly, braced herself, and tried to lift the ball by grabbing it from below. "Argh! It's incredibly heavy. I don't think it'd budge even if I kicked it."

"Hold on, I'm coming. We have proof that it's not dangerous to us." Aureal took a brisk step forward, gasping slightly as she crossed through the invisible barrier surrounding the sphere.

"Yup. Same old magic as the Towers."

Menilmonea nodded, determined. "All right! Let's both push it from this side. On three! One... two... three!"

They put all their strength into it, to no avail. The sphere did not move an inch. Out of breath, Aureal finally declared in discouragement, "What dark wizardry is this? How can such a tiny ball be so heavy?"

Menilmonea crossed her arms, deep in thought. "Let's think.... Maybe we could use a branch as a lever?"

But no sooner had she uttered these words than it began to pour. Soon, it felt as if the heavens were emptying themselves. Both girls were soaked, and Menilmonea's tall pointy hat now looked like a waterfall. She shouted to be heard over the deluge. "Let's find shelter, or we'll end up catching cold."

Aureal nodded and they ran toward Grumf, who had already taken refuge under a large mushroom. Halfway between the sphere and the edge of the forest, they both retched, and stared at each other in disbelief.

"How...?" whispered Aureal, incredulous.

"Yes, me too. Let's find shelter! We can discuss it then," Menilmonea replied hastily.

They ended their sprint and were finally able to catch their breath, sheltered from the storm.

"I'll make a fire. I'm glad I grabbed some branches when we left. I just hope your pile won't miss them," said Menilmonea with a laugh.

With her wet hair plastered all over her face, Aureal smiled broadly and shook herself as best she could.

"Maybe I should consider getting a big hat like yours," she said. "It's bulky, but very practical."

"Oh, yes. I can't count the number of times it started raining when I was in the forest. Without it, I'd have more colds than I already do!"

With help from a few mushrooms, the small fire got off to a slow start. Aureal looked up, satisfied, then asked, intrigued, "Did you notice what happened?"

"Yes! Our gifts returned long before we left the exclusion zone."

"But how is that possible?"

"I have no idea," Menilmonea replied, frowning slightly.

Aureal thought for a moment. "Unless..."

"Yes?" asked Menilmonea, suddenly curious.

"What if the rain has a dampening effect on the sphere's power?"

"That's an interesting theory. With such heavy rain, it must be completely covered in water. That would be an excellent way to neutralize it..."

"If we could move it, maybe we could heave it into the river over there."

"Excellent idea! Let's just wait for the rain to stop completely to see if the negation zone has returned to its original size."

"All right. In the meantime, there should be some of Abigail's strawberry pie left. That'll do us good."

"Yes, with a nice hot cup of tea."

The pair watched the rain in silence and slowly warmed themselves while enjoying their impromptu meal. When the rain began to let up, Menilmonea stood slowly and cautiously approached the negation zone.

"I know a way we can be sure. If I stand just beyond the edge of the negation zone without moving, when the sphere dries, the zone should return to its original size, and I will lose my gift without having to take a step."

Aureal smiled enthusiastically. "What an incredible idea! I love it! I'll stand a little closer to the center of the zone. That way I should lose mine before you do."

Delighted with their clever strategy, the girls took their places.

The rain had long since stopped, and just as the two friends were beginning to lose patience, Aureal let out a little gasp. "It's working! I just heard the animals stop singing."

Menilmonea immediately looked up with a radiant smile. "Perfect! It should be any minute for me now."

A few moments later, she exclaimed enthusiastically, "Bingo! That's it, I'm cut off from the forest's song! There you go, dear friend! Now we know how to block the magic of the Others!"

Jumping up and down for joy, Aureal said determinedly, "All right, now let's try to move it toward the river!"

The two friends rolled up their sleeves and poured all their heart into pushing the sphere toward the river. But it proved much less yielding than expected.

"By all the Titans! It really doesn't want to cooperate!" exclaimed Menilmonea, frustrated.

"No, indeed. Perhaps a lever, as you suggested?" said Aureal.

"Or instead of bringing it to the river," Menilmonea said, thinking out loud, "we could bring the river to it?"

Aureal looked at her in confusion. "What? You want to change the river's course?"

Menilmonea burst out laughing. "Haha, maybe not change it completely, but look: if we dig all around the sphere, we should be able to form a kind of small basin. We might not be able to budge it, but it doesn't float in the air either. If we remove the earth underneath, we can bring it down gently. Then we either wait for the next rain or dig a small channel to bring the river water here and submerge it."

Aureal's eyes opened wide. She exclaimed admiringly, "Menilmonea, you're a genius!"

The mycomanceress blushed slightly. "We're geniuses! It's teamwork through and through! We don't have any tools, however. So this might take a while..."

XXII

After hours of dogged persistence with their bare hands, rocks, pieces of wood, and even their precious frying pan, the two friends finally stepped back and beheld the fruit of their labors with chagrin. The clay soil, saturated with water, had become a sticky paste almost impossible to dig through.

Aureal sighed and let the muddy skillet fall limply to the ground. "Well, this isn't going to work."

Menilmonea nodded, her hands covered in mud and her face smeared with dirt. She absentmindedly wiped a damp strand of hair from her forehead with the back of her sleeve.

"Indeed, it'll take us years at this rate. We'll have to step it up a notch," she announced with a wily grin.

Aureal raised an eyebrow, intrigued but concerned. "Step it up?"

"I'm going to get some detonita."

Aureal gaped at her for a moment, flabbergasted.

"They're amanita mushrooms that explode violently when subjected to stress," Menilmonea explained, suppressing a smile at the alarmed look on her friend's face.

"I usually stay away because they can be very prickly... and sarcastic," she added with a grimace. "But I'll make an effort today. I'll just have to ask the Elders where to find some mature ones."

Aureal seemed to regain her composure and asked hopefully, "Can't the Elders just give you some?"

Menilmonea shook her head with a disappointed pout. "Alas, no, the Elders never mature. They are immortal. Only their offspring have relatively short lives. I'll have to go looking in the woods around the valley."

Aureal straightened up and stretched, grimacing as her every muscle protested. "Well, so be it! Let's go ask them straightaway. We'll take the opportunity to see if there are any fruits or tubers, because we won't last long with what we've left to eat."

Menilmonea nodded vigorously before wrinkling her nose with a soft chuckle. "But first, I wouldn't mind a nice bath... and maybe even doing some laundry!"

Aureal raised her arms, feigning a horrified look as she sniffed herself, before breaking into laughter. "Yes, by all the Titans! Why, I'd even say it's our top priority!"

The river was cool, but the pleasure of feeling clean was enough to lift their spirits. After a vigorous wash-down, they busied themselves scrubbing their clothes against rocks to remove all the accumulated grime.

Suddenly, Menilmonea let out a guffaw. "What awful adventurers we are!"

Aureal looked at her, puzzled. "What? Why?"

"Here we are, standing naked in the river, and neither of us thought to light a fire before jumping in. We haven't even gathered any wood!"

Aureal joined her in hearty laughter.

"You forget, I'm here! Let my ancestral magic do its work," she said, exaggeratedly waving her hands around as if summoning an ancient power.

Menilmonea giggled. "Oh, I see! So that's how you do it?"

"Wait, o ye of little faith!" Aureal replied, feigning indignation.

Amused, Menilmonea made mock apology and obeyed her friend's bidding, all while furiously washing her clothes.

A few minutes later, beavers and a few weasels emerged from the woods overlooking the mushroom valley. They deposited a generous heap of branches before the two friends. Menilmonea looked on, genuinely impressed.

"Well, blow me over!"

Aureal smiled triumphantly.

"Ha! See?" she said with a saucy wink.

Menilmonea quickly got out of the water, grabbed two fire mushrooms, and rubbed them together to light a beautiful blaze. She then leaned toward the animals curiously watching her and said, "Thank you very much. We really appreciate your help!"

Visibly contented, the animals quietly went back to their business.

The two friends spread their clothes out on stones arranged around the fire, sheltering under a giant bolete. The peaceful, pleasant atmosphere provided them occasion for a well-deserved break, and they gave in, letting the warmth of the flames gently dry their skin.

Once dressed and ready, Menilmonea stood up and gently placed her hand against the mushroom's stem. Her gaze grew unfocused as she slowly entered a trance, her body rising to hover ever so slightly over the moss-covered earth.

After a long silence, her eyes opened once again, and her feet settled back on the ground, a radiant smile lighting up her face.

"I told them about our findings, and they're delighted. They directed me to several likely spots and an easy trail for climbing back up to the woods. We'll be able to stock up on detonitas and gather lots of fruit too!"

Aureal sat up gladly, her energy restored.

"Then let's be off! We can leave camp set up here. I'll even put a kettle on to boil so we can make ourselves a nice cup of tea when we get back," Aureal said cheerily.

The two friends followed the westward path the Elders had indicated, gently ascending toward the forest. The canopy was particularly dense, creating an intimate and beguiling atmosphere in the undergrowth. When they reached the amanita mushrooms, Menilmonea stopped.

"All right, I'll do the talking. Stay back in case things go wrong."

Aureal nodded with a smile. "Sure. Grumf and I will gather some berries. We'll also go get some apples from over there. Join us when you're done negotiating?"

"Absolutely," Menilmonea agreed.

The two friends parted ways, and Menilmonea walked toward the group of amanita mushrooms nestled in the natural shelter of mammoth oak roots.

Well, look who's here! If it isn't the girl who talks to mushrooms. This is our lucky day, fellas! said a voice in her mind.

Surprised, Menilmonea replied softly, "Why, you speak very clearly!"

What do you mean? another voice chimed in, annoyed.

She must be used to our country cousins from the far woods, added a third voice, jeering. *Take it from me: spores that fall so far from the cap aren't the freshest anymore!*

Menilmonea gave a nervous giggle. "Um... yes, indeed, I come from far away, and it's true that the mushrooms there don't speak as well as you do here."

You're looking at the cream of the crop, little lady! We are educated and fully sentient! exclaimed another voice proudly.

Menilmonea nodded enthusiastically. "That's excellent news, because I'm going to need your assistance!"

Uh-oh! Who told you about us? asked a curious voice.

"The Elders. They told me where to find specimens of your quality. They assured me that you could help."

Assured you, eh? That's a good one!

Those bluebloods disgust me. What did they ever do to deserve their title, apart from being born first? interjected a cynical voice.

They are immortal, after all... said another voice, somewhat intimidated.

Sure, but what else? the cynical voice persisted.

They're also ginormous, another voice added admiringly.

I'll give you that, too! But apart from all that? You know what I'm trying to say. In the end, they're really no different from you and me.

Amused, Menilmonea reassured them, "Yes, you are all the same! But you're also their children, after all!"

Oh, sure, they love to throw their spores around, but then when we need them, there's no one to be seen!

"I understand," Menilmonea said softly, taking care not to offend her audience. "But would you be willing to help me? I really need to create a big explosion, and your talents would be extremely useful."

I don't see why we'd want to. So you can talk to mushrooms? Big deal! I do that every day! came a sardonic voice.

And honestly, if we wanted to make a big boom, we could just as easily do it right here, another added with a hint of insolence.

Well, not everyone here is mature, so if we could avoid it... interjected a voice of caution and concern.

No, of course not! I meant it metaphorically.

Menilmonea adopted an air of detachment. "No, I understand. It's clearly not easy to make truly impressive explosions."

What exactly are you implying?

"Oh, nothing at all. Everyone feels inadequate now and then. Sometimes we put pressure on ourselves, but nothing good ever comes of that. Besides, the Elders told me about another group further north. Don't worry, I'll go and pop in on them."

Nonsense! We can make explosions so mind-blowing you'll have trouble holding back tears of admiration!

Yeah! And frankly, those fatcaps up north barely even count as Amanitas. Why, a few spores less, and they'd be boletes!

Menilmonea paused dramatically and waited for their reactions.

Fine! Okay! I'll come along. I'll show you what it means to go out with a bang, dammit!

Yeah, me too!

Suddenly, dozens of voices rang out, each eager to prove their honor as detonitas.

After warmly thanking these volunteers, Menilmonea stood and set them very gently on the makeshift wrapping of two large ferns. "Be good, now. I'm off to fetch my friend, and then I'll get you settled."

It'd be a shame to waste our bang on these dumb ol' ferns.

"Exactly! Where I'm taking you will be much classier." Menilmonea gave them a conspiratorial wink.

Knowing that patience was not exactly an amanita's strongest suit, she hastened her step and called out to Aureal, "I'm going to place them around the sphere!"

Her friend replied enthusiastically, "No problem, we're almost done. I've stocked up on goodies. A boar even found me some wild potatoes and chestnuts."

As Menilmonea finished positioning the mushrooms around the base of the sphere, the reality of the situation hit her with a vengeance.

"By all the Titans!" she cried out loud.

Aureal had just arrived. "What's going on?"

"I can't talk to them here! And they've probably all blacked out, anyway."

"Darn, darn, darn! How are we going to blow them up now?"

"We'll give it everything we've got! Bring me as much dry moss as you can."

Meanwhile, Menilmonea took her two ferns and rolled them up into small tubes. As soon as Aureal handed her the moss, she stuffed it inside. She placed these on the ground with one end touching an amanita and the other pointing toward her.

Aureal frowned. "What's that?"

"A wick. Or rather, the somewhat sickly cousin of a wick twice removed."

Aureal smiled, then stepped back when she saw Menilmonea grab two fire mushrooms.

"Stand back. You too, Grumf. Get as far away as you can. Here goes!"

With that, Menilmonea quickly squeezed the two mushrooms and threw them at the closer ends of her makeshift wicks. The girls scampered off, making for camp as quick as they could and, from an excess of caution, opted to hide behind the stem of the overhanging bolete.

The explosion was apocalyptic. A deafening roar tore through the air, followed by a devastating shockwave that shook the whole valley. Bits of clay, propelled with unprecedented force, rose in muddy geysers toward the sky before falling back down in a thick, viscid rain. Their campfire was swept aside like a mere candle snuffed by a storm, while the ground shook violently beneath their feet as if the earth itself were trembling with fear at the cataclysmic explosion.

The detonitas hadn't been lying: they knew how to move earth. When silence had finally returned and the rain of debris came to an end, the two friends cautiously emerged from behind the mushroom stem, working their jaws in an effort to unblock their ears.

"By Tunka's shell, that was impressive!" Aureal exclaimed. "I wonder if it destroyed the sphere itself."

"We should be so lucky!" replied Menilmonea hopefully.

Aureal looked at their demolished camp and grinned, despite it all. "Well, at least we can make some more tea. The teapot's lodged at the base of our bolete."

They began walking toward the sphere, crossing into the zone.

"Nope, still there." Menilmonea sighed. "There goes the forest's song."

Aureal nodded solemnly. "Yes, indeed. The magic of the Others is truly powerful."

Still, their disappointment was short-lived. Although completely intact, the sphere now lay at the bottom of a magnificent crater just over three feet deep and twice as wide across.

"A job well done!" exclaimed Aureal admiringly. "What's more, the heat from the explosion literally fired the clay lining the bottom."

Menilmonea beamed.

"We've made a splendid bowl for our sphere! Now," she added with a smile, "all we have to do is wait for the rain to fall and drown it naturally!"

Aureal nodded enthusiastically. "Let's take a seat. It's been a long day, and we deserve a good meal. And with those clouds in the west, we won't have to wait too long."

After carefully clearing the clay debris and cleaning off their makeshift shelter, they avidly readied their meal: a generous helping of mashed potatoes with a beautiful side of fruit salad. Grumf had returned, still a bit jittery after the explosion, but relieved to be back in their company.

As night slowly fell, the rain began, lightly at first, then gradually intensifying.

"We should get some sleep," Menilmonea suggested, watching the rain run over the ground. "We'll see what happens tomorrow."

XXIII

Menilmonea opened her eyes with a start, awakened by the quiet drumming of the rain's last drops on their makeshift shelter. She stretched slowly, her muscles wooden from the lingering damp. At her side, Aureal had already risen and was busy reviving the fire the night's showers had doused.

"I really hope the sphere was completely submerged," Menilmonea muttered, running a hand through her tangled hair.

"Only one way to find out," Aureal replied with a determined smile, handing her a hunk of bread. "Let's eat quickly and go check."

Grumf kept casting anxious glances toward where the sphere lay, as if sensing something unusual.

"He can tell something's changed," Aureal remarked, watching her furry companion closely.

"Excellent news! Either way, we'll soon find out. If the negation zone is still active, we'll lose our gifts as soon as we get close."

Aureal nodded slowly, reassured. "You're right. Let's finish quickly and go see for ourselves."

Their hearts pounding with a mixture of excitement and apprehension, the two girls quickly rose and made their way to their makeshift basin. The air was thick with moisture, and the rain had made the soil around the sphere particularly muddy, but the joyous birdsong already heralded a milder day.

As they approached, they found the familiar sensation of their gift remained intact. There was no noticeable change. They exchanged a conspiratorial glance, relieved to have won this small victory against the magic of the Others.

At last they reached the pond that had formed in the detonation basin. There, under about three feet of murky water, the sphere seemed completely inert, as if neutralized.

"It's working!" whispered Menilmonea in wonder.

Grumf, meanwhile, had stayed back at the edge of what had been the negation zone. Aureal called out to him softly. "You can come closer. It won't hurt you anymore."

The grizzly growled slightly, hesitating, but finally overcame his apprehension. He approached the muddy puddle with caution, nervously eyeing the shiny object submerged within. Aureal placed a reassuring hand on his thick fur.

"It's okay, Grumf. The water's completely neutralized it."

After a few moments, he finally seemed to relax, convinced its magic no longer posed a threat.

"See? Nothing to worry about," Aureal murmured gently.

Menilmonea whispered a few quick words to the mushrooms around her, trying to pick up their responses. But so loud was the mental tumult that she frowned in frustration.

"All right, then, I'm going to have to make physical contact to make sure they understand we've solved the problem. There are too many of them, and they're too powerful for me to hear their response clearly from here."

"No problem! I'll work on improving our system. I've got an idea," replied Aureal, a gleam in her eye.

Menilmonea gave her a curious, bemused look before returning to their campsite. She sat down, making herself comfortable, shut her eyes, and quickly entered her trance, communing with the Elders. Straightaway, she shared the good news with them.

You have our thanks, human. Your help will not be forgotten. The rumors about you were clearly not unfounded, replied the First Mushrooms, their voices echoing softly in her mind.

"It was our pleasure," replied Menilmonea humbly. "We will now press on eastward. Whoever these Others are, they must have a direct connection to the one we call the Mother. We must find them and ask for their help."

The Elders gave a brief pause before continuing more somberly, *Be wary of them, young girl. They bring nothing but misfortune. Their magic is unholy and artificial. They are not children of Gaia.*

"I understand, but we must attempt the impossible in order to save Tunka and the other Titans."

May Gaia protect you, then.

At these reassuring words, Menilmonea slowly emerged from her stasis and rose to join Aureal.

The sight she returned to flabbergasted her yet again. Her friend seemed to take pleasure in greeting her with farfetched scenes. This time, two large boars were gaily digging a trench connecting the river to the sphere's watery prison. Aureal, seated on Grumf's back, seemed to be attentively supervising their labors.

With a broad smile, Menilmonea said, "All I do is leave you alone for a few moments, and you redecorate the whole place! What exactly are you up to?"

Proud of her idea, Aureal replied with zeal, "I didn't like the idea of depending solely on the rain. Imagine a prolonged dry spell, like in summer. Our basin could completely evaporate. I thought back to our conversation when we first found the sphere, and this morning, it came to me: why not divert the river ever so slightly? Nothing big, just a small channel to maintain a steady supply of water. Anyway, the natural slope will guide the overflow back to the riverbed."

"I'm speechless. That's brilliant! And your friends are giving us a good laugh!"

"Yes, they sure know how to muss up that soil!"

Menilmonea turned gratefully to the boars. "Thank you for your help!"

Without looking up from their work, the two animals replied with high-pitched grunts.

"I don't speak boar, but I'm guessing that was 'You're welcome?'"

Menilmonea ventured, tickled.

"Almost. It was closer to 'Anytime!'" replied Aureal with a cackle.

The girls bid the boars goodbye and continued on their way down the river. The weather was clear and clement, and after about twenty minutes, they emerged from the mushroom valley and returned to the dense wood.

Two hours later, they finally beheld their destination: what the Elders had called the fortress of the Others appeared in all its unsettling splendor below. The river became a roaring waterfall, connecting the woods to the plain surrounding the outlandish structure.

Menilmonea and Aureal froze, mouths agape, unable to utter a word. Where they had expected to find the Mother's sacred Tower, they found instead a behemoth of a pyramid, its gray stone sides streaked with ancient scars. Rust-reddish metal broadly banded the middle like an unhealed wound. At the top, a dazzling flash split the sky, as if the building were capturing lightning. The structure exuded a silent authority, alien to everything around it. It seemed to have been there forever, and yet also to be at utter odds with the world around: a geometric anomaly in the heart of a natural setting. The ground here was bare and rocky, as if nature itself had fled such a presence. The verdant wood and shimmering waters all around formed a backdrop far too alive for this unmoving thing out of time. The disturbing juxtaposition further accentuated the strangeness and hostility of this place.

"Well... it's definitely not a Tower," Aureal acknowledged, eyes wide.

Menilmonea shook her head slowly, just as dumbfounded. "But... what is that thing? Either the Mother really built that structure, or we have to admit that the magic of the Others is even more impressive than we thought."

A heavy silence fell, broken only by the distant thunder of the waterfall plunging into the valley below.

"It's so huge! So... different," Aureal whispered.

"This much is certain: it's nothing like what we were always told. Or at least nothing like how I imagined the Mother's dwelling place to be. Tunka always told us that the Ascension would lead us to her, but he never did specify what it would look like once we got there. Come to think of it, I'm not even sure he ever knew those details."

The two girls exchanged glances full of uncertainty and determination.

"It doesn't matter what it is," Menilmonea finally declared with renewed conviction. "We must go. The answers to all our questions are there."

The pair then spotted a gently sloping path, half overgrown. It seemed to zigzag slowly toward the base of the waterfall, where it then curved to follow the river. Which continued on its way toward the plain, carefully avoiding the area around the pyramid, as if it didn't feel particularly welcome there.

"Judging by the dead zone around it, I bet they also have a sphere of negation... and a really powerful one," said Aureal, scanning the surroundings.

"Oh yes, almost certainly," replied Menilmonea, her gaze still fixed on the massive edifice.

When they reached the boundary between the verdant area and the moribund meadow, Grumf took a step back.

"He's sensed the aura of negation," said Aureal after a moment. "He says the field is extremely powerful."

"Given the size of the structure, I'm not surprised. How can they generate such magic? It's mind-boggling."

"And alarming."

"Yes, that too. Now, please stay here, Grumf. We can't allow you to get hurt."

The bear growled softly but didn't move. He seemed to understand and accept the situation, despite the tension visible in his massive shoulders.

The girls took each other by the hand, glanced confidently at their companion, and stepped onto the yellowish soil.

Mere steps later, Aureal fell to her knees, overcome by sudden dizziness and about to vomit.

"Are you all right?" Menilmonea asked, rushing to her side. "The

shock here is really intense."

Aureal struggled to catch her breath, panting.

"I'll be fine," she finally said. "I've rarely felt so nauseous. Their sphere of negation must be enormous."

As their breathing calmed and they tried to get up, Grumf let out a series of quick, low growls, clearly frightened.

The girls turned toward him, puzzled.

"Sorry, friend," Aureal said softly. "I can't understand you from here. But don't worry, everything will be all right."

The bear, however, did not calm down. His gaze, increasingly tense, seemed directed at something behind them.

The girls followed his gaze—and were seized with terror.

A towering figure had appeared at the foot of the pyramid and just leapt toward them with cataclysmic power, propelling its body through the air like a living projectile ripped from the very earth. Its imposing form preceded the scream of its flight, and the air, rent in its wake, had not yet had time to catch up with titanic roar of its passage. Its body seemed made of gnarled wood, ancient moss, and living vines, as if the forest itself had woken as a single being. Pale blue flowers dotted its coat of verdure, and two glowing golden eyes burned behind a wooden mask from which a beard of foliage sprouted.

Its shadow outpaced its body, already falling over them like an omen of death, long before the breath of its assault reached them.

Menilmonea had no time to speak, and barely even time to think *so this is how we die.*

But just before the imposing mass of this plant golem was upon them, two thick roots sprang from the forest behind Grumf. They wrapped themselves around the girls' waists and yanked them back so violently that they screamed before fainting dead away. In the blink of an eye, the creature crashed to the ground with a deafening clamor but found nothing more than the echo of their presence. The monster let out a primal howl of rage that made the very stones tremble.

From the tall grass, a voice remarked, "Well, now we know. Not even you are allowed to pass."

XXIV

They came to slowly, eyelids heavy and muscles stiff, as if after an evening where too much brandy had flowed from their jugs into their bellies. The moss-covered ground was soft beneath them, almost warm, welcoming as a forgotten bed in the undergrowth. Grumf was lying beside them, calm and relaxed.

Judging by the light, it must have been mid-afternoon, though it was hard to tell with the dense canopy overhead.

The girls stretched, trying to rid themselves of their aches and pains. And then they saw him.

The fox was watching them, perched on a rock just a few paces away, still as a statue sculpted by a roguish genius. His fur blazed orange and white, as if polished with almost supernatural attentiveness. Each hair seemed to have been wind-smoothed. But his long, tapering mane was what really caught their eyes: a cascading shock of fur that stirred and rippled with the breeze in the clearing.

And then there were those... things. Slender growths protruded from his sides: living ribbons, silky, almost translucent, slowly undulating in the air. Too supple for fur, too lively for feathers. They moved independently of the wind in an uncanny choreography, a silent ballet bending only to a tune he alone could hear.

Aureal struggled awkwardly to her feet, all elbows. Without looking away, she whispered, "You see it too, don't you?"

Menilmonea nodded slowly, her eyes wide and fascinated, fixed on the animal. She was sitting down, legs crossed, her back pressed lightly to an old oak tree.

"That's not a normal fox," she said finally.

Aureal smiled slightly, her gaze still fixed on the creature. Just then, she noticed a detail she hadn't seen before: the fox had not one, but three tails. Three sumptuous, swaying, sprightly plumes that swept slowly to and fro like censers of an obscure ritual.

"Is it the three tails, those tentacle-like appendages on its sides, or the fact that it saved us from a brutal death that makes you say that?" Aureal asked with faux-naivete.

Menilmonea straightened up a bit further and said with an embarrassed smile, "Greetings! And... thank you for saving us!"

Then, turning to her friend, she whispered, "Is it talking to you?"

The answer came, clear and calm, though the fox never opened his mouth. "No, I'm not talking to her."

Then, in their heads, like a shared thought, came: Even if I could...

The two friends gasped in surprise.

The fox continued, his voice as calm and mellifluous as ever. "What curious creatures you are... You have shown incredible courage in coming this far, though sometimes I wonder if I'm confusing courage with recklessness."

"Thank you. I... think?" replied Aureal, uncertain.

"But... who are you?" asked Menilmonea, intrigued. "Are you 'the Sentinel'?"

"Yes, some animals like to call me that," the fox said, glancing at Grumf.

He paused briefly before moving on. "I am a Primal, born of our Mother Gaia's desire. I was, in fact, the first."

"A Primal? Like those who fought the Others?" asked Menilmonea, dumbstruck.

"That is correct. I took part in that battle, although unfortunately, I was also the only survivor."

"The Primals were... foxes?" ventured Aureal, frowning.

Visibly amused, the fox replied, "No, we weren't foxes. The shape

you see before you is a mere phantasm. But I'll come back to that a little later. Before all else, I need you to tell me all you know about this entity you call 'the Mother.' In what I have gleaned from echoes of your conversations, she bears a disturbing resemblance to the true Mother. Tell me everything you know of her, and in exchange, I shall tell you who our Mother truly is."

The two friends agreed wholeheartedly.

And so, for a moment that seemed suspended in time, Menilmonea recounted the legends that Tunka had passed down to her since childhood—tales of Ascension, Titans, and blessings, all told with the wonder and fervor of one who had always believed in them. Now and again, Aureal would add a detail, correct a date, or provide clarification.

When they were done, the fox slowly shook his head. "Thank you very much for sharing your stories. It was... informative."

He paused, his tails swaying slowly. "In repayment, I will tell you who I am, and who your Mother truly is."

His voice now sounded deeper, as if hailing from an ancient place forgotten for centuries.

"Gaia, for that is her name, is a supreme entity, a consciousness born of nothingness. When this world was still in its infancy, a spirit woke from the chaos of scattered organic matter. We the living conceive of her essence only with difficulty. It is a little like asking an ant to understand an anthill. We are all elements of our Mother, but her consciousness exists in spheres our minds cannot imagine." He paused for a moment, almost reverently, before going on. "Several thousand rotations ago—or cycles, as you call them—she decided to create the Primals. Seven in all, on our planet Earth: one for each of the great forests on this continent, and one for the aquatic forest that surrounds our world. That was me: born of kelp forests, coral reefs, and hosts of seaweed. When we were born, she entrusted us with the mission of protecting our forests so they could thrive. We were our Mother's immune system."

"Immune system?" asked Aureal, intrigued.

"Yes. Like your body's, in a way. The reason you're not sick all the time is because organisms your body produces are constantly defending it against external attacks."

The blank looks on both girls' faces spoke volumes about how vague it all sounded to them.

The fox blinked slowly, somewhat bemused. "Don't your Titans teach you anything?"

"Nothing like that, in any case. We have... little creatures inside us?" asked Menilmonea, a little disgusted.

The fox said mirthfully, "Yes, but they're so small that even with a magnifying glass, you couldn't see them."

"But how do you know they exist, then?" asked Aureal, raising an eyebrow.

"I feel them. I can feel everything that's alive. In the case of your 'little creatures,' I must really concentrate, but I can sense their activity, their movement in your blood."

The two friends were quiet, trying to digest this revelation.

The fox continued in a voice still calm, almost melodic, "And for hundreds of rotations, everything went well. Using the powers our Mother had granted us, we ensured balance in our ecosystems. We regulated overly invasive animal populations, saw to a fair distribution of resources, and in some cases, even mutated certain species. The goal was always to protect the host."

"What do you mean, 'mutated'?" asked Menilmonea with interest.

"We could physically transform a species to better suit it to its environment. For example, when we noticed that it was becoming increasingly difficult for trees and flowers to pollinate remote areas, we mutated a family of wasps... to create what you now know as bees."

"You created bees?" gasped Aureal.

"Well, sort of, yes," replied the fox with a cheery grin.

"But... you haven't told us what you are. I mean, what do you look like? You mentioned this fox was a..."

"Phantasm. Yes, quite. This fox is me. But for now, it's a bit tricky to explain to humans. Let us simply say that my body is made up of a host of roots, brambles, ivy, and kelp. That said, our primordial self is what we call our heartseed. It is the part that grew from our Mother's desire to create us. My own is located at the bottom of a shallow cove, far away from here, on the southern coast of our continent."

"But you're here with us, aren't you?" asked Aureal, frowning.

"Yes, I am. In this fox. Or rather, my consciousness is in this fox. But I am not this fox. It is only an extension of my body."

The girls stood speechless.

The fox watched them for a moment, then said, "Let me ask you a question to try and help you understand. Suppose I cut off one of your arms and tossed it far away, but thanks to my magic, I could allow you to retain control of and sensation in your limb. If I asked you where you were, what would you say?"

"I would be here," said Aureal, slightly hesitant.

"And not where your arm is?"

"Yes, I... think I understand," whispered Menilmonea.

"And if, by my magic, I cut off all your limbs, your torso, and kept only your head here, with all the other pieces of your body scattered across the plains... where would you be then?"

"Where our heads are," the girls said in unison.

"Well, there you have it. It's pretty much the same for me. Except that in my case, not only do I continue to feel my 'limbs,' but in the case of my phantasm, I can see and act through it."

"And why a fox?" asked Aureal with interest.

"We don't know: every member of my species seems tied to a particular animal. In my case, although I come from the ocean, it's a fox that appears when I summon my phantasm."

"What does your 'head' look like? Your heartseed?" Menilmonea inquired, fascinated.

"I look like a Primal. You've encountered one before... or rather, what's left of him."

"The plant monster?" whispered Menilmonea.

"Alas, yes. He was one of my brothers, but he went mad after our final battle against the Others. I'm much less plant-like, though, and more... aquatic. But the idea is the same: lots of eyes surrounded by a multitude of fibrils and other tentacles that enable us to stretch and grow in all directions."

The two friends paused to form a mental image but, at a loss, soon abandoned the attempt.

"That battle.... What happened?" asked Aureal in a more somber tone.

"We heard about it from the Elders. The big mushrooms, west of here," added Menilmonea.

"Yes. Those mushrooms are all that remain of my five other brothers."

The fox paused at length, gaze lost in the unseen distance, as if he were reliving the horror of that battle.

"The Others have always been here. Or at least, they were here even before the Primals. The moment we were born, we began spreading our network of roots across the world and came across their Towers soon enough. A multitude of Towers, all over the continent. Impenetrable places.

"With patience, we managed to slip a root or two inside now and again, but then it would lose all sensation. Like a numbed limb, if you will, no longer able to feel. But these Towers did not seem to pose a threat. Nothing lived there. So we ignored them. Even the pyramid seemed empty. At that time, there were no negation zones. We could get close, but not inside."

"Wait, all those roots and vines we saw invading the Towers... that was you?" asked Menilmonea.

"Yes, those are mine. Those of my brethren are all dead now," the fox replied.

"But then... you're the one who saved us when the golem tried to jump on us as we left the last Tower!" exclaimed Aureal.

"I'd been tracking him for a while. He was smarter than the others. You were very useful as bait."

"I feel like a worm on a hook now, but... glad to be of service!" Menilmonea smiled.

"But why hunt and destroy the golems?" asked Aureal. "I imagine all the ones we saw dead were your doing."

"Yes, indeed. I hunt and destroy golems because golems are the Others, or at least their soldiers."

This shock knocked the two girls off their feet.

"The golems are the soldiers of the Others?" whispered Menilmonea.

"Yes, they were the ones who fought the final battle against us. It may seem unbelievable, but everything changed in an instant. We had been living in peace for hundreds of cycles when one day, without warning, the pyramid emanated its aura of negation. In a matter of moments, all living things within its sphere of influence died. All our roots were severed from our consciousnesses, and we even lost several descendants."

"What are descendants?" asked Menilmonea.

"Our species does not reproduce like yours. We do not have males and females. We function differently. Each Primal produces half a heartseed, but very slowly compared to your gestation period. It takes about a hundred cycles to create one. We can then fuse it with another's, and from this hybridization, a descendant is born, far less imposing than a Primal, possessing only some of our powers. A bit like your children, perhaps, were they never to grow to more than half their parents' size and strength. They themselves can produce seeds, but that second generation is even smaller and more fragile. And very often, without sentience. Closer to a plant than to a Primal. I think our Mother wanted this limitation to control our expansion. I find it a healthy constraint... even if some descendants did not agree."

He paused, pensive. "When the negation zones first appeared, we sent our phantasms to assess the situation. For several moons, nothing happened. But one morning, there were suddenly hundreds of golems. Some were carrying an object that looked like a large pearl, and the others arranged themselves in circles around them."

"The sphere of negation!" cried Menilmonea.

"Indeed. With its help, they could move outside the zone around the pyramid, and they did so, destroying everything in their path. The situation was serious enough that we decided to relocate our heartseeds, the dwelling place of all our power. When I say 'we,' I mean my six brothers. My own cannot survive outside of water, so I and my phantasm had to stay behind.

"Where the mushroom valley now stands, we gathered all our strength, united in a single breath, a single thought. Our minds merged into a tight web, woven with determination and stifled rage.

"We built ramparts of roots as thick as thousand-year-old tree trunks and hurled our most powerful vines into our assault. But in the magic of negation, our efforts came up against an insurmountable obstacle.

"It was then that the Primal of the Northwest Forest had an idea that would have ensured our victory: tear off entire sections of the mountain and turn them into weapons. In a matter of hours, the front changed. Huge roots lashed the northern cliffs, detaching massive slabs that other roots bore our way, where the outcome of the battle was being decided. And there, in a brutal ballet, we crushed them one by one. The golems fell, mangled, pulverized, reduced to smoking rubble. We had turned the tide of destiny. We had won. Until the unthinkable happened.

"Without knowing why, our mental link was broken, and I found myself back in my heartseed at the bottom of my lagoon, powerless. My consciousness was torn from my phantasm and flung far from the battle. When at last I managed to fashion a new avatar and return, there was nothing left. Five of my brothers were dead. The sixth, I would later discover, had lost his mind."

"We are truly sorry. That must have been terrible," said Menilmonea in a low voice.

"For months, I wandered restlessly, trying to bring my last brother back to his senses, calling upon Gaia for help, seeking to understand what had happened. I then retreated to my forest for countless rotations, not knowing what to do and unable to find out.

"But time, patient sculptor that it is, eases even the deepest wounds. Slowly, I emerged from my mourning. When I returned to the continent, I discovered the villages... and these enormous Titans. Their presence, massive but peaceful, betrayed no hostility. I observed them at length, surprised to find that, apart from the emergence of these curiously peaceable hamlets, the Others had made no further forays.

"For countless rotations, I searched for traces of unholy magic. But there was only you, living in harmony with nature. Deaf to the song of our Mother, certainly, but harmless.

"So I turned my anger, my grief, and what remained of my desire for vengeance toward the Towers... and toward the golems."

The two friends remained silent, deeply moved.

"That's... just awful. I have no words," Aureal finally whispered.

"But why us? Why did you follow us? Why are you interested in us?" asked Menilmonea, troubled.

"Because you are the first to hear the Songs. That is the very reason you understand me and I understand you. You, Menilmonea, even hear the Song of our Mother. This is a wondrous thing. Only those of my kind and our descendants can hear Gaia. I have never known any other species capable of sensing her presence.

"At first, the mushrooms, and then the forest itself, spread word of your feats. Yes, even yours, Aureal, though at the time, you refused the animals' Song. When they told me you had left your village, I couldn't help but come to find out why. Your species is not known for its adventurous nature. I watched the two of you evolve, come to terms with who you are, and above all, refuse to suffer your fate without a fight. When I saw you use the Towers to travel, I knew we could be of help each other."

"What do you mean? Help us meet the Others?" asked Menilmonea, intrigued.

"Exactly. You are capable of surviving the magic of negation. With my help, we will get you into the pyramid. With any luck, you might be able to deactivate the sphere as you did in the mushroom valley. Then I, too, could return to settle scores and no doubt induce the inhabitants of that place to help your Titans."

"Yes, well.... there's still one rather large detail to be ironed out before we can enter that stronghold," Aureal pointed out. "For the record, there's a huge monster that will try to crush us if we show up again."

"Not to mention that we don't know how many are still in the pyramid," added Menilmonea.

"On that score, I don't think there are many left," replied the fox. "There used to be many more golems surrounding the pyramid. But over time, they were sent to protect the Towers, where I was able to silence them."

"That seems a bit silly of them," said Aureal.

"I admit I don't quite understand why they did that," replied the fox. "They must have really wanted your kind to reach the Towers safely."

"But you say you never attacked humans?" asked Menilmonea.

"I haven't. But nature can sometimes be hostile. Some wild animals have been delighted, at times, to devour one of your kind."

"How awful!" whispered Aureal.

"They have to live, don't they? What's so different about eating slices of bacon?"

Aureal didn't know how to respond.

The fox added placidly, "It's the natural order of things. Healthy, even. It helps maintain the balance of the ecosystem. That said, you're in no danger, Aureal. Your gift protects you."

"So much the better," she said, casting a gentle glance at Grumf. "Actually, all this talk has made me hungry. Would you mind if we built a fire to cook a meal... and make some nice tea?"

"No, not at all," the fox replied.

"Would you like to join us?" asked Menilmonea, curious.

The fox smiled in amusement.

"I don't eat like you. In that respect, I'm much closer to the trees. My roots, which connect me to the earth, are my source of energy."

While Aureal gathered a few branches, Menilmonea asked, "Even if there are no more golems, how do you plan to get us past the Guardian?"

The fox gave a slight shrug. "I haven't the faintest idea."

XXV

The Primal had advised them to get some rest. He had to leave to deal with a golem wandering around a distant Tower to the north. He promised they would discuss their next steps in the morning, once their minds were clearer and their hearts calmer. And, truth to tell, the two friends were in dire need of rest and peace. After the shock of their encounter with the pyramid's Guardian, their nerves were stretched close to snapping.

They had made themselves a cozy space around a modest fire, whose languid flames gently licked a blackened log. The resinous smell of the crackling wood mingled with the herbal scent of their tea, creating an almost soothing atmosphere despite the circumstances. The girls each held a warm cup in their hands, lost in contemplating the steam that rose from it. Grumf dozed peacefully nearby, enjoying the warmth of the fire, his steady breath forming little clouds in the cool evening air.

"So the Mother as we know her is just a figment of our imagination," Aureal finally said, blowing on her cup. "We've been manipulated by the Others our whole lives. I don't know if I want to scream or curl up in a ball and cry my eyes out."

"Save all that energy for confronting them," replied Menilmonea, her eyes fixed on the embers. "If the Primal is right and they've used up almost all their golems, we might have a chance to get into their lair and find out why they did this to us."

Aureal shook her head slowly, throat tight with a mixture of anger and disbelief. "It's mind-boggling to think that we believed, even lived our entire lives, according to the precepts of a lie. What about Ascension? Was that a lie too? What happened to all those who left? Our parents?"

"I-I don't know. But I can promise you that we'll do everything we can to get to the bottom of this. And besides, I tell myself that not everything had to be completely untrue. There is a Mother. She's just not the chimera that the Titans sold us. We can still believe in her. She's out there somewhere. And watching over us, through her creations."

A long pause ensued, punctuated by the crackling of wood and the faint sounds of night falling. The first stars pierced the veil of twilight, twinkling faintly above their heads.

"I just hope the Titans didn't know either," Menilmonea continued, her gaze lost in the flickering glow. "I want to believe that Tunka was sincere and that he, too, was deceived."

"By... by... I don't even know who anymore," Aureal groaned. "Yes, let's hope Tunka wasn't manipulating us too. That said, you're right. I find it comforting to know that our goddess really does exist, even if we've been praying to a pale imitation for so long. I'm sure she heard our voices anyway."

"Her Song is so sweet, so pure," added Menilmonea in a whisper. "She embodies everything we've always believed in: kindness, love, gentleness, and boundless empathy."

"With all that's going on, I don't even miss our simple little life anymore," said Aureal, her voice filled with suppressed rage. "I'm so angry we were kept under control like that! I could burn the world down!"

"Oh, yes, I understand. I never imagined that when we left home, we'd end up... here."

They surrendered to their thoughts, each trying as best they could to come to terms with their new reality. At long last, Menilmonea broke the silence.

"Let's get some sleep. Or at least try to. We need to be in good shape tomorrow for the fox's return."

The night was restless. Sleep eluded them, replaced by insidious doubts, unanswered questions, and anxieties as vast as the night sky. The girls tossed and turned on their makeshift beds so often that they ended up wearing through what had once been a thick layer of moss.

When the sun finally rose, only by a stretch of imagination could the pair have been described as well-rested. Their faces were marred by dark circles, their eyes red, their eyelids heavy as if they'd been carrying the weight of the world for hours. Even their movements seemed mired in concentrated, clinging fatigue.

The Primal arrived a few moments after they woke. Or rather, he appeared from the ground, as if sprouted from the earth itself, which made Aureal raise an eyebrow.

"Excuse me, but you just grew out of the ground, didn't you? I ask because after the night we just had, I'm not sure I can fully trust my eyes."

The fox laughed heartily, though nothing on his face indicated that he had made a sound.

"Yes, that's a pretty good description of what just happened. My phantasm can grow from any of my branchings, which cover a vast swath of the continent and the surrounding abyssal plain."

Aureal said, stammering slightly, "Y-you stretch across the entire world?"

"The continent, yes. It wasn't always so. Once upon a time, my brothers looked after the terrestrial forests. But now that task falls to me."

"Are you... a god?" asked Aureal, eyes still squinty with sleep, though her mind was suddenly wide awake.

The fox tilted his head slightly, as if he found the question entertaining.

"The only goddess in the mythical sense of the word is our Mother. That said, I share certain characteristics with the concept of divinity. But I would say that I am, at best, a demigod. I am far from the magnificence of Gaia."

"Are you immortal?" asked Menilmonea, curious.

213

"Also... in a way. Gaia is a truly immortal being. Nothing can destroy her, nothing can even touch her. In my case, if you destroyed my seedroot, I would disappear. Look at what the Others have done: they killed five immortals. Almost six."

"And your 'children'?"

"It depends. They can live much longer than you, or any animal. It often has to do with the quality of the hybridization, and... a little luck. But they all end up dying after a few thousand rotations. Again, this too is vital. Stagnation must be avoided."

"I'm not sure the dying would agree with you," Aureal muttered.

"No, indeed," replied the fox with a hint of humor. "But that's how Gaia wanted the world to be."

Changing the subject, Menilmonea asked, "Well, Primal, how are we getting in there? And by the way, what would you like us to call you?"

The fox smiled quietly.

"'Primal' is fine. I have had many names over the years, but that one suits me best." He turned slightly toward the mycomanceress, his eyes glinting with a singular brilliance. "Before I answer your other question, Menilmonea, there is something I would like to give you. Something rare... and powerful."

"A... gift?" she asked cautiously.

"Yes, indeed. I'm not yet sure you'll be able to use it, but it's worth a try. We're going to have to face the Guardian, and anything that might help is welcome."

The two friends remained silent, eyes fixed on him, hanging on his every word, their fatigue completely forgotten.

The fox took a few steps back, then stared at a spot on the ground between himself and Menilmonea. She followed his gaze and saw a small half-sphere emerge from the earth, like half a seed. It glowed with a soft green light.

"This is a half-heartseed," said the fox. "In ancient times, I used it to hybridize with my brothers. Today, Menilmonea, I wish to entrust it to you. If your gift truly comes from our Mother, then you should be able to make the power contained within this seed your own."

"The power?" whispered Menilmonea, taken aback.

"Yes. It contains a portion of my power... which I myself received from Gaia. Your gift, even if I don't yet understand where it comes from, should allow you to talk to her. To tame her. And perhaps to harness her strength."

"About our gifts, there's something you need to know. Just before he fell into his endless sleep, Tunka confessed to me that he had given them to us at birth, when our parents presented us to him," said Menilmonea.

The fox turned to her with an intrigued look.

"That can't be. Titans can't hear the Song. They are the Others' creations. Nothing could be more distant or alien."

"I understand, but... he seemed sure of himself when he told me. He didn't understand how it was possible himself, or whence the impulse came. But he was certain that he had passed a part of himself on to me. And to Aureal, as well."

"I don't see how..."

"If Gaia is the goddess of all creation," Aureal interjected, "then even the creatures of the Others are her children, aren't they? Even if they are cut off from her, lost, and no longer hear her Song. After all, the animals, and even I myself, cannot hear her, and yet you say she is indeed the Mother of us all. It's not so illogical to think she might have wanted to give destiny a helping hand through Tunka."

The fox remained thoughtful, his eyes half-closed, his tails gently sweeping the ground in a hypnotic rhythm. Then, his voice barely audible above the whisper of the wind in the leaves, he added softly, "That's a very nice way of looking at things. I'm not saying you're wrong. But Gaia rarely interferes in our affairs. She dwells on a higher plane, and we are but small things in her eyes. Still, whatever the source of your gift, if you are well connected to our Mother, you should be able to feel the seed. Ask it to wrap itself around your neck."

"Ask... it?" repeated Menilmonea, a little taken aback.

"Yes, like when you speak to mushrooms," the fox clarified.

"I see..." murmured Menilmonea, before staring at the half-seed with all the intensity that the situation demanded. "Would you come around my neck, please?"

Aureal couldn't repress a quick giggle.

Menilmonea glared at her, but her anger faded at once as two tiny roots shot out lightning-swift from the half-seed and joined at the nape of her neck. Before she could blink, her new medallion was proudly displayed above her breast.

"I was expecting something like this, but I must admit I'm impressed," said the fox. "It reacted immediately. With at least as much alacrity as if a Primal had asked it. This bodes well indeed... I'm starting to think you were right, Aureal. Perhaps our Mother did give us a little helping hand via your Titan after all."

Menilmonea was transfixed, completely stunned by what had just happened. The sensation was indescribable, as if a new consciousness had nestled against her own, vibrant and responsive.

"It's incredible! I can feel it in my mind... It's not really talking to me. I'd say it's more... singing softly."

"Yes. It's pleased with your communion," replied the fox.

"And what are its abilities?" asked Menilmonea, delicately touching the medallion with her fingertips, feeling its living warmth pulsing against her skin.

"Ah. That... only it can tell you. When we grow our half-seeds, part of our essence flows into them, but which part, we never know. It's completely chaotic. This allows us to mingle our skills for as much variety as possible."

"And I should talk to it out loud?"

"As you wish. Talk to it, or else project your thoughts. The two of you are in symbiosis now; it will understand you. Go on, try."

Menilmonea whispered, "Grab my cup, please."

Immediately, a thin moss-covered vine sprouted from her plant necklace and seized the designated target. To an outside observer, the entire operation would have seemed completely instantaneous.

Aureal couldn't contain her amazement. "That's miraculous!"

The fox nodded, ears twitching slightly. "The better you come to know the seed, the easier it will be to communicate your requests. But be careful—even though it contains only a small portion of my power, and above all, our Mother's, it is still a living entity. It, too, needs rest. You will learn its limits."

"I don't know what to say, Primal," whispered Menilmonea. "This is a wonderful gift. I will make the best use I can of it."

"Exactly," replied the fox. "It will be very handy in defeating the Guardian."

"Can it cross the negation zone?"

"No. The magic of negation will completely deactivate the half-seed, as it does everything else closely or even distantly related to our Mother," replied the fox.

"But then... How did you catch us during the attack yesterday?" asked Aureal, intrigued.

"I am powerful enough to send tendrils a few paces into the dead zone. I lose almost all sensation in those extremities, but I can still control them. Unfortunately, not for more than a few moments. But that was just enough to save your lives."

"But then what can we do?" Aureal asked worriedly.

"We need to lure it outside," suggested Menilmonea.

"If only it were that simple. This Guardian is far smarter than all the golems put together. It is truly different. More... organic, I would say. The Others have outdone themselves with this creature," replied the fox gravely. "I've spent so many moons looking for a way to lure it out. But none of my traps have ever worked. It knows full well that without the protection of the negation magic, it would be at my mercy."

"But then what was your strategy in saving us and wanting to team up?" asked Aureal.

The fox, visibly amused, replied, "Why, my dear, I don't rightly know. I just went with my gut. You didn't seem stupid to me. After all, you made it this far with next to no outside help. Given your ability to adapt, I supposed you might think differently than I do. Come up with new ideas. After all, look what you managed to do with the sphere of negation."

He then shot Grumf a glance, a twinkle in his eye. "And besides, had I not saved you, I'd have gotten into big trouble with our friend the grizzly bear."

While the fox and Aureal were talking, Menilmonea marveled at the powers of her medallion. She had just asked it to make a chair, which had woven itself from roots and vines before her widened eyes. She couldn't help but exclaim, "Unbelievable!"

Without turning around, the fox said, "And that's only a tiny fraction of what it can do."

Projecting her thoughts as if she were blowing on a soap bubble, Menilmonea thought quietly, *You may stop.*

No sooner had she finished forming the thought in her head than the chair had already returned to oblivion. All the fibers retracted with a soft click into the half-seed, leaving behind a faint smell of damp earth.

"The Others don't stand a chance against us!" exclaimed Menilmonea with almost childlike fervor.

"Well, not to be a killjoy, but I think it's more like they don't stand a chance *if* we can get to them," replied Aureal with a hint of pragmatism.

Menilmonea, however, had already tuned her out, completely absorbed by the endless possibilities her gift offered.

Aureal turned to the fox, "She'll come back down to earth soon, I'm sure of it."

"We're in no rush. Let's give her time to get to know the half-seed. We'll need all her power when we face them," the fox replied placidly.

With those words, a light rain began to fall. And before the first drops hit the ground, Menilmonea had already conjured up, over the trio, an umbrella of wood and roots intertwined.

"I must admit, that's extremely handy," said Aureal with a broad smile.

"At your service, my dear! It would have put me out if you'd gotten wet."

At this, Aureal's expression abruptly altered, as if the Mother had just appeared before her.

"Aureal? Are you all right? What's the matter?" asked Menilmonea, instantly worried.

Her friend replied with a triumphant smile. "I know *exactly* how we're going to beat that Guardian!"

XXVI

The rain kept up its drumming on their conjured umbrella as Menilmonea and the fox exchanged a knowing look. Both stared at Aureal with palpable interest, hanging on her every word.

"We'll do exactly as we did with the sphere of negation," Aureal resolutely declared. "Wait for a heavy rain, something close to a torrential downpour. That should drastically reduce the pyramid's influence and shrink the boundaries of the negation zone."

"Except that the Guardian won't be able to tell!" Menilmonea finished with a smile of satisfaction. "And then the Primal will be able to use all his power."

The fox nodded, giving his body a brisk shake in approval.

Amused, Aureal raised her eyebrows. Then, feigning nonchalance, she jerked a thumb at her furry companion. "Grumf here would like to kindly remind you that you can count on him too!"

It was an excellent plan. The Primal peered up at the heavens laden with black clouds. Then, after a long moment, he declared in a grave voice, "We won't have to wait long. A big storm is moving in this afternoon, early evening at the latest. Let us be ready. Here's what I suggest: you venture into the dead zone. Not too far, but far enough to lure the Guardian out. If you still sense the magic of negation's baleful influence, I'll fetch you back like last time. Otherwise, give me a slight wave to say it's safe to proceed. As soon as the Guardian rushes you, I'll grab him, and the rest is up to me."

"Good!" said Menilmonea with determination. "Perhaps I can help too?"

The fox shook his head slowly. "I'd rather not get you involved in the fray. You're already the bait. On the contrary, I'd ask you to stay as far away as you can, to keep from getting hurt. I don't want to have to worry about you while focusing on the fight."

"Suits me just fine!" added Aureal with a gleeful grin.

They spent the remaining time in preparation.

The fox sank into a deep silence, barely stirring, as if immersed in some form of deep meditation and no longer really with them.

Aureal, meanwhile, helped Menilmonea practice using her half-seed, tossing various objects her way to be caught in midair. By day's end, as dusk began to fall, Menilmonea was able to catch everything her friend threw at her flawlessly.

"You've really got the hang of it now," Aureal remarked, impressed. "I think it's getting smoother all the time."

"Yes," replied Menilmonea with a soft smile. "I speak less and think more. It improves our symbiosis, I find. I feel more than I sense."

The rain that had been falling all day had turned into a storm, and a wall of water was approaching their position. In an instant, the fox came out of his trance and announced, "It is time. Let's get closer to the pyramid. The storm won't last long."

The two friends looked at each other and took each other's hands. At that moment, all their doubts, all their fears, everything that could have held them back was swept away by a keen sense of pride and confidence in their destiny. The Songs of the Mother and the animals rang mighty in their heads, like a war march carrying them forward.

When they reached the dead zone, they tightened their grip on each other's hands and stepped forward.

Nothing happened. They were still connected to their gifts.

The two friends advanced cautiously, each footfall resounding within them with an almost unbearable intensity, the deluge hitting their bodies like tiny shards of ice.

Hearts pounding, they saw that the barrier of rain was doing its job well.

Menilmonea planted her feet firmly in the soggy mud and slowly raised a trembling hand to signal the fox. Alert, he stationed himself at the border's edge, bright eyes piercing the darkness. He was ready to unleash his power at the right moment. He didn't want to enter the so-called negation zone and tip the Guardian off.

Grumf, breathing quickly, muscles tense, also hung behind. He paced nervously alongside the Primal.

Steadfastly clenching her jaw, Aureal turned her gaze to her friend, eyes shining with emotion in the pouring rain.

"Menil, if we must go through with this, know that I am grateful to you for showing me the light. I am happy. I know who I am at last, all thanks to you, and I am proud of it." Aureal's voice trembled with restrained emotion, eyes sparkling with rain and tears.

"Hush, silly! You'll make me weep. No one's dying here except that thing." No sooner did Menilmonea utter these words than a violent wind rent the air before them, whipping their hair back. The monster had spotted them and came cleaving through the rain with terrifying swiftness. In an instinctive act of utter surrender, the girls shut their eyes, abandoning themselves entirely to their fate and the Primal's protection.

The Guardian was approaching at full tilt when a tangle of vines and thick brambles sprang from the ground with colossal force, violently stopping it in its tracks. So brutal was the collision that several vines snapped with a sharp, tearing sound. The colossus staggered, trapped in this raging mass of vegetation, but managed to remain standing, its muffled fury making the air, saturated with wild electricity, shudder.

Aureal opened her eyes with a start and shouted loudly, "By all the Titans! Quick, run!"

The two friends spun sharply around and broke into headlong flight. They had gone no more than a few yards when a gigantic shadow abruptly looming overhead stopped them dead in their tracks. Grumf had hurled himself heroically in front of a deadly vine hurtling straight for them. A vine the Guardian had thrown!

"What...?" cried Menilmonea, her voice choked with horror.

Powerful and robust though he was, the grizzly was swept aside by the ferocity of the attack, flung unceremoniously from the zone with a pained roar. He did not get up.

Aureal let out a heart-rending cry, but a second attack was already bearing down on them. Reacting instinctively, Menilmonea wrapped her arms tightly around her friend, knelt down, and breathed a desperate whisper. "Protect us..."

In an instant, hundreds of fibers shot out from her medallion, forming a cage of wood, roots, and vines around them. The roots dug deep into the ground with untamed vigor. With a series of sharp pops, small purple mushrooms sprouted by the dozen, lending the cage a supernatural glow. When the Guardian's root struck this shield, a shower of burning acid from the spores repelled it, forcing the enemy to retreat with a furious cry of pain. In the confines of their safe space, the two friends caught their breath, aware that they had narrowly escaped death.

Meanwhile, more and more plant tentacles launched themselves at the Guardian. Barely visible through the rain, the fox seemed bathed in a soft green light.

"But how can the golem also shoot out roots?" whispered Menilmonea, completely lost.

"I don't know," Aureal said, "but we have more pressing issues right now."

"Yes! Sorry. The cage is protecting us, but if the Primal doesn't kill him quickly, my half-seed won't last long. There aren't many acid mushrooms left."

As if to prove her right, two vines as thick as tree trunks aggressively smashed into their shield, the air around them ringing with the impact.

All at once, the fox's voice echoed in their minds. *The rain quells much of the Others' magic, but alas, not all of it. I can't fully extend my fibers, unfeeling as they are. And this creature is incredibly powerful. I'm trying to drag it from the sphere of influence, but it's resisting me.*

Several sharp cracks were heard. More of the Primal's restraints had snapped. He swiftly wove new ones, but the Guardian wouldn't budge.

Completely panicked, Aureal cried, "Can you get us out of here?"

No, replied the fox gravely. *I would have to undo your defenses, and you would be vulnerable for too long. All my strength is focused on holding him back. I won't have time to react quickly enough.*

With no acid to slow them now, the vines rattled the cage forcefully with their repeated assaults.

Menilmonea remained silent, weighing her options.

She concentrated on Gaia's song. Even found herself praying, much to her surprise, to the goddess, beseeching her help. Time stood still, and all at once everything became clear in her mind.

She then whispered softly to her necklace, almost in a sigh, "I know you're exhausted, but can you grow two detonita plants?"

The music echoed in her head, soft and reassuring, as if to say, *You can count on me.*

Slowly, almost painfully, two amanita mushrooms sprouted inside the cage, close to Menilmonea's hand. She gently plucked them and whispered her request.

Aureal, surprised, exclaimed, "You have a plan!"

"Yes. And I'm going to need your help."

Hurriedly, she filled her friend in on her idea. When Aureal nodded with a big grin, the mycomanceress immediately addressed the Primal. "We're going to try something. Get ready to pull with all your strength and drag him into the forest."

The fox's voice rang out loud and clear despite his exhaustion. *Understood. But whatever you plan to do, do it quickly! The rain is letting up, and I've lost almost all feeling in my extremities.*

Aureal closed her eyes, concentrated, then whispered a few words. Her friend watched her closely, searching for a sign, a trace of confirmation. Aureal responded with a simple nod, firm and unequivocal.

Moments later, two magnificent gray wolves emerged from the woods and cautiously approached the cage, keeping a close eye on the colossus wrestling against the Primal's strength.

The Guardian's plant tentacles kept pounding violently on the cage, completely ignoring the wolves.

With extreme caution, Menilmonea slipped the detonitas between their fangs, emphasizing how carefully they had to be handled. Aureal confirmed that her message had been understood and directed their new friends toward the monster's legs.

The wolves delicately deposited their precious cargo near the feet of the Guardian struggling against the Primal's hold. Then they turned and fled. As soon as they were at a safe distance, the mycomanceress shouted, "Detonate!"

The amanitas exploded with all their might, jolting the earth up to the edge of the woods. Thrown to the ground by the blast, the Guardian had not a moment to react.

Instantly the fox tightened his grip, summoning every last ounce of his strength. Roots, vines, creepers, and every other part of the plant kingdom able to grab or pull shot toward the giant's body.

In a matter of seconds, it was torn from the ground with unforgiving ruthlessness, then catapulted far from the dead zone.

It came crashing to the ground in a muffled din of splintering wood. The Primal gave it no time to figure out what was going on, covering it with branches, fibers, and everything else his magic could invoke. Drawing on all his suffering, all his anger, all his regrets, he created a cocoon around the colossus.

Then he crushed it all to pieces.

At that moment, Menilmonea felt Gaia's Song change abruptly. It hummed with vengeance, it was martial; it was final.

There was a sinister crack, as if several deities had split a mountain asunder. Amidst the maelstrom of wood and vines, nothing whatsoever remained of the mighty warrior.

It took a moment for everyone to realize that it was all over.

Menilmonea placed her fingers on her medallion and thanked it softly. In response, the cage came apart, roots slowly withdrawing under the ground. Slower than usual, she noted. The half-seed must have been exhausted. It displayed nothing like the alacrity from that very afternoon.

She whispered to it, "You've been wonderful. I can't thank you enough."

In return, the necklace sang softly, a tender and gentle lament.

Aureal, meanwhile, rushed over to Grumf. Kneeling down beside him, she cried out with vibrant relief, "He's alive! Just knocked for a loop, I think!"

The fox remained motionless. He stared at his enemy's final resting place, his eyes somber and worn with fatigue. Then he turned to the girls and, with deep respect, declared, "In the name of the forests and our mother Gaia, I thank you with all my heart. You were magnificent."

Menilmonea bowed and joined her friend. She confirmed that poor Grumf was fine; he was even starting, slowly, to stir. But he would need rest.

"As will we all," replied Aureal, gently stroking the grizzly's fur.

"True indeed, for the next step is now within our reach," declared Menilmonea. "We'll finally be able to enter that accursed pyramid... and have a serious conversation with the Others."

XXVII

Returning from the sodden plain, the two friends reached the edge of the wood with its rain-laden foliage and slowly made their way in, followed by the fox and Grumf, whose tired paws slipped from time to time on the waterlogged ground. The downpour had let up but not come to a complete stop, and patter played a piercing melody on the thick leaves. Still heavy, the sky gave off a lifeless glow, twilight-tinged, that signaled the unassuming advance of night.

Menilmonea stopped at the foot of a gnarled old oak whose canopy offered excellent shelter. They set their belongings down with a sigh of relief. Menilmonea then began gathering a few branches the foliage had miraculously kept dry. A few deft gestures, two well-chosen fire mushrooms, and a flame was born, timid at first, then more confident.

Soon the fire crackled merrily, warming air and hearts. Menilmonea took out a handful of wrinkled but valiant potatoes, swiftly peeled and boiled them, mashed them in a small pot, and added a pinch of dried herbs that she kept in a thin cloth bag. A soothing aroma immediately filled the air, promising a modest but comforting meal.

Meanwhile, Aureal watched Grumf out of the corner of her eye. Her worried expression betrayed a concern she made no effort to hide.

"You should rest by the fire," she whispered softly, placing a hand on his massive shoulder, his still-damp fur quivering at her touch. "You've been heroic enough for one day."

The bear gave a soft growl, then finally gave in to fatigue. He hunkered down close to the flames, slowly lowering his imposing bulk. He let his gaze grow lost in their orange dance until his eyelids gently shut.

When she was certain he was asleep, Aureal turned to the fox and asked in a voice little louder than a whisper, "Why don't we go straight to the pyramid while the way is clear? Before they send another guard?"

The fox shook his head slightly. His golden eyes shone with a calculating gleam. "Because I want to be sure they're out of options. If they don't replace the guard by tomorrow morning, my suspicions will be confirmed. I haven't seen any new golems for some time now.... And that plant colossus we killed was one of a kind."

Menilmonea nodded attentively. "I agree. This way, we'll be more or less certain that no other golems await us inside."

"Exactly. And remember, once you're in, you'll have no connection to the Songs. You will be completely alone."

Aureal knit her brow, pensive. Then she nodded slowly. "Yes, when you put it that way, it's probably wiser to wait. An ounce of patience to keep from disaster!"

An intimate silence set in, broken only by the crackle of flames and the rain's steady patter on the leaves.

Menilmonea emerged from her thoughts, gaze still a bit unfocused, and turned to the fox.

"Primal, I wanted to ask... How was the guardian able to manipulate roots and vines so well? I find it truly strange. So unlike all the other golems. After all, the Others' structures, with their stones and metal, are far removed from nature."

The fox tilted his head, ears twitching slightly. "I think that Guardian was a Titan. A very aggressive one, quite different from the others, but a Titan all the same. That's the only explanation I can come up with for now. Titans seem to be the only creatures of the Others capable of communing with nature. Rather powerfully, even. And despite the fact that they cannot hear our Mother's song."

Aureal nodded, growing thoughtful in turn. "True, the Titans all seem to exist in symbiosis with plants. I've always loved watching every sort of flower thrive on Tunka's shell."

"Yes," added Menilmonea, "the ones we've encountered seemed deeply rooted in nature, as if an intrinsic part of it."

The fox nodded slowly. "The question has always intrigued me since I started observing them. How can they be in such harmony with their environment without communing through the Song? Their symbiosis with nature is undeniable, and yet they evolve outside of our connection with Gaia. This is a mystery I hope we shall be able to solve once inside the pyramid."

Menilmonea frowned slightly, deep in thought. "Are we so sure we know all the Mother's ways? If everything that lives comes from her, even the creations tainted by the Others, then perhaps she has connections completely foreign to us."

"Indeed... as with your gifts. I am likely too arrogant in thinking I know all there is to know about Gaia." He paused, as if to brood on this bit of soul-searching. "On that note, your priority now is to locate the sphere of negation. If you find a way to deactivate it, do so, but only if it's safe. Otherwise, come back to me and we shall think up a solution together. Do not take any unnecessary risks."

Aureal gave a weary smile and a slight shrug. "Don't worry, we won't. You can count on us for that! I think we've had our fill of risks until Ascension. Or at least, er... for a good long while."

Menilmonea answered with a mischievous grin, eyes twinkling in the dim light. "We'll be as quiet as mice!"

She then straightened up, giving her tunic a brisk and spirited dusting-off. "I'll just stock up on mushrooms before going to sleep."

As she walked off to start her harvest, the fox lifted his snout. "You could ask your half-seed, you know. It wouldn't take much effort for it to grow a few mushrooms."

"Oh, yes! What an excellent idea."

She leaned down slightly and whispered a few words to her necklace. In response, a few fine fibers escaped the half-seed, worming their way into the ground before her. Within seconds, beautiful specimens sprang up, mature and ready to be picked.

Charmed, Aureal crossed her arms and shook her head gently.

"Pretty handy, I'll say!"

Night fell without incident, stretching its silent veil over the woods. Comforted by this final touch of familiar magic, Menilmonea and Aureal fashioned themselves a thick bed of moss beneath the shelter of the great oak. Then, without further ado, they snuggled up against Grumf, whose thick, warm fur made an ideal pillow. No sooner had their eyes closed than they fell into a deep, dreamless sleep.

When morning came, the two friends awoke peacefully, still nestled in the grizzly's reassuring warmth. The sky was overcast as ever, but the rain had finally stopped. After some modest stretching, they decided to go and freshen up at the nearby river, letting the water coax them gently back to reality and a welcome semblance of cleanliness.

When they returned, the fox was waiting for them, a small pile of colorful fruits carefully placed on a large leaf. Had he picked them? Or summoned them? It was impossible to say. In any case, they were delicious, juicy, and surprisingly sweet for the season.

Once they'd had their fill, they gathered their belongings and the little band set off, leaving the shelter of the great oak to resume their journey across the plain.

When they reached the forest's edge, the two girls stopped. The time had come to part ways. They gave Grumf a long hug, their arms lost in his comforting folds of fur, then turned to the fox.

"Good luck to you both," he said simply, his voice soft but serious.

"Thank you for your help, Primal," said Aureal.

Menilmonea nodded. "We'll be careful and return as soon as we can."

Without another word, the girls stepped through the invisible veil. The magic of negation immediately enveloped them, wrenching the usual retch from them, now familiar and almost bearable.

They turned back one last time to their companions. But without their gift, they could communicate only in broad gestures now.

"Well! Let's be off, my dear!" Aureal said in a falsely solemn tone.

"You took the words right out of my mouth."

The two friends set off as quickly as they could toward the massive, gaping black mouth at the base of the pyramid. The entrance didn't seem to be guarded. At least not for the moment.

Without hesitation, they dashed in.

Once their eyes had adjusted to the darkness, Aureal whistled softly through her teeth. "Well, I wasn't expecting this."

At the end of a long, paved road, a colossal metropolis rose before them, unlike anything they had ever seen. It bore no resemblance to their village, with its modest dwellings and dirt paths. Beneath the pyramid's immense vault, it sprawled in a complex network of elegant edifices, illuminated by hundreds of windows from which warm light poured into the darkness like molten metal.

The refined domes, slender towers, and suspended walkways between the buildings all seemed both spectacular and oddly delicate. This unique architecture struck them as wondrous and deeply alien at once, almost intimidating. Each structure gave the impression of obeying an arcane logic far removed from the familiar simplicity of their own world.

The two friends advanced cautiously, impressed by the captivating setting, but aware that this beauty concealed a reality they were as yet unsure they wished to face. They had entered an unknown universe: admittedly fascinating, but by no means harmless.

"This place must have thousands of inhabitants," whispered Menilmonea.

"Yes, but don't you find it bizarre that we can't hear a sound? The city seems completely silent," replied Aureal, her brow slightly furrowed.

"They must be here. All those lights aren't just to welcome us."

"I really wonder what they look like."

"Good question. Let's try to get closer while not drawing attention to ourselves."

"Yes, well, there's a huge open avenue leading into the city. You'd have to be blind, with your back turned, to miss us," Aureal pointed out.

Menilmonea giggled nervously, more so than she would've liked.

"Right. I was hoping for, I don't know, hallways or something where we might have remained less obtrusive, but now... Oh well!

Let's at least make our way forward without seeming aggressive."

They advanced warily toward the entrance to the city, and as its layout became more apparent, a detail struck them.

"These doors, these windows... every part of these buildings could have been built for humans," whispered Menilmonea, intrigued.

"Yes, look! Knobs on the doors. So they have hands," Aureal added.

"And they're clearly the size of adult men and women..."

Upon reaching the base of the city, they approached the first building.

"It looks like a house," observed Menilmonea. "The style is eccentric, but a house nonetheless."

"Do you think it's open?"

"I don't know. This is madness. There's not a soul in sight. The streets are empty. Even that one over there, the one leading to the city's summit. It's clearly an important road. And yet it's deserted."

"Look, between that and having golems attack us, I'd pick empty streets any day," Aureal remarked with a half-smile.

"Do you want to go in?" asked Menilmonea, staring at the door.

Without waiting, Aureal put her hand on the knob and turned. "Unlocked! Imagine that!"

The two friends entered, ready for anything, but what they found took them by surprise. The interior was almost unreal in its cleanliness, bathed in a soft light that seemed to emanate from the very walls. No wood, no cloth: everything was polished metal and smooth stone with pearly glints. The walls were decorated with framed paintings depicting alien landscapes of cold, distant beauty, or scenes of unfamiliar but clearly human life.

Everything seemed to have its place: immaculately tidy shelves, a table set with plates and glasses as if a meal had been interrupted. A family had lived here. Or still did.

"It's very... utilitarian," Menilmonea murmured. "But beautiful, in its way."

"Definitely human," Aureal breathed, placing a finger on a carved chair that was just the perfect height for them. "It's as if someone had just stepped out for a moment."

"It's bright, but I can't tell where the light is coming from. Fascinating…"

As they were about to leave, Aureal lingered over one of the paintings. "Did you see the frame? There are words written in our language."

She turned to Menilmonea, a mixture of astonishment and confusion in her eyes. "Do the Others speak the same language we do?"

Menilmonea remained silent for a moment, deep in thought. "I think we're the ones who speak like them. It makes sense, after all. They created the Titans, who in turn taught us to read and write. They must simply be passing their language on to us."

"By Tunka's shell! Mind-boggling. And here we thought we spoke the language of the Mother."

"If the Others also created or invented the concept of the Mother, that wouldn't be so far off the mark," Menilmonea replied with a bitter smile. Then she turned back to the board. "What does this say? The… 'Exodus'?"

Aureal squinted, studying the painting intently. "It looks like some kind of city on an island. Interesting… Clearly a painting, but I've never seen such detail. It's quite simply stunning. The artist who did this is a genius. How vexed poor Maëlle would be if she saw it! She does think of herself as the village artist…"

Menilmonea smiled with amusement. "Indeed, her drawings would pass for a child's beside these. And look at that wave. The way the water's rendered is incredible."

She reached out to touch the rough surface. "Such mastery!"

"Well… if this painting depicts an actual event, I don't think that island exists anymore, given how big the wave is," Aureal concluded.

With that, they left the house, making for the central avenue that climbed to the city's heights.

"Now, if we had to store a sphere of negation, we wouldn't put it in a house, would we?" asked Menilmonea.

"No, decidedly not. I'd put it somewhere important. Maybe one of those weird buildings over there, with a huge dome?"

"Why don't we give them a try? I wasn't expecting to end up

wandering around an underground city, so I have to admit I'm a bit short on ideas."

"To be honest, I don't know what I was expecting either. But I feel that at every turn along this journey, our improvisations have left us better off."

Menilmonea burst out laughing. A little too loudly. She clapped both hands over her mouth.

"Honestly, Menil, I think you could scream as loud as you want and it wouldn't make a difference. This city is deserted."

"Hmm... Quite recently, though. It would be in far worse shape than this without maintenance."

"Who's to say the Others don't have magic that takes care of maintenance too? A sphere just for cleaning?"

Menilmonea laughed again, eyes twinkling. "If we find that, we're taking it back to the village, end of story!"

They pressed on toward the temple Aureal had pointed out. On the way, they passed silent shops, abandoned houses, and even stranger buildings at whose purpose the two friends could not even guess.

At an intersection with a street that descended toward a small square, a statue caught their eye. It seemed to invite them to join it, standing in the quiet space nestled between surrounding houses.

"Amazing! Look at that!" exclaimed Aureal. "A sculpture... made of stone! How did they manage to do that?"

"I don't know, but they're clearly much more advanced than we are. Look around! Our villages seem like they're thousands of cycles behind in comparison," replied Menilmonea, a little dazed. Then, after a few moments of silence, she added, frowning, "But wait... that sculpture is clearly a human woman. A woman in some kind of robe, pointing at her temples with both hands. That must mean the Others are humans... unless it's some kind of joke of theirs to make statues that look like us?"

"Yes, you're right," replied Aureal, suddenly troubled. "It's clearly human. Like us."

They hurried down to the square, mesmerized by their discovery.

Aureal read the plaque at the base of the statue aloud. "Obinaelle,

High Magistrix of the Core."

"What?" asked Menilmonea, eyebrows raised. "That's her name?"

"Yes. And her title, no doubt."

"Aureal, Great Whisperer to Animals."

"Oh yes! If we make it out of here and back home, I want that on my front door."

"Of course we'll get through this. Let's keep going. We have to find that sphere. I'll feel better when the Primal can join us."

The girls resumed walking, eventually reaching the large building topped by an immense dome. Its majestic entrance was framed by tall columns of a sober but impressive style, similar to those they'd seen in the Towers. The entire structure seemed to vibrate with an ancient gravity, as if it had been built not for use but remembrance, crafted to defy the centuries, even millennia. It was a place whose very silence weighed heavily.

"What an impressive building!" Menilmonea whispered. "It'd be perfect for keeping a sphere of negation!"

They went in. At once, their footsteps rang out on the marble floor, echoes reverberating throughout the building.

What they found left them speechless. The interior was an immense circular library that rose several stories high. A central spiral staircase, suspended from an elegant structure of smooth pale metal, connected the various levels. Each floor was encircled by gigantic bookshelves lined with thousands of books. Some were within reach, while others could only be accessed using ladders that slid smoothly on rails along the walls.

"By all the Titans!" whispered Aureal. "I've never seen so many books!"

"Imagine how long it took to make all that paper!" said Menilmonea, eyes wide with wonder.

"The Others are..." began Aureal.

"Or... were?"

"Yes, maybe. Were incredibly well organized. Look at all these shelves!" She approached a panel above a stack of books and read aloud, "Necropreservation... Culture... Textiles... Hah! Even cooking!"

Menilmonea didn't know where to look first. "Imagine what we could learn here."

"Yes... Although I'm not sure I want to know what necropreservation means."

"Ha ha, no. Of course not... But look here, for instance: '*Caring for Ailments*,'" said Menilmonea, pulling out a book at random. "'*The Art of Using Flux to Cure Toothache*.' Why, I could spend months here!"

"If only we weren't about to be caught out like thieves by the owners. They could turn up at any moment, just like that. And they'd no doubt be ecstatic to find two intruders in their temple to knowledge," Aureal sighed.

Reluctantly, Menilmonea let go of the book. Then she thought better of it.

"Just a moment," she said. "I know we must move on, but... this town is empty, Aureal. And it hasn't been empty for very long. Look around. Nothing's broken, nothing's overgrown. We have a rare opportunity to learn here. We'd be foolish to leave without at least trying to understand who we're dealing with."

"Menil... we don't have time. What if they come back?"

"Then we'll only linger a little while. We'll quickly check every floor. If we don't find anything, we'll move on to another building. Agreed?"

Aureal sighed, resigned. "You're probably right. What exactly are we looking for?"

"Anything that could tell us more about the Others. Who they are. Where they come from. What they want. Or better yet: how to heal a sleeping Titan!"

Menilmonea was already scanning the shelves, a new fire in her eyes.

Aureal nodded, but kept her eyes fixed on the door. "All right... let's search. But quickly."

The two friends split up, each taking a part of the circular ring and reading the names of the sections they came across out loud.

"Astrology!" Aureal called out.

"Theory of Flux," replied Menilmonea, walking along a shelf filled

240

with leather-bound volumes.

"Planar Confrontation!"

"Storage... and here, Preservation..."

As Aureal finished browsing her shelves, Menilmonea climbed the metal steps of the wide central staircase to tackle the floor above.

"Aha! Already, topics more interesting to us! I see 'History'!" she exclaimed.

"Coming," replied Aureal, quickening her pace.

Menilmonea approached the first volumes on the shelf and picked out a massive tome with symbols etched on the cover. "*Exodus and Renaissance: The End of the Curse.* Hmm... that one sounds promising."

"Sounds like a good candidate," replied Aureal, joining her. "What's it about?"

Menilmonea opened the volume but immediately let out a small cry. "The pages... they're blurry! I can't see what it says!"

"What do you mean?"

Menilmonea handed her the book. "Go on, try reading it."

Incredulous, Aureal took the volume in her hands. Her gaze fell on the open page, but right away she took a step back.

"What kind of witchcraft is this? I thought I saw words, but my vision blurs as soon as I look at the page."

They took other books from the same shelf, with the same result. Every time, the letters seemed to vanish before their eyes.

"Unbelievable!" Menilmonea sighed with frustration. "So much knowledge, and we can't access it!"

She moved away to explore another shelf. "Let's see... *Mind Control of Indigenous Entities.* No idea what that means, but let's see if I can read it."

She opened the book, then shook her head in exasperation. "No such luck."

"I'm going back downstairs to see if it's the same down there," said Aureal.

She headed for the Cooking section, opened a volume at random, read a few lines, then called out to Menilmonea. "Well, I can read this one! It looks like they only put a spell on the important books!"

"What a nightmare!" Menilmonea groaned. "I'll go up to the upper floors to see if it's the same everywhere."

When she reached the next level, she exclaimed in amazement. "By the Mother! There's a section called Religion!"

At these words, Aureal rushed up the stairs to join her.

Menilmonea was inspecting the spines of the books lined up on the shelves. "*Origin of the Source... Flux and Source... Conjuration of Major and Minor Orbs of Power.*"

"May the Titans grant us the ability to read these," whispered Aureal, snatching a volume entitled *Divinity and Humanity: The End of the Cycle*. No sooner had she cracked it open than she slammed the book shut and put it in its place without a word.

"What happened?" asked Menilmonea, taken aback.

"I-I don't know. I was able to pull the book out, but as soon as I tried to read it, I lost control of my movements. The book forced me to put it back."

"By the Titans!"

"Guess these books are really important," Aureal muttered.

"I can't imagine what's upstairs," replied Menilmonea, looking up at the library's silent heights.

"Let's just hope the warding spells aren't dangerous."

"We'll see," replied Menilmonea, starting back toward the stairs.

She began climbing the final flight, followed by Aureal, who was feeling a bit lost but determined not to leave her alone.

Once at the top, they discovered new sections.

"'Religious Control'... 'Population Evolution'... 'Growth through Mutation'," read Menilmonea. "Charming."

"There!" Aureal suddenly exclaimed. "'Village Establishment!'"

Menilmonea scowled. "Strangely, I don't like the looks of this..."

"And if we assume that the higher it is, the more important it is... I, too, am getting a bad feeling," admitted Aureal, cautiously approaching the shelves.

They took a few steps toward the section in question, but couldn't go any further. A searing pain shot through their skulls and sent them tottering back.

"Well, there you go! I should have known. We'll never find out," Menilmonea groaned, rubbing her temples.

"Let's go, Menil. We won't get anything out of this accursed place," said Aureal, still reeling.

Reluctantly, Menilmonea nodded, and they slowly made their way down the floors to the exit.

"What a waste!" whispered Menilmonea, turning back. "We had so much to learn. So much to understand!"

"I know. But for now, we need to focus on our goal: finding and deactivating the sphere of negation!"

As they left, Aureal pointed to another building similar to the library.

"Let's try that one." Then, pointing to the biggest such building atop the city, she added, "And if all else fails, we still have that behemoth over there. It doesn't dominate the entire city for nothing. It must be an important place."

Menilmonea followed her in silence, then whispered, "Given their power and magic, I'm sure there's a book somewhere about the Titans... and how to cure them!"

"We'll come back! I promise!" replied Aureal. "But first we must complete our mission. Then we can explore their knowledge in peace. And maybe even figure out how to break their spell."

"You're right," Menilmonea admitted with a slight smile. "After all... we did manage to counter their magic of negation!"

XXVIII

The two friends approached the building, whose exterior oddly resembled the library they had just left. Here too, the circular structure was surrounded by a collar of columns supporting an imposing dome, whose perfect curve stood out against the dark backdrop of the pyramid's inner wall.

They exchanged glances, then cautiously stepped over the threshold.

Inside, a single round chamber, bathed in gentle gloom, received them. The floor, smooth and cold beneath their feet, echoed their every step. In the middle of the room, bathed in a subdued glow, stood a large circular bench upholstered in plush, plum-colored fabric, like a hushed invitation to rest.

"What is this place?" breathed Menilmonea, her voice lost in the chamber's murmurous vastness.

No sooner had she spoken than a soft, warm female voice rang out, seeming to come from nowhere and everywhere at once.

"Welcome to the Chamber of Memory."

The two friends jumped, shoulders tensing with fright, eyes wide and scanning walls and ceiling. They could spot no figure, no visible source.

"Where are you, Lady?" Aureal ventured.

"Oh! I see that your reincarnation must not have gone smoothly. But have no fear, I'm here to help you remember. What you are

245

experiencing is perfectly normal. You have woken from a long slumber, in a healthy body, but one not yet entirely your own.... All this is quite customary. Come forward, please. Find a comfortable spot."

Visibly uneasy, Aureal took a step back. "But... who are you, Lady? And where exactly are we?"

The voice let out a theatrical sigh, almost amused. "Well, this may take a little longer than expected! I am all around you. I am the Spirit of the Chamber. You, strictly speaking, are inside of me."

"Oh..." said Menilmonea and Aureal in unison, mouths half open and eyebrows raised.

"There you are. That's good, now come and sit down. We've work to do."

The two friends exchanged astonished glances, but in unspoken agreement complied and took their places on the circular bench, letting their bodies slowly relax into the unexpected comfort of the plush fabric.

"To help you reconnect with reality," the voice continued, "I'm going to tell you your story. This should activate the memories buried in your minds and help you feel better."

At these words, a section of the wall lit up. A painting, splendid as the one they had encountered in the first house, appeared, as if sprung from the marble itself.

"To complement my story and activate the right areas of your memory," added the voice, "you will see paintings related to what I am about to tell you."

A shiver ran down Menilmonea's spine as the image took shape: a human figure, standing over a pile of skulls and skeletons, drawing a swarm of blue lightning bolts toward herself.

"Charming," Aureal whispered.

Menilmonea, however, remained transfixed by the intensity of the scene.

"It all began with the Breaking of the Pact," said the voice. "It was this event that unleashed the Source's wrath."

A new tableau slowly surfaced on the adjacent wall. Her gaze fixed on this fresco, Menilmonea murmured, "Look! It's like a variation on the one in the house."

The voice continued impassively, "The first plague to strike us was the Curse. It made our bodies fragile, mortal, and vulnerable to the sun's rays."

"You say 'us'… Were you there when the curse struck?" Menilmonea asked.

"Ahem, no… What an odd question. It's more of a figure of speech," the entity clarified, almost humorously. "I'm not Arkandian, as you might guess. Your Mind Mages created me. But, shall we say, I feel like a member of your people. And it's warmer to say 'we' rather than 'you.'"

"Oh…" replied Menilmonea and Aureal, completely lost.

"So, as I was saying: the first plague was the Curse, quickly followed by the Flood, which threatened to destroy our beautiful city."

A third tableau blossomed from the stone.

"Aware of the tragedy to come, High Magistrate Obinaelle gathered the most powerful Flux Manipulators from the Core and the First Circle. She hatched a desperate rescue plan: she would teleport a large section of the heart of Arkandis to safety from the wrath of the Source. The city proved too large, too sprawling to be transferred, and Obinaelle was forced to make a choice. Better to save part of the population than to let everyone die without lifting a finger. The lands of Landria were chosen, for though they had never yet been colonized, we had already established a network of Flux Capture Towers there, and most importantly of all, built a confluence pyramid. It was the perfect place to bring part of the city back to life. Our people would be sheltered from the sun while still having access to high flux density."

Another scene slowly formed on the wall, revealing a resplendent depiction of the pyramid surrounded by lines of energy radiating outward to unseen lands far beyond.

"This transfer drew on the last resources of Arkandis and our Mages. And we also had to pay an immeasurable price: exhausted by the incredible amount of flux she'd had to channel to control the transport spell, Obinaelle died moments after accomplishing the feat of saving what remained of our civilization."

The voice then took on a solemn, almost religious tone. "Glory to her spirit."

A theatrical pause followed, pregnant with meaning. The two friends exchanged a puzzled glance.

"So... you don't even remember that?" sighed the voice. "Well, my poor dears... we must have had to extract you just before the affliction reached your brains."

Then, more calmly, the voice stated, "You must answer, 'Praise be unto her for all time.'"

"Praise be... praise be," the girls repeated in unison, hesitantly.

"Very good," the voice approved.

A new tableau appeared, radiating a pale glow that made the shadows on the circular walls flicker.

"Alas, despite all our efforts," the voice went on, "the Curse continued to claim victims. We could not afford to lose any more lives. The remaining Core Magisters then made a difficult decision: they asked the Jar Keepers to extract the minds of those whom the Curse had too greatly weakened... and to preserve them for as long as possible."

The image that formed before the girls' eyes showed a procession of hunched figures carrying dark urns with red reflections as they advanced through a twilit landscape.

"For eons, we fought relentlessly against the magic of the Source. But we were simply not powerful enough. Despite our best efforts, our bodies rotted. We had to preserve more people every year. That was probably when you were put into slumber in a jar: when your old body could no longer be healed."

The voice paused dramatically. A new scene arose, bathed in a pale light.

"Our people were almost extinct. We were on our knees," the entity continued solemnly. The minds of our greatest spellcasters had to be extracted and preserved, reduced to a dormant state. Only a handful of Jar Keepers and Spirit Mages still remained. However, when all seemed lost, hope was reborn... with the arrival of the Traitor."

Menilmonea frowned, but the voice continued without giving her time to interrupt as a final image appeared in a shimmer of blue light.

"Thanks to our magic and its powers, we finally had healthy, un-corrupted vessels. And patiently, over the centuries, we were able to reincarnate the minds we had stored away. The most difficult to bring back were, of course, those capable of manipulating the flux. But we are patient! And soon we shall be able to rebuild Arkandis! Soon we shall take our revenge and regain our immortality!"

The voice lingered on this last sentence, as if to emphasize its gravity, then emphatically concluded, "This has been the story of the Exodus of the Arkandian people."

Their eyes still fixed on the final glimmers of light fading from the wall, the girls sneaked a quick peek at each other. Then, unable to wait any longer, Aureal asked, "But… you did succeed, then? The streets are empty.... Has everyone moved on to Arkandis and left you behind?"

"And what do you know about the villages? And the Titans? Do you know why they won't wake up anymore?" Menilmonea continued, frowning.

"And the Mother? What do you know about her? Does she really exist?"

A silence fell, as if the chamber itself were hesitating. Then the voice replied, more confused than it had ever been. "I do not understand a word of what you're saying. Truly… I am sorry. What's all this about villages and a Mother? Usually, the reincarnated are much quicker to remember. This has never happened to me before."

A note of distress began to enter its tone. "I'm not qualified to treat you. My duty consists simply of telling the tale. You really ought to go see the Spirit Mage who woke you. Something must have gone wrong…"

Then, as if she had further pondered the question, the voice said, "But wait—when you say the streets are empty, do you mean that literally? There's no one left?"

"Yes. We saw not a soul," confirmed Aureal.

"But then who woke you? You can see that what you're saying doesn't make sense, my dears."

"Yes, you're right," Menilmonea finally said. "We must have been half asleep. We'll go find that wizard right away. Sorry to bother you."

Then, taking Aureal by the arm, she ran as fast as she could toward the exit without even waiting for a reply.

Once outside, she stopped behind a pillar, panting. "It clearly thought we were Others, back from who knows where. I feared it would divine the truth from our questions and sound the alarm."

"Yes, although I can't see whom it might have called for help. That said, the story left a strange taste in my mouth, even if I can't say why yet," replied Aureal, still peering vacantly into the darkness of the chamber.

"I agree. Let's locate that damned sphere and be quick about it. With any luck, it's in that huge building up top. I don't really care for this most recent turn of events."

XXIX

As they continued up the city's main avenue, the two friends tried their best to gather their thoughts, still shaken by their unsettling encounter with the Chamber of Memory.

"The Others seem to have suffered greatly as a people," Aureal murmured, staring up at the gigantic arches above them.

"Yes, and they're so ancient. To think this pyramid has been here for thousands of cycles!"

"What I find bizarre is that the spirit never once mentioned the war with the Primals."

"Nor the Titans, nor the villages," Menilmonea commented. "However, I don't believe it was from ill intent. The voice sounded sincere. If you ask me, it told us everything it had been taught."

"That's obvious. Her reaction to our questions was convincing, to say the least."

"Their mastery of magic is astonishing! They can manipulate minds, store them, transport entire cities..." She trailed off.

The street had turned a corner and abruptly opened on their destination.

Before them stood a monumental building, so vast it could not be taken in all at once. A majestic dome ringed with tall alabaster columns dominated the structure, which emanated a soft, warm light as if gently breathing. Elegant spires rose from the roofs, each topped with enigmatic sculptures. The building appeared open, with no real walls: the immense columns alone delineated its boundaries, describing in the air a geometry that was all circles. The street gradually transformed into an imposing staircase of pale stone, its wide steps worn smooth by time, that led directly to the base of the building.

The two girls stopped dead in their tracks, their headlong momentum halted.

"Beautiful…" whispered Menilmonea.

"Like a heavenly sanctuary," Aureal breathed, eyes wide, unable to tear her gaze away.

They paused to take in the scale of the structure. Exchanging determined glances, they began moving once more, scaling the unending steps one after another, their pace slowed only by the solemnity of their surroundings.

When they reached the top, their eyes instantly zeroed in on a source of light coming from the center of the sanctuary. There, above a gold-veined marble pedestal, a perfectly smooth radiant sphere hung as if suspended in the air. It glowed softly with an unreal silver light.

"There it is!" cried Aureal, breathless.

"Praise the Titans!" replied Menilmonea, unknowingly clasping her hands together.

But just as they were about to enter the temple, a low, rasping sound, like stones being scraped together, rose through the air. It was coming from the far side of the building.

They could not tell what was causing it: the source of the noise was concealed by the broad marble base of the sphere's pedestal.

A gravelly voice rang out. It seemed to speak with some difficulty and gave the two friends the impression that an ancient boulder was trying to imitate human speech.

"Greetings, Mages. I am delighted to see you. I won't hide the fact that I was beginning to worry when I hadn't seen anyone for several days. I like to believe that my last harvest pleased you. It is so rare to find so many candidates sensitive to the flux at once."

The two friends looked at each other, unsure of how to respond. Menilmonea took the lead.

"Greetings."

Immediately, the voice changed its tone. "Oh! What a curious accent you have. Not that I'm really in any position to criticize. Please come closer, dear Mages... You know quite well that I can't move."

Aureal gave Menilmonea a long stare, as if searching her friend's eyes for a clue as to what to do next. Finally, she whispered, "Are we going inside?"

The mycomanceress hesitated, then nodded. "Yes. We didn't come all this way for nothing!"

They entered the sanctum, on guard, their eyes alert for the slightest trap. The source of the voice continued to emit stone-like noises but did not seem to move. This reassured them somewhat, and they continued their cautious advance.

When they reached the central pedestal, a massive shadow fell over them. In a heartbeat, the creature that cast it was looming over them. With his spherical central body seemingly composed of an amalgam of dark rock and fossilized wood, streaked with emerald veins of thick moss, he looked like a neglected relic. From beneath this sphere, four colossal tentacles emerged, formed of cubic segments of stone of varying sizes, jointed by twitching blue energy like a network of captive lightning bolts. Ancient runes appeared on some segments of his appendages, thrumming to the rhythm of some unfathomable power. In the middle of what must have been his head, six luminous eyes glittered with supernatural brilliance. And just above, on what might, with a little imagination, have been called a forehead, an intense green emerald pulsed gently.

Shocked by this sudden apparition, the two friends fell backward, victims of an all-too-familiar feeling of nausea.

"You're not Mages, are you? Or else you would have known that I can move about without difficulty, at least within the confines of this accursed temple," the voice boomed knowingly. And then, without even giving them time to respond, he said. "Ho ho ho! Why, I'd say you're not even from this city. But what's the matter? Are you all right? Did I scare you? Why are you sitting on the ground?"

The creature seemed to think for a moment, then went on, his voice still grating. "You humans are so hard to read. You're all ugly, each uglier than the last, and I can never tell if you're happy or dying. And what's more, you all look alike!"

He proceeded to inspect them from head to toe. "Well, in your cases, you've made it a bit easier for me: there's one with a hat, and the other with just hair on her head."

He paused again, adopting an almost pensive tone, as if talking to himself. "Not like those damn Arkandians. They're all covered up in the same fashion, it's absolute hell trying to tell them apart."

The girls slowly got back to their feet, frightened but determined. Menilmonea turned to Aureal to signal that everything would be all right. Aureal gestured back to convey something, but the myco-manceress whispered, "Yes, I know. I felt it too."

Then she turned back to the creature and stated, "My name is Menilmonea, and this is Aureal. Who are you?"

Instead of even feigning to attempt a reply, the creature simply went on, "I was right, wasn't I? What a genius I am! Allow me to continue, I love this game. I'll wager you must be from the villages. Am I correct? Am I?"

Stunned, the two friends nodded in confirmation.

"But wait. There's just one thing… Why, or how, did the Arkandians let you pass and get this far? And even before that, their golems or my Guardian should have sensed you. What's your secret, little things?"

Aureal turned to Menilmonea with a shrug, silently asking, "What now?"

The latter put a finger to her lips, signaling her friend to remain silent and let her speak. Then she straightened slightly before declaring. "There's no one else here. The area around the pyramid is empty, as are the streets and houses of this city. We haven't seen anyone. You are the first living being we've come across."

At these words, the creature became carried away, his voice increasingly difficult to understand. "But that's poppycock! Impossible! They can't do that! Not after everything I've done for them…. You're lying! They wouldn't have left without keeping their promise!"

And with that, it lunged toward their faces at lightning speed.

The two friends were terrified, but Aureal managed tremblingly to reply. "I promise you it's true! As you said, we'd never have been able to reach you otherwise."

"No, no, they'll definitely come back! I'm certain of it. You're just putting thoughts into my head. After all, they've kept all their promises so far! Almost...."

He paused. "Yes, they'll come back. They must have tried that damn magic experiment they were always talking about. They were always short of people for it, but with the thirty or so potential Mages I found for them, they must have succeeded. Yes, it's obvious! And now that it's worked, they'll be happy and come back to pay their debt."

He paused again, even longer this time, muttering incoherently. "And besides, when they arrive, they'll probably appreciate that I captured two little mice who thought they could get away with whatever they wanted.... Yes, that'll make a nice welcome back present!"

He paused one last time, muttering something incomprehensible, then added, "But back to our game! We must busy ourselves while we wait."

He drew closer to them once more, startling the two friends. "Now, now! Don't be afraid. I'm not going to eat you. I don't have a digestive system, anyway. That said, I could crush your limbs. It might be entertaining...."

"That could actually kill us, you know," Menilmonea pointed out. "And I'm sure the Arkandians would rather us whole and alive. For when they come back."

"Wise words from our friend in the pointy hat!" With that, he leaned forward even closer, as if trying to smell them. "I see, I see.... No, not the frog Titan, or the badger.... No, I'd wager the turtle. Yes, that's it, you come from the village of the turtle Titan. Am I right?"

"How did you know that? Do you know our Titans? Do you know how to wake them up?" asked Menilmonea incredulously.

"By Tunka's shell, who are you?" Aureal continued, her voice tenser than ever.

The creature seemed to snicker, clearly delighted with its effect on them.

"Why, you poor fools, don't you understand? I am the Mother, of course."

XXX

Aureal squeezed Menilmonea's hand so tightly that she let out a small muffled cry. But already, the creature had burst into its gravelly, grating laugh, like stones tumbling down an unsound mountainside.

"Yes, that's right! It's me, your beloved goddess of love and happiness! And this... is your paradise!" he declared in a theatrical tone, dripping with sarcasm.

His laugh rang out again, dry and shattered, an echo of disaster.

"I had to concoct a beautiful tale to make you progress, make you obey. It was so easy. Why, I could promise you anything, your people are so gullible! You devoted your lives to us in exchange for an unverifiable promise. You're worse than sheep."

Menilmonea frowned. When she spoke, her voice quavered. "'Us'? Who do you mean, 'us'? You obey the Arkandians? Why? Why make a pact with those who destroyed your people? Why betray your own kind?"

The creature seemed to squint its countless eyes almost tenderly. "Oho! I see you haven't told me everything, you secretive little mice. You met our friend the wee fox, didn't you? His Lordship the Primal has stooped so low as to learn your language. He must be truly desperate. How delectable."

The two friends looked at each other without saying a word. Paying no attention to their silent exchange, the Traitor continued, "So he told you about our people. Or rather, his people. Well, I'm not like them anymore! The Others wed me to their stones. These tentacles might have fooled you. How did you figure it out? Oh, I see—it's my eyes, isn't it? Yes? Of course, a classic of my kind. Hard to hide, indeed.... So he sent you to do his dirty work for him. What did he promise you? Come, do tell, I'm truly interested."

"Nothing at all, you monster!" roared Aureal, eyes flashing. "He just helped us. We wanted to come here to ask your aid for our Titans. The Primal helped us destroy your pathetic Guardian!"

The creature froze for a moment, as if surprised, before bowing slightly, a sneer on its lips. "How... sad. If only you'd known that poor creature was descended from the Primals."

Menilmonea stood frozen, her throat tight. "What? What... are you talking about?"

The laughter resumed, lower, deeper—even gravellier, if that were possible.

"Ha! You're good for a laugh, at least. Time passes faster when you're having fun, doesn't it? How I relish your reactions."

Aureal clenched her fists. "Why did you say that Guardian was a descendant?"

"Simply because he was. And I'll tell you an even bigger secret—why not? All the Titans, every last one, are descended from children of the Primals. And I am the one who enslaved them. All!"

Satisfied with this proclamation, the Traitor let his gaze linger on the two friends. Then his voice rose again, sharper than before. "I, who was to have died, for I was not worthy of immortality, oh no! Only the Primals, the Lords of Nature, have that right. I, a miserable Second Generation, barely able to move—I should have died. They wanted me dead! But in the end, why, look at me! I'm still here! I destroyed them all! And those I didn't destroy, I made into slaves, subject to my will alone."

He paused. Deliberately. For a long time. "Fascinating, isn't it?"

"I don't believe a word of it," Menilmonea countered. "The Others slew the Primals. As for the Titans, they look like nothing your people.

Your psychological torture won't work."

"Oh, you think so? Allow me to tell you my story, then, and you can judge for yourself. I wouldn't want my audience to take me for a liar."

Without waiting for their reply, he barreled on. "When I was hybridized, I knew I wasn't strong enough to stay alive. Second Generation beings are normally much stronger than I was. I was a mistake, and the law of the Primals were clear on my account: I had to let myself perish to preserve the natural cycle. Except that I existed. I had a life. It meant nothing to them, but it was everything to me. I didn't want to die! Admittedly, I was without abilities, but still, I could have helped. I wanted to be part of the greater whole, I wanted to protect our Mother. But the Primals had no use for a weakling like me. I had to die."

He seemed to gaze into the distance for a moment, lost in ancient regrets.

"And surprise you though it may, I had accepted my fate. But I didn't want a slow death, left to rot away against an old tree trunk, turning into fertilizer for the rest of the forest. No! I wanted to go quickly.... So I found myself facing a difficult question."

"How to commit suicide?" asked Aureal, her voice full of gravity.

"Exactly! Astonishing, how your people can be so stupid and so brilliant all at once. Anyway, yes! So how could I kill myself? A difficult question. Well, of course, no one wished to lend me a hand. It wasn't what nature's law dictated. Fortunately, my intellect hadn't been diminished like the rest of my body. Finally, then, I found a solution: the pyramid! If I went inside, my death would be instantaneous. A slight numbness, and goodbye, no protracted suffering...."

He cackled, almost moved by his own story.

"It took me months to get here, for of all the disabilities Gaia had decided to bestow upon me, among the worst was that I could only budge my limbs very slightly. Nor could I grow any new ones. Needless to say, I didn't cover much ground on a daily basis."

"But then where did these tentacles come from?" Menilmonea asked in surprise.

"My dear, they are a gift from the Arkandians. Which is why, to answer your question from earlier: no, I don't obey them. We work together toward a common goal, which will allow both them and me to secure what we desire."

"Yes, well, you seem to be a prisoner here, don't you?" Aureal asked skeptically.

"Not a prisoner, you poor ninny! These stone artifacts only work within the confines of this temple, but they are temporary. The Arkandians are working to regrow my fibers, my limbs! Then I will be free again."

"You must be patient, because if you've been here since before the war with the Primals, that's hundreds of cyc—rotations, I mean," said Aureal.

"Yes, patient I am. And what's more, I can afford to be, because they have given me another gift: I am immortal, like a Primal! I, the detritus meant to perish, have obtained what even the First Generations never had."

"Bravo! But I'm sorry, I don't see the connection between your gifts and the fact that the Titans are hybrids of the Primals," said Menilmonea.

"That is because my tale has only just begun, child," replied the Traitor, his voice sliding through the air with soft menace. "Allow me to continue recounting my odyssey! So, as I was dragging myself toward certain death, the Arkandians sent a golem to retrieve me and bring me here, where we now stand."

"But how? You should have died as soon as the sphere of negation took effect on you!" exclaimed Aureal, incredulous.

"Well, well, haven't we done our homework! Yes, that should have been the case. But they gave me something that enabled me not to feel the effects of what they call their 'orb of power.'"

With one of his tentacles, he tapped lightly, almost affectionately, on the emerald embedded in his forehead.

"I must confess, I didn't understand what was happening. Why save me? Me, of all creatures.... I had no value, no power."

He paused, his many eyes flickering slightly.

"Or so I thought. When they brought me here, they summoned their Mind Mages, who rapped at the door of my consciousness with their magic. I didn't know what to do. And anyway, I wanted to die. So I let them in."

His sudden silence brimmed with suspense.

"They asked me what I wanted. Why I was there. Who my people were. What we wanted. They had never left their pyramid and weren't really aware of what was going on outside. I told them everything. After all, I was talking to a people who didn't judge me, who didn't want me to die, who seemed genuinely interested in me. I even learned their language without using their magic to facilitate communication."

His voice softened, as if lulled by a distant memory.

"They were fascinated by our abilities, especially the one that enables us to mutate species. They told me of their curse, their bodies falling apart, their desperate attempts to save themselves. They revealed their powers to me, in particular their ability to manipulate consciousness. They even offered to use their stone magic to give me temporary tentacles."

He let out a joyless laugh.

"After several days, one of their greatest Mages came to me. He was one of the few who had not been affected by the curse. He asked me many questions about the role the Primals played, about Gaia.... And he offered me a deal: if I helped them capture the Primals, they would heal my appendages and make me immortal. All I had to do was act as a conduit to reach the consciousness of those they captured. They had rightly anticipated that my people, unlike me, would not let them in. And without direct, willing access, their magic would not work. I would be the key that opened those doors. My people's ability to unite their minds would be the cause of their demise."

"You sold out your own kind in order to live?" Menilmonea gasped. "What kind of monster are you?"

"That's where you're wrong, little human. I no longer had a people. I was dead to my own kind. And so I was free. I betrayed no one, for I had no one left to betray."

The Traitor paused, then continued with calculated slowness,

"Their plan was to capture several Primals and subjugate them with their mind magic. They wanted to force them to mutate diseased bodies to extract the curse. Not a bad idea in and of itself, except that the Primals proved far more powerful than the Arkandians had anticipated. What's more, they had only a few spheres of negation, and they needed their main one to protect the pyramid."

Saying this, he pointed to the artifact behind the two friends.

"The Primals literally crushed the Arkandian offensive. They lost the vast majority of their golems in a single afternoon."

His eyes narrowed, glinting with twisted pride.

"But guess who came up with the idea that turned the tide? Me! Of course! I'd never really brought it up, but it turned out that despite all my shortcomings, there was one thing I did exceptionally well. I could extend my consciousness over vast distances. Perhaps as far as a Primal. I suggested that they use me to infiltrate the collective consciousness that the Primals and the First Generations had established to wage war. Through me, their Mind Mages would project, directly into my people's consciousness, a magical attack so potent it would leave them in a brief coma. Just long enough to destroy the most powerful Primals by exposing them to a sphere of negation, and to capture the others."

He paused for a moment, quivering with a sick satisfaction.

"They channeled all the magic this place could produce and focused it all on my mind. The suffering was unspeakable. It burrowed into my soul; I was on the verge of madness, but I held fast. I would not allow myself to falter. I clung to my revenge. I would show them all how wrong they were. With my help, the Arkandians were able to render the Primals unconscious. So powerful was the attack that their descendants' memories were instantaneously erased! What golems were left easily rounded them up like a flock of bewildered sheep."

His tone was calm now. Triumphant.

"The battle was over in a heartbeat. The spheres had destroyed five Primals. One of the mightiest did not fall unconscious but sank instead into madness. The last of them, that coward only present through his phantasm, was spared. And you know the rest of his story better than

I, no doubt."

"How horrible!" Aureal whispered.

"You disgust me," Menilmonea spat, her voice vibrating with anger.

"Come, come! I don't think you're in any position to say such things. Show some respect for your goddess," he simpered, before bursting into gravelly laughter. "But what of the Titans, you ask? I'm getting there, I'm getting there... You're so impatient!"

He pretended to clear a throat he didn't have.

"Once the war was over, the Others asked a descendant—again, with my help as a talented interpreter—to mutate the body of one of their sickest members, and the mutation worked. Almost. The body was healed, but the mind... had vanished. The original consciousness had been erased, replaced by a blank slate."

A mocking silence, and then he went on.

"And I must admit, the Arkandians have one quality: they don't give up easily. Faced with this setback, they spent days devising plans. They were even courteous enough to include me in some of their discussions. Then their Jar Keepers had a brilliant idea. An idea that would change everything."

He paused dramatically.

"They were going to cultivate bodies. Create farms of... you. Since they couldn't heal their own bodies, they were going to make brand new ones."

Aureal and Menilmonea looked at each other in disbelief.

"Oh, yes, you understood correctly! The Arkandians raised you like cattle. It was excellent, as ideas went. They would build villages, populate them, and harvest the bodies they needed as vessels for all the minds they had extracted. They had to sacrifice the most diseased to give birth to the first bodies untouched by the Curse, those of the original villages. But once in place, the system was self-sustaining."

A wicked smile accompanied his next revelation.

"And that's where I stepped in again to perfect my masterpiece. I suggested using the descendants we had captured to speed up production. All we had to do was force these descendants to stay near the villages to make the bodies grow twice as fast. We even tried to go faster, but human bodies couldn't handle it. Unpleasant things started happening."

"The Arkandians were making us grow? Grow faster?" whimpered Menilmonea, on the verge of tears.

"Wonderful, no? Faster growth means more bodies! Yes, as apparently not all bodies are compatible, they say. Certain conditions I don't have a grasp of must be met to enable the safe transfer of a saved consciousness to a new body. I must admit I never paid much attention to that part. I merely acted as a relay when the Arkandians went to fiddle with the mind of a descendant in charge of a village, looking for the right 'vessel.' You know... to offer them Ascension."

He slammed a tentacle against the floor excitedly.

"But how can we grow... faster? I-I don't understand," replied Menilmonea.

"In the name of our Mother, how can you be so dimwitted? All right, then: how old are you?"

"Thirteen cycles," she stammered.

"And ten for me," whispered Aureal.

"*Wrong!* You are twenty-six and twenty rotations old, respectively. Your bodies have twenty-six and twenty rotations, to be precise. You have only lived thirteen and ten rotations, but your kind turtle used all the energy from its heartseed to accelerate your growth."

"But did Tunka know?" asked Menilmonea, her heart completely shattered.

"No, of course not! He thought he was serving his 'goddess.' He had no inkling he was draining his life force to make you grow faster. It's even more satisfying that way, isn't it? Thanks to the magic of my Arkandian friends, I had total control of his actions. Well, I won't conceal the fact that it was difficult at first; their spells had a hard time fighting against the descendants' unconscious will and, above all, against Gaia's hold. And I got violent migraines with each attempt, for their magic often rebounded back on me. But they finally found a solution: their understanding of what they call 'flux' enabled them to cut the descendants off from the Song. Thus severed, they became brave little puppies, ready to believe anything."

There was a flash of cruelty in his voice.

"The only side effect, and one that ultimately without impact, at least on our plans, was that this severing proved so painful and traumatic that the subjects either died or retreated into a dream world and were physically transformed. They became crude versions of their totem animals, or at least some combination of their fantasies and their former bodies."

"How awful..." whispered Aureal, stunned.

"Exactly!" concluded the Traitor, delighted. "Now, sprinkle all that with my story of a goddess who whispers in the Titans' ears, and you have the final recipe: for hundreds of rotations, the Arkandians selected and sent your people to Ascension as vessels for their minds. The minds that previously occupied these bodies were tossed on the dungheap. Delectable, isn't it? See how clever I was about it. Your 'goddess' wanted to see the villages prosper. It was her sacred wish that families be fruitful and multiply. The more children, the more bodies to offer..."

The revelation hit the girls like a shockwave. The world around them seemed to totter, warp, lose all meaning. Menilmonea felt her legs buckle beneath her, as if the Earth itself refused to bear her weight any longer. Her breath caught abruptly in her throat, snatched away by the sheer horror of what she had just heard. She brought a trembling hand to her mouth, unable to utter anything but a silent moan.

Aureal staggered in turn, eyes wide, staring at the creature as if beholding death incarnate. Cold sweat beaded on her forehead, her fingers grasping at thin air, casting about for an anchor that no longer existed. She wanted to shrink back, run away, to scream, but no sound came from her mouth.

An unbearable iciness had seeped into them, deeper-seated than fear, more dreadful than hatred. It was utter collapse. The slow, merciless erosion of their every belief, of all that had brought them this far.

At last, the truth was theirs. And that truth hurt more than anything they had ever known before.

"Hah! And there you have it!" exclaimed the Traitor. "I no longer sense your mistrust, your disdain! You believe me at last."

He drew up himself to his full height, towering over them.

"How I love this feeling of having snapped you like pathetic twigs. Just as I broke all those pitiful Primals and their arrogance! Where are your convictions now, little humans? You see? I am your goddess after all!"

XXXI

Menilmonea staggered. Her head was spinning and her stomach churned with almost unbearable violence. The urge to vomit took hold of her, brutal and coercive, but she managed to keep control. Her voice was no more than a faint whisper.

"But how could they kill all those people? People of their own kind?"

The Traitor slammed a tentacle against the ground, almost as if to cut her off.

"Tsk tsk! Not kill. Well... not their bodies! Their minds, on the other hand.... Ah, yes, that made for quite a nice collection of sacrificed consciousness. But do you think twice when you crush an ant? No? Well, it's the same for them. You're just... meat."

He raised a tentacle with a vaguely philosophical air. "And some even got a little reprieve."

"How so?" whispered Aureal, her voice almost stifled.

"At first, we used the poor Second Generation sorts to keep the Towers fed with minds. They were still wandering aimlessly about, lost without their beloved 'parents.' But, alas, that isn't, to put it bluntly, the kind of resource that grows on trees. So the supply soon dwindled."

"By all the Titans! The Spirits of the Towers are also descendants."

"For the most part, yes."

"But… why?"

"Ah, my dear! Your people are so simpleminded that we had to instruct you on how to reach this place. At first, I tried to pass it off as part of my 'religion,' you see. I explained the procedure using parables. But the loss rate was too high. People would arrive at the Towers and wander off who knows where. I still can't convince myself that you and the Arkandians are of the same species. But at any rate! In short, we had to give you a helping hand. But as I was saying, I didn't have enough descendants left under my tentacle, so some of your beloved Chosen Ones had their consciousness conscripted to serve as guides. After being 'wiped,' of course, if you know what I mean."

He burst out in a deep, guttural laugh, a sound that seemed to crawl up their arms and creep into their pores. They shivered, the icy sensation almost painful.

Despite her disgust, Menilmonea dared ask one more question, voice trembling. "But… why kill the Titans?"

The Traitor made a mocking, almost weary clucking sound. "Oh, that? No, that wasn't me. Well, not directly. It's just that, since they exhaust their own resources to speed up your growth, and they can't reconnect with our Mother, well… they end up dying. Shame, isn't it?"

When he paused, a cruel smile could be heard in his voice.

"The best part is that they could recharge, but they've forgotten how. Life is so unfair."

"Then… you could save them?"

"Oh yes, it would be child's play! Well, for those still awake. For the others, it's already too late. But the real question is: why on earth would I ever want to?"

Menilmonea shuddered inside but didn't let it show.

"Don't you think you've had enough revenge?"

"Oh no, my dear—far from it! I want to see them all quietly rotting away, just as they intended for me to do. Then, and only then, will my revenge be complete… They could have helped me, you know. They could have put me out of my misery, helped me die quickly and with dignity. But no, not one of them lifted so much as a fibril. 'That's just the natural order of things,' they said, or 'That would go against Gaia's wishes.' But I only wished to serve her and adore her! Despite everything she put me through! I just didn't want to suffer in pain and die miserably."

As if aware of the gravity of what he was about to say, he paused, then added, "We are nothing but grains of sand to her, mere pawns she moves about or crushes according to her unfathomable whims. We don't matter! But today, with the help of the Arkandians, I can finally hold up a mirror to her. Show her the reflection of her crimes. Scream what she has done to me right back at her. Perhaps by upending her works, by annihilating everything she has so arrogantly built, she will deign to see me, hear me. Perhaps then, just for a moment, I will exist in her eyes. Even if it means burning everything, corrupting everything, desecrating everything. Even if it means becoming the scourge of her creation."

Eyes brimming with tears, Menilmonea seized Aureal's hand and gave her a determined look. Her face had become a resolute mask. Without a word, Aureal stared back at her and nodded, her pupils filled with the same desire for revenge.

Menilmonea leaned in slightly and whispered something barely audible.

"What? What did you say?" growled the Traitor. "Speak up, for heaven's sake! I'm already making an effort to use your archaic means of communication."

With that, he slowly approached and pressed his face close to Menilmonea's. "It would be a shame if I lost patience and I no longer found our little game diverting, wouldn't it?"

Without warning, Menilmonea's voice whispered directly into the Traitor's mind. *It's probably better this way, isn't it?*

The creature recoiled, as if from an electric shock, tentacles quivering, eyes wide.

"What?" he replied, panicked. "What spell is this? How can you speak to me through the Song? What is this abomination? I don't—"

He didn't have time to finish his sentence.

"Get the gem," Menilmonea whispered.

In a fraction of a second, dozens of fibers surged forth from her medallion. Some took root around her, forming solid footholds, while others, driven by the mycomanceress' anger and hatred, leapt straight for the descendant's forehead.

With a terrifying screech of crushed stone and broken wood, the tendrils forcefully pierced the creature's mineral flesh, extracting the emerald in a blinding flash.

The operation was so swift and brutal that the Traitor had no time even to recover from the shock of the mental contact before the stone was torn out. The violence of the broken link hurled him backwards, and he collapsed with a crash to the ground, body wracked by fleeting spasms.

The medallion brought the gem back to Menilmonea's chest. She grabbed it straightaway. Already on her feet, she pulled Aureal with her and, without waiting, they both dove around the other side of the pedestal that bore the sphere of negation.

Her heart pounding, Menilmonea glanced over her shoulder, panting. She saw the Traitor regaining his senses. Deprived of his jewel, he was unsteady on his feet, but pure rage seemed to course through him. The emerald began to pulse faster, as if agitated by the chaos all around.

"What have you done, you wretched creatures?" he shouted, his voice ringing out like an echo of pure anger. "Who are you?"

He roared again, tentacles frantically lashing the ground as he struggled to get back on his feet.

"I'll tear you limb from limb! You'll surrender all the secrets of your power! You'll give me that half-seed! The Primal made a huge mistake entrusting it to you. I'll put it to so much better use! Why, with it, I could even leave this miserable place behind!"

The two friends were at a loss.

"How can this be?" gasped Menilmonea. "I checked carefully. Whenever he was more than a few steps away from us, we lost our powers. How can he still be alive?"

"I don't know. But we have to get out of here! If we can reach the stairs—"

"We'll never make it to the entrance before he does. He's incredibly fast!"

She had barely finished her sentence when Aureal shouted, "Here he comes!"

The Traitor had finally gotten back to his feet, limbs quavering with the effort, but his hatred seemed to give him wings. He came hurtling toward them at full speed.

Menilmonea stood up then and turned toward her fate, one hand clenched around her half-seed, eyes closed.

"Stop him!"

At her words, a wave of power spread through the ground. Numerous thick roots sprang up and sank deep into the stone slabs, while several others came darting out like giant serpents and launched themselves at the Traitor's tentacles.

The impact was titanic. The creature was immobilized. His gnarled appendages struggled, their runes glowing with a blinding blue light, but the plant-like bonds held firm. The harsh, fibrous grating of stone on vine could be heard, along with the hiss of contained energy.

The Traitor screamed in rage, eyes wild, voice steeped in a blend of pain and contempt.

"You insignificant piece of filth! You are no match for me! I am a god! I will crush you, reduce you to dust, and dance on your remains!"

Menilmonea struggled to maintain the roots' grip, her face contorted with effort.

"I can't hold him off much longer!" she cried, panicked. "Flee! There's no way we can both stay here! Flee, Aureal, save yourself!"

"Never!" her friend replied, eyes aflame with fierce loyalty. "Even if I'm scared to death, my fate is tied to yours, no matter what!"

"Go! Don't leave me with your death on my conscience. Please, Aureal!"

"If we both die, you won't have to bear it for long! Anyway, when it comes to muleheadedness, I don't think you can beat me! Focus on him instead!" said Aureal, a smile trembling on her lips.

Menilmonea swallowed hard and reluctantly gave in. "You're so stubborn!"

"Great! Now use that pretty frustration against him!"

Muffled booms echoed around them: wood creaked, stone groaned. Sweat beaded on Menilmonea's brow, her every muscle taut as a drawn bow. A huge crack resounded through the room. One of the Traitor's tentacles, mighty with fury, managed to break free, tossing the roots that had bound it skyward.

"He's incredibly strong!"

With a wrathful roar, the Traitor swung his freed tentacle with all his might in an effort to crush Menilmonea. But he was still too far away: his attack only shattered a few slabs, sending fragments of stone flying around him.

"You won't be able to hold me back for long, you wretched insects!" he thundered.

Gasping for breath, Menilmonea cried out, "Why continue to spread misery? You've had your revenge! The Primals are almost all dead! You've destroyed and humiliated the last of your kind! You've sent your message to Gaia! What more do you want?"

The Traitor paused for a moment, his eyes burning with a new intensity.

"What do I want? I want her attention! I want her to regret what she did to me! I want her to talk to me!"

"But perhaps she already has!" Menilmonea replied, her voice vibrant with feeling. "What if you just can't hear her? Who's to say we're not her message? Who's to say she didn't give us our gifts and allow us to make this journey just to reach you? To speak to you?"

The Traitor growled, his tentacles quivering with contained doubt. "And what would that message be?"

"Stop the cycle of suffering. Save the remaining Titans. She heard you. You are no longer a grain of sand on the beach. You matter to her."

Just then, with an impressive crash, a new tentacle broke its chains. A loud bang shook the entire room. The stones trembled.

"A valiant attempt, my young friend," the Traitor sneered. "But I don't believe a word of it. I don't know where you got your powers, but I doubt Gaia is behind them. You are insignificant. You are nothing.

Gaia will not come down to me. I will raise myself up to her!"

And with that, he thrust his two appendages forward, exerting considerable pressure on the last roots still hobbling him.

He pounded the ground with insane violence, each blow making it rumble as if thunderstruck. Fragments of stone flew in all directions, turning the atmosphere into a chaos of dust and debris.

Menilmonea whispered softly through clenched teeth to her half-seed, enveloping it in a murmur of gentle supplications. In response, the seed seemed to vibrate with a green glow before making one last-ditch effort. Before the two friends unfolded a barrier of green, woven tightly of foliage, branches, thick vines. It managed to stop most of the flying rock shards, which hit the freshly formed bark with sharp snaps.

The mycomanceress gave Aureal a desperate look. "We're done for. I can't ask any more of my medallion. It's used up all its energy, and the Traitor shows no sign of slowing down."

Utterly lost, Aureal could not hold back her tears. She pressed herself against Menilmonea's back and hugged her as tightly as she could. "You are my family. You are my forever friend. I have no regrets."

Her embrace brought tears to Menilmonea's eyes. The mycomanceress dropped the emerald and placed her hand on her friend's, her trembling fingers seeking the warmth of one last unbreakable bond.

"In the end, I don't think there will be anything left for the Arkandians when I'm through with you," said the Traitor venomously. "Unless I keep you alive just long enough to make you watch as I drain your precious Titans of their substance. Oh, decisions, decisions...."

With a hideous crack of splintering wood, a third tentacle broke free. The creature was inexorably gaining ground.

Awaiting her fate, Aureal looked down at the emerald fallen to the stone floor. It was pulsing at a phenomenal rate, as if trying to convey an urgent message. In a desperate attempt to blot out the reality around her, she tried to focus on it: how could the Traitor still move when he was no longer carrying the stone? There was no doubt but that he was well out of its sphere of influence. And why was the gem blazing so brightly?

Just then, her gaze fell on the sphere of negation, and she froze.

"By the Mother!" she cried.

"Unngh?" was all Menilmonea said, grimacing in pain.

"We're too close to the sphere! I mean, the emerald is too close to the sphere!"

"Sorry, Aureal, I-I don't understand what you mean," Menilmonea gasped, on the verge of fainting. Her face was a mask of agony.

"The emerald is acting like a magical water orb!" exclaimed Aureal. "Its nullification zone encompasses the sphere! Which must be completely drowning out its powers! The sphere isn't working!"

"By all... the Titans.... I-I'm going to let go, the half-seed is... spent," whispered Menilmonea, shaky.

At these words, her friend leaned forward, grabbed the stone, and flung it away with all her strength.

And as the emerald traced a magnificent parabolic arc beneath the temple dome, a terrible noise rang out. A mixture of crushed rock and dry wood shattering under unbearable pressure.

The Traitor had just died.

Menilmonea collapsed in turn, drained of all strength. Her body fell to the ground as if felled by the wind. All the roots and vines that the half-seed had sprouted dropped limply, sapped of energy, slowly disintegrating with a leafy rustle.

Aureal went to help her friend up, but realized she had one last task left to accomplish and rushed to retrieve the precious stone. She ran and pressed it, hands shaking, against the sphere of negation.

"There!"

She hurried back and knelt beside Menilmonea, whose nerves had finally given way. Aureal took her in her arms without a word, offering her friend a shoulder to pour out her overflowing emotions. Huddled against her, Menilmonea wept, letting her body loosen, tremble, and expel the accumulated tension. She could let out all her fatigue and grief at not having been able to save her Titan.

After a long moment, Aureal whispered, "You were magnificent, Menil. A true heroine. Tunka would have been so proud of you."

Between sobs came the mycomanceress' voice, fragile but sincere. "Thank you. I could never have done it without you. The two of us, together, against the world."

Menilmonea then focused on the Song and called the Primal.

He was quick to respond. A low rumbling shook them from their stupor. They stood as quickly as they could manage, alerted by the unsettling vibration that shook the temple's very foundations.

They made their way to the stairs and saw hundreds of roots sprouting from all sides, crawling in from the entrance of the pyramid. They wound into alleys and buildings, engulfing every corner of the city. The entire city was changing hands.

The Primal had received the message.

Menilmonea tried to send another message through the Song, as loudly as she could. "Don't destroy the city, please.... We have so much to learn from them."

No sooner had she formed this thought than a familiar figure seemed to sprout but a few paces away, rising from a large root that had already conquered the broad steps.

"I didn't plan to destroy everything, my dear," the fox said lightly. "But still, we must be wary of their magic, and I would like, let us say, to have as much presence in this place as possible."

His gaze then fell on the sphere. "How did you manage to deactivate it?"

"It was the emerald," Aureal replied proudly. "It blocks the magic of negation."

"I see. I'll make sure those two stay as close as can be, then."

With that, thick bundles of roots emerged from the temple floor, slowly forming a sturdy shell of wood and vines around the sphere of negation and its companion.

"I used the sturdiest wood I could produce. It should no longer be possible to separate the gem from the sphere." Then, turning to Menilmonea, the Primal asked, "Are you all right?"

"Yes, Primal. We were just shaken by what the Traitor told us."

"The Traitor?"

"Yes... How about we eat and rest, and then I'll fill you in on everything?"

Before she could finish her sentence, the Primal had already conjured up a magnificent carpet of moss at their feet.

"Rest. The grizzly shouldn't be long. I'll let you build a fire—it's not my forte, but I know you need it," he said with a laugh. "I won't hide the fact that I can't wait to find out what this place really is."

"You won't be disappointed," replied Aureal with a tired smile.

XXXII

The two young women took turns recounting their journey, one voice filling in or picking up where the other left off. Each incident that had befallen them took shape in the solemn calm of their surroundings. The Primal sat motionless, not saying a word. Now and then, however, he turned his inscrutable gaze toward what had once been this temple's occupant, and one of his own kind.

When their story came to an end, he finally spoke. His tone was sorrowful and laden with pain. "That one of our own could do such a thing horrifies me beyond words. He wiped out an entire race, his own, out of pure vengeance. I never thought my kind capable of such evil."

He fell silent again, this time at length. A suspended eternity, which the young women dared not disturb.

Then, with a sigh that was almost human, he said, "I am truly sorry for your Titan. I share your grief."

"Thank you, Primal," replied Menilmonea. "But we can still save those who are not yet asleep. If a descendant could reconnect them to Gaia.... That shouldn't be hard for you, right?"

"Have you ever tried?" asked Aureal in a moment of naivete.

The Primal shook his head slowly. "Alas, no. It never occurred to me. Did you try talking to the stones when you arrived here? It's somewhat like that. They weren't part of the Song. There was no reason for me to try projecting my thoughts into their minds."

"Yes," Aureal said after a moment, "it makes perfect sense now that you put it that way."

"What worries me right now," the Primal continued, "is what has become of those Arkandians. They remain dangerous, even if they seem to have left our continent."

"After all the horrors they put us through for hundreds of cycles, I dare hope they'll finally leave us alone," replied Menilmonea.

"I hope so too. But I'm going to strengthen my presence here as much as possible. If they come back, I want to know," said the fox firmly.

"The question that's been on my mind for a while," Aureal admitted, "is how they ever left in the first place."

"Through the transport rings?" ventured Menilmonea.

"I don't know. I'm no expert, really," said Aureal, "but it would definitely be worth taking a look at their library to try and break through their protective spells. The less we know, the more vulnerable we are."

"It's fascinating," said the Primal. "They were a people who accumulated so much knowledge, so many wonders... only to reveal themselves to be so selfish and ignorant of the simplest moral principles."

"As the Traitor said," added Menilmonea bitterly, "they thought we were ants. Less than nothing.... I hope they pay someday for all the harm they've done."

"For my part," she went on, "I wonder most of all what we will be able to tell the villagers."

"Indeed," concurred the Primal, "as you will never again have the promise of Ascension. Your people have spent their entire existence working toward that goal. I'm not sure that telling them the unvarnished truth is a good idea."

"I agree," said Menilmonea. "We'll also have to explain why we're all going to start aging more slowly."

"And therefore live twice as long.... By the Titans, Menil!" Aureal exclaimed. "Are we really going to live to at least eighty cycles?"

"It would seem so.... I'm not sure if it's a gift or a curse."

"Come now, my dear children!" exclaimed the Primal. "You will be able to live longer, flourish, explore the fruits of Gaia's labors. A new world is opening up to you. The fetters that this monster forged about you are no more! Our Mother now offers you twice the lifespan! The one for which she created you! This is obviously an incredible opportunity. Imagine what your people will be able to accomplish now that they are free!"

The two friends remained pensive, trying to absorb the immensity of their new reality.

"We'll have to go home now," said Menilmonea. "But first I'd like to stop by the village of Opponka to warn Abigail and Aboren."

Aureal nodded.

"You mean the serpent Titan, don't you?" asked the Primal. "He's very far west of here, likely three or four moons' walk."

"Moons? By Tunka's shell!" Aureal gasped.

"We'll use the Towers," replied Menilmonea. "After all, they're still there."

"Exactly. Except we still have the problem of knowing where we'll come out."

"We'll finally put our map together," said Menilmonea. "It'll take as long as it takes, but we'll find them. And our village too."

"A map?" asked the Primal in surprise.

"Yes. Inside the Towers, there's a magical system that seems to represent the world, with the Towers visualized as glowing glyphs. Touching one of these glyphs activates the transport magic. We plan to draw them on a scroll so we can find our way around and proceed by process of elimination. We just need to find the right one among the dozens that are there."

"I see. I should be able to help you, then. If your 'map' corresponds to the reality of the world, I'll have no trouble telling you who's where," he said with a hint of humor in his voice.

"That would be perfect!" exclaimed the two friends in unison.

"Great! Let's head for the Tower beyond the mushroom forest, then," Aureal said.

"I can't wait to see our crotchety friend there again," replied

Menilmonea with a smirk.

"Oh yes, I'd forgotten.... Let's ignore him. He already learned his lesson when the Primal destroyed his golem."

"We'll also have to do something about those Spirits locked up in the Towers," added the Primal in a serious tone. "It just won't do to leave them there for all eternity."

"I agree wholeheartedly," replied Menilmonea. "Let's add that to our list of tasks. Why, having twice as long to live may prove useful after all!"

The journey to the Tower proceeded without incident, but not without emotion. Grumf had offered to carry them on his back, and this simple gesture turned a walk into a ride across the world. Over the plains, through the woods, and down half-overgrown paths, the girls sped along at a pace their legs could never have sustained. The trees seemed to part reverently before them, and the forest sang beneath the grizzly's paws. The friends laughed, enjoying the wind in their hair and their protector's quiet power.

When they neared the Tower, the Primal was already waiting for them a few paces from the entrance. Grumf slowed, nervous. He ventured no closer.

Aureal, attentive to his emotions, closed her eyes for a moment, then turned to Menilmonea. "He can't stay. He's already too far from his territory."

They huddled against him in silence, their hearts heavy.

"We will never forget you," whispered Aureal, her voice breaking with emotion.

In her mind, the deep, familiar voice echoed one last time. *Goodbye, dear friend. The inhabitants of this territory will always remember you. You are strong.*

Grumf turned away and headed toward the forest in silence. His massive shape gradually vanished among the trees.

Aureal wiped away a tear, grabbed Menilmonea's hand, and with a determined step, entered the Tower.

The interior was still in working order, bathed in an otherworldly light. As expected, their gifts disappeared as soon as they crossed the threshold.

Almost immediately, a quavering voice rang out. "You again! Have you come to torment me?"

"Why no, of course not! We mean you no harm," replied Menilmonea in a calm tone.

Without waiting, she took out her parchment and a small piece of charcoal sharpened to a point. After selecting the local rune, she began to copy the map that appeared before her eyes.

"We have killed the Mother," Aureal said sharply.

"Aureal!" said Menilmonea, frowning.

"But it's true, isn't it?" she continued. "We defeated a traitor to his own kind, who kept us all in unwholesome ignorance for an eternity, just to glorify himself and satisfy his petty need for revenge."

"What are you talking about?!" choked the voice. "You killed the Mother? You poor humans, you killed the goddess? You're even crazier than I thought!"

"But you saw what we did to your guardian, didn't you? Doesn't that give you pause?"

"No, why—no.... I don't believe you!"

"I just want to spare you from living a lie any longer. We are all victims. This horror must end."

"Poor girl! I don't know who you think you are, but you won't get me with your schemes. The Mother will punish you. Ascension will never be yours!"

"Yes, you couldn't be more right about that," Menilmonea said ironically. "All right, I'm done. I've gotten it all down, even if it's not perfect. I didn't realize the ring's map was on a half-sphere. But let's place our trust in the Primal's powers of visualization."

"Good, let's be off, then," Aureal concurred. Then she turned to address the voice one last time. "Think carefully, dear Spirit. Ask yourself if the Mother would really have let us do all this if she were still around."

With that, she turned on her heel and followed Menilmonea out of the Tower.

"You were hard on him, weren't you?" said Menilmonea.

"Maybe, but his arrogance reminds me of too many awful things."

The fox was waiting outside, as serene a figure as ever. Menilmonea unfolded her parchment.

"Here you are, Primal. The crosses represent the Towers, and this arrow points north."

"Hmm.... Let me try to get my bearings," he murmured.

At these words, several thin vines shot out of the ground and delicately grasped the map. The fox shut his eyes. Several roots rose up in front of him, gathering to form a rectangle of wood the span of an adult forearm, with finely chiseled edges. Almost immediately, tiny red flowers began to bloom on its surface.

"Oh!" whispered Menilmonea. "It's beautiful! But is that... my map?"

"It is!" confirmed Aureal. "The flowers are arranged in roughly the same pattern as your crosses."

The Primal's magic continued its work. Under some of the flowers, small ideograms appeared, graven in the very wood.

Aureal approached, squinting, and a broad smile lit up her face. "Look! There's a rabbit drawn under that flower! And oh—there, a snake! It's Opponka!"

Menilmonea joined her, speechless. "Unbelievable!"

Some of the flowers changed color, turning a deep purple. Under one of them, the wood formed the shape of a turtle.

"Tunka..." whispered Menilmonea.

"Yes. These flowers represent the dead Titans," Aureal whispered, her voice filled with sadness.

And with those words, a lizard appeared beneath another purple flower.

This ballet went on hypnotically for a long time. It ended with the appearance of a tiny mushroom, obviously representing the Valley of the Ancients.

At last, the Primal broke his silence. "There. That corresponds to the reality of our world. I entrust it to you."

With these words, the roots that had formed the wooden map slowly retracted, leaving their work lying on the ground.

"This should help you find your way during your travels between Towers," added the fox.

Aureal bent down and picked up the map, surprised by how light it was.

"We can't thank you enough, Primal. This will be incredibly useful to us," she said sincerely.

"How do you wish to proceed with the Titans?" asked Menilmonea. "Could we start with Opponka?"

"Yes, let us start with the serpent," the Primal replied. "I'll wait for you outside his village. It would probably be best if I approached him at night to avoid witnesses, even though I don't think any other humans besides you two can understand me."

"Yes, a wise choice. I don't know how he'll react, but that will inform how we proceed with the villagers," Menilmonea agreed.

Armed with their map, the two friends returned to the Tower and headed for its ring. This time, no voice greeted them, and they made no comment. Once they were standing in the transport liquid, they took their time examining their wooden map of the world, comparing it with the magical version projected around them. After exchanging glances and carefully studying the surroundings, they finally chose a rune, confident of their selection.

The magic worked, and they appeared in a new Tower.

"Well, well, well, who do we have here?" exclaimed a clearly amused voice. "What a pleasant surprise to find you both still alive!"

"The pleasure's all ours," replied Menilmonea with a chuckle. "We must hurry to your village, but I promise I'll be back very soon!"

"At least tell me if you met the Mother."

"Oh, we met her all right," said Aureal with a smile.

"And we'll come back and tell you all about it soon! Promise!" added Menilmonea, already turning toward the exit.

"I'm counting on you! I... I have a feeling I'm going to like your story!" cried the Spirit as they disappeared into the light. "What a time to be alive!"

They reached the village at nightfall, taking the same little path they'd followed on the way there.

The fox was seated on a tree stump, waiting for them.

"Glad to see you again, my friends," he said calmly.

"Likewise, Primal! Ready to save one of your descendants?" asked Aureal.

"Indeed. I gently probed his mind while waiting for you. He is asleep."

"Oh no!!"

"No, no, just sleeping," he clarified, amused. "Nothing unusual. I'll let you wake him, and I'll do the rest once he's conscious."

Noiselessly, they made their way toward where the Titan lay. As soon as they arrived, Aureal took a deep breath and pretended to clear her throat loudly.

Menilmonea shot her an impish look. "Opponka? We apologize for waking you, but we need to speak with you urgently."

Slowly, the Titan woke, his long form cautiously uncurling from his slumbering coils. Faint waves rippled up and down his scaly body, setting the grass and plants on his back gently asway. Two pale eyes opened halfway, slow and cloudy, seeking to pierce the darkness. His deep voice rose, stretched by the torpor of awakening and tinged with surprise.

"Why, what are you doing here, my dear little ones? Abigail told me you had gone back to pray to the Mother in your village."

"Yes, that was our idea at first, but there have been a few twists and turns along the way," replied Menilmonea with a cautious smile.

"I'm glad no ill has befallen you." He stopped abruptly, frozen.

"Opponka?" asked Menilmonea, worried.

The fox had just appeared behind them. His voice was soft but confident. "I am with him. Have no fear. Thank you for your help. I shall look after him now."

The two friends exchanged hesitant glances, frozen in place, not daring to speak or move.

Time seemed to stretch out, then at long last, Opponka slowly moved. His body undulated with a strange torpor, as if he were trying to find his bearings. He seemed lost, as if he had just emerged from a dream.

Then, all of a sudden, he looked up at the fox. "Primal?"

Thank you for reading Menilmonea's story!

If you enjoyed this book, please don't hesitate to post your thoughts online. A few words, even a review—it doesn't have to take long but can prove tremendous in helping this book reach more readers.

Thanks in advance for your support!

And if you're interested in what happens next, or receiving digital wallpapers, please don't hesitate to subscribe to my newsletter:

https://list.deltakosh.link